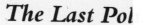

"A solidly plotted whodunit with strong characters and excellent dialogue . . . the impending apocalypse isn't merely window dressing, either: it's a key piece of the puzzle Hank is trying to solve. This memorable tale is the first of a planned trilogy."

—*Booklist*

"This thought-provoking mystery should appeal to crime fiction aficionados who like an unusual setting and readers looking for a fresh take on apocalypse stories."

—*Library Journal*

"A promising kickoff to a planned trilogy. For Winters, the beauty is in the details rather than the plot's grim main thrust."

—Kirkus Reviews (starred review)

"Ben H. Winters spins a wonderful tale while creating unique characters that fit in perfectly with the ever-changing societal pressures. . . . [This] well-written mystery will have readers eagerly awaiting the second installment."

—*The New York Journal of Books*

"Extraordinary—as well as brilliant, surprising, and, considering the circumstances, oddly uplifting."

—*Mystery Scene Magazine*

"Exhilarating. . . . do not wait for the movie!"

—*E! Online*

THE

LAST

POLICEMAN

The

Last

Policeman

By Ben H. Winters

QUIRK BOOKS
PHILADELPHIA

Library of Congress Cataloging in Publication Number: 2013935622
ISBN: 978-1-59474-674-1

Printed in Canada
Typeset in Bembo and OCRA

Designed by Doogie Horner
Production management by John J. McGurk
Cover photographs: (hanged man) © Jonathan Pushnik;
(farmhouse) © Ocean/Corbis; (comet) © Shutterstock

Quirk Books
215 Church Street
Philadelphia, PA 19106
quirkbooks.com
10 9 8 7 6 5 4 3

To Andrew Winters,
of the Concord Winters

"Even for Voltaire, the supreme
rationalist, a purely rational suicide
was something prodigious and
slightly grotesque, like a comet or
a two-headed sheep."

—A. Alvarez, *The Savage God:*
A Study of Suicide

——————

"And there's a slow,
slow train comin',
up around the bend."

—Bob Dylan, "Slow Train"

PART ONE

....

Hanger Town

....

Tuesday, March 20

Right ascension 19 02 54.4
Declination -34 11 39
Elongation 78.0
Delta 3.195 AU

1.

I'm staring at the insurance man and he's staring at me, two cold gray eyes behind old-fashioned tortoiseshell frames, and I'm having this awful and inspiring feeling, like holy moly this is real, and I don't know if I'm ready, I really don't.

I narrow my eyes and I steady myself and I take him in again, shift on my haunches to get a closer look. The eyes and the glasses, the weak chin and the receding hairline, the thin black belt tied and tightened beneath the chin.

This is real. Is it? I don't know.

I take a deep breath, demanding of myself that I focus, block out everything but the corpse, block out the grimy floors and the tinny rock-and-roll Muzak from the cheap speakers in the ceiling.

The smell is killing me, a pervasive and deeply unpleasant odor, like a horse barn that's been splashed with French-fry grease. There are any number of jobs in this world still being efficiently and diligently accomplished, but the late-night cleaning of twenty-four-hour fast-food-restaurant bathrooms is not among them. Case in point: the insurance man had been slumped over in here, lodged between the toilet and the dull green wall of the stall, for several hours before Officer Michelson happened to come in, needing to use the john, and discovered him.

Michelson called it in as a 10-54S, of course, which is what it looks like. One thing I've learned in the last few months, one thing we've all learned, is that suicides-by-hanging rarely end up dangling from a light fixture or a roof beam, like in the movies. If they're serious, and nowadays everybody is serious, would-be suicides fasten themselves to a doorknob, or to a coat hook, or, as the insurance man appears to have done, to a horizontal rail, like the grab bar in a handicapped stall. And then they just lean forward, let their weight do the work, tighten the knot, seal the airway.

I angle farther forward, readjust my crouch, trying to find a way to share space comfortably with the insurance man without falling or getting my fingerprints all over the scene. I've had nine of these in the three and a half months since I became a detective, and still I can't get used to it, to what death by asphyxiation does to a person's face: the eyes staring forward as if in horror, laced with thin red spiderwebs of blood; the tongue, rolled out and over to one side; the lips, inflated and purplish at the edges.

I close my eyes, rub them with my knuckles, and look again, try to get a sense of what the insurance man's appearance had been in life. He wasn't handsome, that you can see right away. The face is doughy and the proportions are all just a little off: chin too small, nose too big, the eyes almost beady behind the thick lenses.

What it looks like is that the insurance man killed himself

with a long black belt. He fastened one end to the grab bar and worked the other end into the hangman's knot that now digs brutally upward into his Adam's apple.

"Hey, kid. Who's your friend?"

"Peter Anthony Zell," I answer quietly, looking up over my shoulder at Dotseth, who has opened the door of the stall and stands grinning down at me in a jaunty plaid scarf, clutching a steaming cup of McDonald's coffee.

"Caucasian male. Thirty-eight years old. He worked in insurance."

"And let me guess," says Dotseth. "He was eaten by a shark. Oh, wait, no: suicide. Is it suicide?"

"It appears that way."

"Shocked, I am! Shocked!" Denny Dotseth is an assistant attorney general, a warhorse with silver hair and a broad, cheerful face. "Oh, geez, I'm sorry, Hank. Did you want a cup of coffee?"

"No, thank you, sir."

I give Dotseth a report on what I've learned from the black faux-leather wallet in the victim's back pocket. Zell was employed at a company called Merrimack Life and Fire, with offices in the Water West Building, off Eagle Square. A little collection of movie stubs, all dating from the last three months, speaks to a taste for adolescent adventure: the *Lord of the Rings* revival; two installments of the sci-fi serial *Distant Pale Glimmers;* the DC-versus-Marvel thing at the IMAX in Hooksett. No trace of a family, no photographs in the wallet at all. Eighty-five dollars in fives and tens. And a driver's license, with an address here in town: 14 Matthew Street Extension, South Concord.

"Oh, sure. I know that area. Some nice little town houses down that way. Rolly Lewis has a place over there."

"And he got beat up."

"Rolly?"

"The victim. Look." I turn back to the insurance man's distorted face and point to a cluster of yellowing bruises, high on the right cheek. "Someone banged him one, hard."

"Oh, yeah. He sure did."

Dotseth yawns and sips his coffee. New Hampshire statute has long required that someone from the office of the attorney general be called whenever a dead body is discovered, so that if a murder case is to be built, the prosecuting authority has a hand in from Go. In mid-January this requirement was overturned by the state legislature as being unduly onerous, given the present unusual circumstances—Dotseth and his colleagues hauling themselves all over the state just to stand around like crows at murder scenes that aren't murder scenes at all. Now, it's up to the discretion of the investigating officer whether to call an AAG to a 10-54S. I usually go ahead and call mine in.

"So what else is new, young man?" says Dotseth. "You still playing a little racquetball?"

"I don't play racquetball, sir," I say, half listening, eyes locked on the dead man.

"You don't? Who am I thinking of?"

I'm tapping a finger on my chin. Zell was short, five foot six maybe; stubby, thick around the middle. Holy moly, I'm still thinking, because something is off about this body, this corpse, this particular presumptive suicide, and I'm trying to figure out what it is.

"No phone," I murmur.

"What?"

"His wallet is here, and his keys, but there's no cell phone."

Dotseth shrugs. "Betcha he junked it. Beth just junked hers. Service is starting to get so dicey, she figured she might as well get rid of the darn thing now."

I nod, murmur "sure, sure," still staring at Zell.

"Also, no note."

"What?"

"There's no suicide note."

"Oh, yeah?" he says, shrugs again. "Probably a friend will find it. Boss, maybe." He smiles, drains the coffee. "They all leave notes, these folks. Although, you have to say, explanation not really necessary at this point, right?"

"Yes, sir," I say, running a hand over my mustache. "Yes, indeed."

Last week in Kathmandu, a thousand pilgrims from all over southeast Asia walked into a massive pyre, monks chanting in a circle around them before marching into the blaze themselves. In central Europe, old folks are trading how-to DVDs: *How to Weigh Your Pockets with Stones*, *How to Mix a Barbiturate Cocktail in the Sink*. In the American Midwest—Kansas City, St. Louis, Des Moines—the trend is firearms, a solid majority employing a shotgun blast to the brain.

Here in Concord, New Hampshire, for whatever reason, it's hanger town. Bodies slumped in closets, in sheds, in unfinished basements. A week ago Friday, a furniture-store owner in East Concord tried to do it the Hollywood way, hoisted himself from an overhanging length of gutter with the sash of his bathrobe, but the gutter pipe snapped, sent him tumbling down onto the patio, alive but with four broken limbs.

"Anyhow, it's a tragedy," Dotseth concludes blandly. "Every one of them a tragedy."

He shoots a quick look at his watch; he's ready to boogie. But I'm still down in a squat, still running my narrowed eyes over the body of the insurance man. For his last day on earth, Peter Zell chose a rumpled tan suit and a pale blue button-down dress shirt. His socks almost but don't quite match, both of them brown, one dark and one merely darkish, both loose in their elastic, slipping down his calves. The belt around his neck, what Dr. Fenton will call the ligature, is a thing of beauty: shiny black leather, the letters B&R etched into the gold buckle.

"Detective? Hello?" Dotseth says, and I look up at him and I blink. "Anything else you'd like to share?"

"No, sir. Thank you."

"No sweat. Pleasure as always, young man."

"Except, wait."

"Sorry?"

I stand up straight and turn and face him. "So. I'm going to murder somebody."

A pause. Dotseth waiting, amused, exaggerated patience. "All righty."

"And I live in a time and a town where people are killing themselves all over the place. Right and left. It's hanger town."

"Okay."

"Wouldn't my move be, kill my victim and then arrange it to appear as a suicide?"

"Maybe."

"Maybe, right?"

"Yeah. Maybe. But that right there?" Dotseth jabs a cheerful thumb toward the slumped corpse. "That's a suicide."

He winks, pushes open the door of the men's room, and leaves me alone with Peter Zell.

* * *

"So what's the story, Stretch? Are we waiting for the meat wagon on this one, or cuttin' down the piñata ourselves?"

I level Officer Michelson a stern and disapproving look. I hate that kind of casual fake tough-guy morbidity, "meat wagon" and "piñata" and all the rest of it, and Ritchie Michelson knows that I hate it, which is exactly why he's goading me right now. He's been waiting at the door of the men's room, theoretically guarding the crime scene, eating an Egg McMuffin out of its yellow cellophane wrapper, pale grease dripping down the front of his uniform shirt.

"Come on, Michelson. A man is dead."

"Sorry, Stretch."

I'm not crazy about the nickname, either, and Ritchie knows that also.

"Someone from Dr. Fenton's office should be here within the hour," I say, and Michelson nods, burps into his fist.

"You're going to turn this over to Fenton's office, huh?" He balls up his breakfast-sandwich wrapper, chucks it into the trash. "I thought she wasn't doing suicides anymore."

"It's at the discretion of the detective," I say, "and in this case, I think an autopsy is warranted."

"Oh, yeah?"

"Yeah."

He doesn't really care. Trish McConnell, meanwhile, is doing her job. She's on the far side of the restaurant, a short and vigorous woman with a black ponytail jutting out from under her patrolman's cap. She's got a knot of teenagers cornered by the soda fountain. Taking statements. Notebook out, pencil flying, anticipating and fulfilling her supervising investigator's instructions. Officer McConnell, I like.

"You know, though," Michelson is saying, talking just to talk, just getting my goat, "headquarters says we're supposed to fold up the tent pretty quick on these."

"I know that."

"Community stability and continuity, that whole drill."

"Yes."

"Plus, the owner's ready to flip, with his bathroom being closed."

I follow Michelson's gaze to the counter and the red-faced proprietor of the McDonald's, who stares back at us, his unyielding gaze made mildly ridiculous by the bright yellow shirt and ketchup-colored vest. Every minute of police presence is a minute of lost profit, and you can just tell the guy would be over here with a finger in my face if he wanted to risk an arrest on Title XVI. Next to the manager is a gangly adolescent boy, his thick mullet fringing a counterman's visor, smirking back and forth between his disgruntled boss and the pair of policemen, unsure who's more deserving of his contempt.

"He'll be fine," I tell Michelson. "If this were last year, the whole scene of crime would be shut down for six to twelve hours, and not just the men's john, either."

Michelson shrugs. "New times."

I scowl and turn my back on the owner. Let him stew. It's not even a real McDonald's. There are no more real McDonald's. The company folded in August of last year, ninety-four percent of its value having evaporated in three weeks of market panic, leaving behind hundreds of thousands of brightly colored empty storefronts. Many of these, like the one we're now standing in, on Concord's Main Street, have subsequently been transformed into pirate restaurants: owned and operated by enterprising locals like my new best friend over there, doing a bustling business in comfort food and no need to sweat the franchise fee.

There are no more real 7-Elevens, either, and no more real Dunkin' Donuts. There are still real Paneras, but the couple who owns the chain have undergone a meaningful spiritual experience and restaffed most of the restaurants with coreligionists, so it's not worth going in there unless you want to hear the Good News.

I beckon McConnell over, let her and Michelson know we're going to be investigating this as a suspicious death, try to ignore the sarcastic lift of Ritchie's eyebrows. McConnell, for her part, nods gravely and flips her notebook to a fresh page. I give the crime-scene officers their marching orders: McConnell is to finish collecting statements, then go find and inform the victim's family. Michelson is to stay here by the door, guarding the scene until someone from Fenton's office arrives to collect the corpse.

"You got it," says McConnell, flipping closed her notebook.

"Beats working," says Michelson.

"Come on, Ritchie," I say. " A man is dead."

"Yeah, Stretch," he says. "You said that already."

I salute my fellow officers, nod goodbye, and then I stop short, one hand on the handle of the parking-lot-side door of the McDonald's, because there's a woman walking anxiously this way through the parking lot, wearing a red winter hat but no coat, no umbrella against the steady drifts of snow, like she just ran out of somewhere to get here, thin work shoes slipping on the slush of the parking lot. Then she sees me, sees me looking at her, and I catch the moment when she knows that I'm a policeman, and her brow creases with worry and she turns on her heel and hurries away.

* * *

I drive north on State Street away from the McDonald's in my department-issued Chevrolet Impala, carefully maneuvering through the quarter inch of frozen precipitation on the roadway. The side streets are lined with parked cars, abandoned cars, drifts of snow collecting on their windshields. I pass the Capitol Center for the Arts, handsome red brick and wide windows, glance into the packed coffee shop that someone's opened across the street. There's a snaking line of customers outside Collier's, the hardware store—they must have new merchandise. Lightbulbs. Shovels. Nails. There's a high-school-age kid up on a ladder, crossing out prices and writing in new ones with a black marker on a cardboard sign.

Forty-eight hours, is what I'm thinking. Most murder cases that get solved are solved within forty-eight hours of the commission of the crime.

Mine is the only car on the road, and the pedestrians turn their heads to watch me pass. A bum leans against the boarded-up door of White Peak, a mortgage broker and commercial real-estate firm. A small pack of teenagers is loitering outside an ATM vestibule, passing around a marijuana cigarette, a kid with a scruffy goatee languorously exhaling into the cold air.

Scrawled across the glass window of what used to be a two-story office building, at the corner of State and Blake, is graffiti, six-foot-tall letters that say LIES LIES IT'S ALL LIES.

I regret giving Ritchie Michelson a hard time. Life for patrol officers had gotten pretty rough by the time I was promoted, and I'm sure that the fourteen subsequent weeks have not made things easier. Yes, cops are steadily employed and earning among the best salaries in the country right now. And, yes, Concord's crime rate in most categories is not wildly elevated, month against month, from what it was this time last year, with notable exceptions; per the IPSS Act, it is now illegal to manufacture, sell, or purchase any kind of firearm in the United States of America, and this is a tough law to enforce, especially in the state of New Hampshire.

Still, on the street, in the wary eyes of the citizenry, one senses at all times the potential for violence, and for an active-duty patrol officer, as for a soldier in war, that potential for violence takes a slow and grinding toll. So, if I'm Ritchie Michelson, I'm bound to be a little tired, a little burned out, prone to the occasional snippy remark.

The traffic light at Warren Street is working, and even though

I'm a policeman and even though there are no other cars at the intersection, I stop and I drum my fingers on the steering wheel and I wait for the green light, staring out the windshield and thinking about that woman, the one in a hurry and wearing no coat.

*　*　*

"Everybody hear the news?" asks Detective McGully, big and boisterous, hands cupped together into a megaphone. "We've got the date."

"What do you mean, 'we've got the date'?" says Detective Andreas, popping up from his chair looking at McGully with open-mouthed bafflement. "We already have the date. Everybody knows the goddamned date."

The date that everybody knows is October 3, six months and eleven days from today, when a 6.5-kilometer-diameter ball of carbon and silicates will collide with Earth.

"Not the date the big meatball makes landfall," says McGully, brandishing a copy of the *Concord Monitor*. "The date the geniuses tell us where it's gonna hit."

"Yeah, I saw that," nods Detective Culverson, settled at his own desk with his own paper; he reads the *New York Times*. "April 9, I think."

My own desk is in the far corner of the room, by the trash can and the little fridge. I have my notebook open in front of me, reviewing my observations on the crime scene. It's actually a blue book, the kind college students use to take their exams. My father was a professor, and when he died we found about twenty-five boxes of these things up in the attic, slim paper books of robin's-egg blue. I'm still using them.

"April 9? That seems so soon." Andreas slumps back down in his chair, and then he echoes himself in a ghostly murmur. "Seems soon."

Culverson shakes his head and sighs, while McGully chortles. This is what remains of the Concord Police Department's division of Criminal Investigations, Adult-Crimes Unit: four guys in a room. Between August of last year and today, Adult Crimes has had three early retirements, one sudden and unexplained disappearance, plus Detective Gordon, who broke his hand in the course of a domestic-violence arrest, took medical leave and never came back. This wave of attrition has been insufficiently countered by the promotion, in early December, of one patrolman. Me. Detective Palace.

We're pretty fortunate, personnel-wise. Juvenile Crime is down to two officers, Peterson and Guerrera. Tech Crime was disbanded entirely, effective November 1.

McGully opens today's *New York Times* and begins to read aloud. I'm thinking about the Zell case, working through my notes. *No signs of foul play or struggle // cell phone? // Ligature: belt, gold buckle.*

A black belt of handsome Italian leather, emblazoned "B&R."

"The crucial date is April 9, according to astronomers at the Harvard-Smithsonian Center for Astrophysics in Cambridge, Massachusetts," reads McGully from the *Times*. "Experts there, along with legions of other astronomers, astrophysicists, and dedicated amateurs following the steady progress of Maia, the massive asteroid formally known as 2011GV$_1$—"

"Jesus," moans Andreas, mournful and furious, jumping up again and hurrying over to McGully's desk. He's a small guy, twitchy, in his early forties, but with a thick head of tight black curls, like a cherub. "We know what it is. Is there anyone left on the planet who doesn't know all of this already?"

"Take it easy, pally," says McGully.

"I just hate how they give all the information over and over again, every time. It's like they're rubbing it in or something."

"That's just how newspaper stories are written," Culverson says.

"Well, I hate it."

"Nevertheless." Culverson smiles. He's the only African American officer in the Criminal Investigations Unit. He is in fact the only African American officer on the Concord force and is sometimes lovingly referred to as "The Only Black Man in Concord," though this is not technically true.

"All right, all right, I'll skip ahead," says McGully, patting poor Andreas on the shoulder. "Scientists have been . . . I'll skip, I'll skip . . . some disagreement, now largely resolved, as to . . . skip skip skip. Here: 'On the April date, with only five and a half months remaining until impact, sufficient points of declination and right ascension will have been mapped to pinpoint the precise location on the surface of Earth where Maia will land, to an accuracy of within fifteen miles.'"

McGully gets a little hushed at the end there, his baritone bluster softening, and he gives out a whistle, low and long. "Fifteen miles."

A silence follows, filled by the small clanging noises of the radiator. Andreas stands at McGully's desk, staring down at the newspaper, his hands balled in fists at his side. Culverson, in his comfortable corner, picks up a pen and begins tracing long lines on a piece of paper. I close the blue book, tilt my head back, and fix my eyes on a point in the ceiling, near the scalloped light fixture in the center of the room.

"Well, that's the gist of it, ladies and germs," says McGully, bluster recovered, sweeping the paper closed with a flourish. "Then it gets into all the reaction and so on."

"Reaction?" howls Andreas, flapping his hands angrily in the direction of the newspaper. "What kind of *reaction*?"

"Oh, you know, the prime minister of Canada says, hey, hope it lands in China," says McGully, laughing. "President of China says, 'Listen, Canada, no offense or anything, but we've got a different perspective.' You know. Blah blah blah."

Andreas growls in disgust. I'm watching all this, sort of, but really I'm thinking, eyes focused on the light fixture. Guy walks into a McDonald's in the middle of the night and hangs himself in a handicapped stall. Guy walks into a McDonald's, it's the middle of the night . . .

Culverson solemnly lifts his paper, reveals it to be crosshatched into a large simple chart, X axis and Y axis.

"Official Concord Police Department asteroid pool," he announces, deadpan. "Step right up."

I like Detective Culverson. I like that he still dresses like a real detective. Today he's in a three-piece suit, a tie with a metallic sheen, and a matching pocket square. A lot of people, at this point, have wholly given themselves over to comfort. Andreas, for example, is presently wearing a long-sleeve T-shirt and relaxed-fit jeans,

McGully a Washington Redskins sweatsuit.

"If we must die," Culverson concludes, "let us first collect a few bucks from our brothers and sisters in the patrol division."

"Sure, but," Andreas looks around uneasily, "how are we supposed to predict?"

"Predict?" McGully whacks Andreas with the folded-up *Monitor*. "How are we supposed to collect, goofus?"

"I'll go first," says Culverson. "I'm taking the Atlantic Ocean for an even hundred."

"Forty bucks on France," says McGully, rifling through his wallet. "Serve 'em right, the pricks."

Culverson walks his chart to my corner of the room, slides it on the desk. "What about you, Ichabod Crane? What do you think?"

"Gee," I say absently, thinking about those angry lesions beneath the dead man's eye. Someone punched Peter Zell in the face, hard, in the recent-but-not-too-recent past. Two weeks ago, maybe? Three weeks? Dr. Fenton will tell me for sure.

Culverson is waiting, eyebrows raised expectantly. "Detective Palace?"

"Hard to say, you know? Hey, where do you guys buy your belts?"

"Our belts?" Andreas looks down at his waist, then up, as if it's a trick question. "I wear suspenders."

"Place called Humphrey's," says Culverson. "In Manchester."

"Angela buys my belts," says McGully, who's moved on to the sports section, leaned way back, feet propped up. "The hell are you talking about, Palace?"

"I'm working on this case," I explain, all of them looking

back at me now. "This body we found this morning, at the McDonald's."

"That was a hanger, I thought," says McGully.

"We're calling it a suspicious death, for now."

"We?" says Culverson, smiles at me appraisingly. Andreas is still at McGully's desk, still staring at the front section of the paper, one hand clapped to his forehead.

"The ligature in this case was a black belt. Fancy. Buckle said 'B&R.'"

"Belknap and Rose," says Culverson. "Wait now, you're working this as a murder? Awfully public place for a murder."

"Belknap and Rose, exactly," I say. "See, because everything else the victim was wearing was nothing to write home about: plain tan suit, off the rack, an old dress shirt with stains at the pits, mismatched socks. And he was *wearing* a belt, too, a cheap brown belt. But the ligature: real leather, hand stitching."

"Okay," says Culverson. "So he went to B&R and bought himself a fancy belt for the purposes of killing himself."

"There you go," puts in McGully, turns the page.

"Really?" I stand up. "It just seems like, I'm going to hang myself, and I'm a regular guy, I wear suits to work, I probably own a number of belts. Why do I drive the twenty minutes to Manch, to an upscale men's clothing store, to buy a special suicide belt?"

I'm pacing a little bit now, hunched forward, back and forth in front of the desk, stroking my mustache. "Why not, you know, just use one of my many existing belts?"

"Who knows?" says Culverson.

"And more important," adds McGully, yawning, "who cares?"

"Right," I say, and settle back into my seat, pick up the blue book again. "Of course."

"You're like an alien, Palace. You know that?" says McGully. In one swift motion, he balls up his sports section and bounces it off my head. "You're like from another planet or something."

2.

There is a very old man behind the security desk at the Water West Building, and he blinks at me slowly, like he just woke up from a nap, or the grave.

"You got an appointment with someone here in the building?"

"No, sir. I'm a policeman."

The guard is in a severely rumpled dress shirt, and his security-guard cap is misshapen, dented at the peak. It's late morning, but the gray lobby has a gloaming quality, motes drifting listlessly in the half light.

"My name is Detective Henry Palace." I display my badge—he doesn't look, doesn't care—I tuck it carefully away again. "I'm with the Criminal Investigations Division of the Concord Police Department, and I'm looking into a suspicious death. I need to visit the offices of Merrimack Life and Fire."

He coughs. "What are you, anyway, son? Like, six foot four?"

"Something like that."

Waiting for the elevator I absorb the dark lobby: a giant potted plant, squat and heavy, guarding one corner; a lifeless White Mountains landscape above a row of brass mailboxes; the centenarian security man examining me from his perch. This, then, was my insurance man's morning vista, where he started his professional existence, day in and day out. As the elevator door creaks open, I take a sniff of the musty air. Nothing arguing against the case for suicide, down here in the lobby.

* * *

Peter Zell's boss is named Theodore Gompers, a jowly, pallid character in a blue wool suit, who evinces no surprise whatsoever when I tell him the news.

"Zell, huh? Well, that's too bad. Can I pour you a drink?"

"No, thank you."

"How about this weather, huh?"

"Yep."

We're in his office, and he's drinking gin from a short square tumbler, absently rubbing his palm along his chin, staring out a big window at the snow tumbling down onto Eagle Square. "A lot of people are blaming it on the asteroid, all the snow. You've heard that, right?" Gompers talks quietly, ruminatively, his eyes fixed on the street outside. "It's not true, though. The thing is still 280 million miles from here at this point. Not close enough to affect our weather patterns, and it won't be."

"Yep."

"Not until afterward, obviously." He sighs, turns his head to me slowly, like a cow. "People don't really understand, you know?"

"I'm sure that's true," I say, waiting patiently with my blue book and a pen. "Can you tell me about Peter Zell?"

Gompers takes a sip of his gin. "Not that much to tell, really. Guy was a born actuary, that's for sure."

"A born actuary?"

"Yeah. Me, I started out on the actuarial side, degree in statistics and everything. But I switched to sales, and at some point I sort of drifted up to management, and here I have remained." He opens his hands to take in the office and smiles wanly. "But Peter wasn't going anywhere. I don't mean that in a bad way necessarily, but he wasn't going anywhere."

I nod, scratching notes in my book, while Gompers continues in his glassy murmur. Zell, it seems, was a kind of wizard at actuarial math, had a nearly supernatural ability to sort through long columns of demographic data and draw precise conclusions about risk and reward. He was also almost pathologically shy, is what it sounds like: walked around with his eyes on the floor, muttered "hello" and "I'm fine" when pressed, sat in the back of the room at staff meetings, looking at his hands.

"And, boy, when those meetings ended he would always be the first guy out the door," Gompers says. "You got the feeling he was a lot happier at his desk, doing his thing with his calculator and his statistics binders, than he was with the rest of us humans."

I'm scratching away, nodding encouragingly and empathetically to keep Gompers talking, and I'm thinking how much I'm starting to like this guy, this Peter Anthony Zell. I like a guy who likes to get his work done.

"The thing about him, though, about Zell, is that this craziness never seemed to affect him too much. Even at the beginning, even when it all first started up."

Gompers inclines his head backward, toward the window, toward the sky, and I'm guessing that when he says "when it all first started up," he means early summer of last year, when the asteroid entered the public consciousness in a serious way. It had been spotted by scientists as early as April, but for those first couple months, it only appeared in News-of-the-Weird kinds of reports, funny headlines on the Yahoo! homepage. "Death from Above?!" and "The Sky is Falling!"—that sort of stuff. But for most people, early June was when the threat became real; when the odds of impact rose to five percent; when Maia's circumference was estimated at between 4.5 and 7 kilometers.

"So, you remember: people are going nuts, people are weeping at their desks. But Zell, like I said, he just keeps his head down, does his thing. Like he thought the asteroid was coming for everyone except him."

"And what about more recently? Any change in that pattern? Depression?"

"Well," he says. "You know, wait." He stops abruptly, puts one hand over his mouth, narrows his eyes, as if trying to see something murky and far away.

"Mr. Gompers?"

"Yeah, I just . . . Sorry, I'm trying to remember something." His eyes drift shut for a second, then snap open, and I have a moment of concern for the reliability of my witness here, wondering how many glasses of gin he's already enjoyed this morning. "The thing is, there was this one incident."

"Incident?"

"Yeah. We had this girl Theresa, an accountant, and she came to work on Halloween dressed as the asteroid."

"Oh?"

"I know. Sick, right?" But Gompers grins at the memory. "It was just a big black garbage bag with the number, you know, two-zero-one-one-G-V-one, on a name tag. Most of us laughed, some people more than others. But Zell, out of nowhere, he just *flipped*. He starts yelling and screaming at this girl, his whole body is shaking. It was really scary, especially because, like I said, he's normally such a quiet guy. Anyway, he apologized, but the next day he doesn't show up for work."

"How long was he gone?"

"A week? Two weeks? I thought he was out for good, but then he turned up again, no explanation, and he's been the same as ever."

"The same?"

"Yeah. Quiet. Calm. Focused. Hard work, doing what he's told. Even when the actuarial side dried up."

"The—I'm sorry?" I say. "What?"

"The actuarial end. Late fall, early winter, you know, we stopped issuing policies entirely." He sees my questioning expression and smiles grimly. "I mean, Detective: would *you* like to buy life insurance right now?"

"I guess not."

"Right," he says, sniffs, drains his glass. "I guess not."

The lights flicker and Gompers looks up, mutters "come on," and a moment later they glow brightly again.

"Anyway, so then I've got Peter doing what everyone else is doing, which is inspecting claims, looking for false filings, dubious claims. It seems loony, but that's what our parent company, Variegated, is obsessed with these days: fraud prevention. It's all about protecting the bottom line. A lot of CEOs have cashed in their chips, you know, they're in Bermuda or Antigua or they're building bunkers. But not our guy. Between you and me, our guy thinks he's going to buy his way into heaven when the end comes. That's the impression I get."

I don't laugh. I tap the end of the pen on my book, trying to make sense of all the information, trying to build a timeline in my head.

"Do you think I might speak to her?"

"To who?"

"The woman you mentioned." I glance down at my notes. "Theresa."

"Oh, she's long gone, Officer. She's in New Orleans now, I believe." Gompers inclines his head, and his voice peters down to a murmur. "A lot of the kids are going down there. My daughter, too, actually." He looks out the window again. "Anything else I can tell you?"

I stare down at the blue book, spiderwebbed with my crabbed handwriting. *Well? What else can he tell me?*

"What about friends? Did Mr. Zell have any friends?"

"Uh . . ." Gompers tilts his head, sticks out his lower lip. "One. Or, I don't know what he was, I guess he was a friend. A guy, kind of a big fat guy, big arms. Once or twice last summer I saw Zell having lunch with him, around the corner at the Works."

"A large man, you said?"

"I said a big fat guy, but sure. I remember because, first of all, you'd never see Peter out to lunch, so that was unusual in itself. And second, Peter was such a small person, the two of them were kind of a sight, you know?"

"Did you get his name?"

"The big man? No. I didn't even talk to him."

I uncross and recross my legs, trying to think of the right questions, think of the things I'm supposed to ask, what else I need to know. "Sir, do you have any idea where Peter got the bruises?"

"What?"

"Under his eye?"

"Oh, yeah. Yeah, he said he fell down some stairs. A couple weeks ago, I think?"

"Fell down some stairs?"

"That's what he said."

"Okay."

I'm writing this down, and I'm starting to see the dim outlines of the course of my investigation, and I'm feeling these jolts of adrenaline shooting up my right leg, making it bounce a little bit where it's crossed over the left one.

"Last question, Mr. Gompers. Do you know if Mr. Zell had any enemies?"

Gompers rubs his jaw with the heel of his hand, his eyes swimming into focus. "Enemies, did you say? You're not thinking that someone *killed* the guy, are you?"

"Well. Maybe. Probably not." I flip closed my blue book and stand up. "May I see his workspace, please?"

* * *

That sharp jolt of adrenaline that shot up my leg during the Gompers interview has now spread throughout my body, and it lingers, spreading up my veins, filling me with a strange kind of electric hunger.

I'm a policeman, the thing I've always wanted to be. For sixteen months I was a patrol officer, working almost exclusively on the overnight shift, almost exclusively in Sector 1, cruising Loudon Road from the Walmart at one end to the overpass on the other. Sixteen months patrolling my four-and-a-half-mile stretch, back and forth, 8 p.m. to 4 a.m., breaking up fights, scattering drunks, rolling up panhandlers and schizophrenics in the Market Basket parking lot.

I loved it. Even last summer I loved it, when things got weird, new times, and then the fall, the work got steadily harder and steadily stranger and I loved it still.

But since making detective I've been befogged by a frustrating unnamable sensation, some dissatisfaction, a sense of bad luck, bad timing, where I got the job I've wanted and waited for my whole life and it's a disappointment to me, or I to it.

And now, today, here at last this electric feeling, tingling and fading at my pulse points, and I'm thinking holy moly, this might just be it. It really might be.

* * *

"So what are you looking for, anyway?"

It's an accusation more than a question. I turn from what I'm doing, which is sorting methodically through Peter Zell's desk drawers, and I see a bald woman in a black pencil skirt and white blouse.

It's the woman I saw at the McDonald's, the one who approached the door of the restaurant and then turned away, melting back into the parking lot and out of sight. I recognize her pale complexion and deep black eyes, even though this morning she was wearing a bright red wool cap, and now she is hatless, her smooth white scalp reflecting the harsh overhead lights of Merrimack Life and Fire.

"I am looking for evidence, ma'am. A routine investigation. My name is Detective Henry Palace, from the Concord Police Department."

"Evidence of what, exactly?" she asks. The woman's nose is pierced, one nostril, a single understated golden stud. "Gompers said that Peter killed himself."

I don't answer, and she steps the rest of the way into the small airless office and watches me work. She's good-looking, this woman, small and strong-featured and poised, maybe twenty-four, twenty-five years old. I wonder what Peter Zell must have made of her.

"Well," she says, after thirty seconds or so. "Gompers said to find out if you need anything. Do you need anything?"

"No, thank you."

She's looking over and around me, at my fingers pawing through the dead man's drawers. "I'm sorry, what did you say you were looking for?"

"I don't know yet. An investigation's proper course cannot be mapped in advance. It follows each piece of information forward to the next one."

"Oh, yeah?" When the young woman raises her eyebrows, it creates delicate furrows on her forehead. "It sounds like you're quoting from a textbook or something."

"Huh." I keep my expression neutral. It is in fact a direct quote, from Farley and Leonard, *Criminal Investigation*, the introduction to chapter six.

"I actually do need something," I say, pointing to Zell's monitor, which is turned backward, facing the wall. "What's the deal with the computers here?"

"We've been all-paper since November," she says, shrugging. "There's this whole network system where our files here were shared with corporate and the different regional offices, but the network got incredibly slow and annoying, so the whole company is operating offline."

"Ah," I say, "okay." Internet service, as a whole, has been increasingly unreliable in the Merrimack Valley since late January; a switching point in southern Vermont was attacked by some kind of anarchist collective, motive unclear, and the resources haven't been found to repair it.

The woman is just standing there, looking at me. "So, I'm sorry—you're Mr. Gompers's executive assistant?"

"Please," she says, rolling her eyes. "Secretary."

"And what's your name?"

She pauses, just long enough to let me know she feels that she could, if she chose, keep the information to herself, and then says, "Eddes. Naomi Eddes."

Naomi Eddes. She is not, I am noticing, completely bald, not quite. Her scalp is gently feathered with a translucent blonde fuzz, which looks soft and smooth and lovely, like elegant carpeting for a doll's house.

"Do you mind if I ask you a few questions, Ms. Eddes?"

She doesn't answer, but neither does she leave the room; she just stands there regarding me steadily as I launch in. She's worked here for four years. Yes, Mr. Zell was already employed when she started. No, she did not know him well. She confirms Gompers's general portrait of Peter Zell's personality: quiet, hardworking, socially uncomfortable, although she uses the word *maladroit*, which I like. She recalls the incident on Halloween, when Peter lashed out at Theresa from Accounting, though she doesn't recall any subsequent weeklong absence from the office.

"But to be totally honest," she says, "I'm not sure I would have noticed him not being here. Like I said, we weren't that close." Her expression softens, and for a split second I would swear she's blinking back tears, but it's just a split second, and then her steady, impassive expression recomposes itself. "He was very nice, though. A really nice guy."

"Would you have characterized him as being depressed?"

"Depressed?" she says, smiling faintly, ironically. "Aren't we all depressed, Detective? Under the weight of all this unbearable imminence? Aren't you depressed?"

I don't answer, but I'm liking her phrase, *all this unbearable imminence*. Better than Gompers's "this craziness," better than McGully's "big meatball."

"And did you happen to notice, Ms. Eddes, what time Mr. Zell left the office yesterday, or with whom?"

"No," she says, her voice dipping down a half register, her chin pressing against her chest. "I did not notice what time he left the office yesterday, nor with whom."

I am thrown for a moment, and then by the time I realize that her sudden pseudoserious intonation is meant to tease me, she's continuing in her regular voice. "I left early myself, actually, at about three. We've got kind of a relaxed schedule these days. But Peter was definitely still here when I took off. I remember waving good-bye."

I have a sudden and vivid mental image of Peter Zell, three o'clock yesterday afternoon, watching his boss's beautiful and self-possessed secretary leave for the day. She gives him a friendly indifferent wave, and my man Zell nods nervously, hunched over his desk, pushing his glasses up the bridge of his nose.

"And now, if you'll excuse me," says Naomi Eddes abruptly, "I have to go back to work."

"Sure," I say, nodding politely, thinking, *I didn't ask you to come in. I didn't ask you to stay.* "Oh, Ms. Eddes? One more thing. What were you doing at the McDonald's this morning, when the body was discovered?"

In my inexperienced estimation, this question flusters Ms. Eddes—she looks away, and a trace of a blush dances across her cheeks—but then she gathers herself and smiles and says, "What was I doing? I go there all the time."

"To the McDonald's on Main Street?"

"Almost every morning. Sure. For coffee."

"There's a lot of places closer to here, for coffee."

"They have good coffee."

"Then why didn't you come in?"

"Because—because I realized at the last minute that I had forgotten my wallet."

I fold my arms and draw myself up to full height. "Is that true, Ms. Eddes?"

She folds her own arms, mirrors my stance, looks up to meet

my eyes. "Is it true that this is a routine investigation?"

And then I'm watching her walk away.

* * *

"It's the short fella you're asking about, is that correct?"

"Pardon me?"

The old security officer is exactly where I left him, his chair still swiveled to face the elevator bank, as if he's been frozen in this position, waiting, the whole time I was working upstairs.

"The fella who died. You said you were on a murder, up at Merrimack Life."

"I said I was investigating a suspicious death."

"That's fine. But it's the short fella? Little squirrelly? Spectacles?"

"Yes. His name was Peter Zell. Did you know him?"

"Nope. Except I knew everybody who worked in the building, to say hello to. You're a cop, you said?"

"A detective."

The old man's leathery face contorts itself for a split second into the distant sad cousin of a smile. "I was in the Air Force. Vietnam. For a while, when I got home, I used to want to be a cop."

"Hey," I say, offering up by rote the meaningless thing my father always used to say, when confronted with any kind of pessimism or resignation. "It's never too late."

"Well." The security officer coughs hoarsely, adjusts his battered cap. "It is, though."

A moment passes in the dreary lobby, and then the guard says, "So last night, the skinny guy, he got picked up after work by someone in a big red pickup truck."

"A pickup truck? Running gas?"

No one has gas, no one but cops and army. OPEC stopped exporting oil in early November, the Canadians followed suit a couple of weeks later, and that was it. The Department of Energy opened the Strategic Petroleum Reserve on January 15, along with strictly enforced price controls, and everybody had gas for about nine days, and then they didn't anymore.

"Not gas," says the guard. "Cooking oil, by the smell of it."

I nod, excited, take a step forward, smooth my mustache with the heel of one hand. "Did Mr. Zell get in the truck willingly or unwillingly?"

"Well, no one pushed him in there, if that's what you mean. And I didn't see any gun or anything."

I take out my notebook, click open a pen. "What did it look like?"

"It was a performance Ford, an old model. Eighteen-inch Goodyears, no chains. Smoke billowing out the back, you know, that nasty vegetable-oil smoke."

"Right. You get a license plate?

"I did not."

"And did you get a look at the driver?"

"Nope. Didn't know I'd have a reason to." The old man blinks, bemused, I think, by my enthusiasm. "He was a big fella, though. Pretty sure of that. Heavyset, like."

I'm nodding, writing quickly. "And you're sure it was a red pickup?"

"It was. A red, medium-body pickup truck with a standard bed.

And there was a big flag airbrushed on the driver's side wall."

"What flag?"

"What flag? United States," he says diffidently, as if unwilling to acknowledge the existence of any other kind.

I write quietly for a minute, faster and faster, the pen scratching in the silence of the lobby, the old man looking abstractedly at me, head tilted, eyes distant, like I'm something in a museum case. Then I thank him and put away my blue book and my pen and step out onto the sidewalk, the snow falling on the red brick and sandstone of downtown, and I'm standing there for a second watching it all in my head, like a movie: the shy, awkward man in the rumpled brown suit, climbing up into the shotgun seat of a shiny red pickup running a converted engine, driving off into the last hours of his life.

3.

There's a dream I used to have, pretty consistently once or twice a week, going back to when I was right around twelve years old.

The dream featured the imposing figure of Ryan J. Ordler, the long-serving chief of the Concord Police Department, long-serving even back then, whom in real life I would see every summer at the Family and Friends Picnic Potluck, where he would awkwardly tousle my hair and flip me a buffalo-head nickel, like he did for all the children present. In the dream, Ordler stands at attention in full uniform, holding a Bible, on which I place my right hand, palm down, and I'm repeating after him, pledging to enforce and uphold the law, and then he's solemnly presenting me with my gun, my badge, and I salute him and he salutes me back and the music swells—there is music in the dream—and I am made detective.

In real life, one brutally cold morning late last year, I returned to the station at 9:30 a.m., after a long night spent patrolling Sector 1, to find a handwritten note in my locker instructing me to report to the office of the DCA. I stopped in the break room, splashed water on my face, and took the stairs two at a time. The Deputy Chief of Administration at that time was Lieutenant Irina Paul, who had held the post a little more than six weeks, after the abrupt departure of Lieutenant Irvin Moss.

"Good morning, ma'am," I say. "Did you need something?"

"Yeah," Lieutenant Paul says, looks up and then back down at what's in front of her, a thick black binder with the words U.S. DEPARTMENT OF JUSTICE stenciled on the side. "Gimme one sec, Officer."

"Sure," I say, looking around, and then there's another voice, deep and rumbling, from the far end of the office: "Son."

It's Chief Ordler, in uniform but no tie, collar open, shrouded in semidarkness at the small office's only window, arms crossed, a sturdy oak tree of a human being. A wave of trepidation washes over me, my spine straightens, and I say, "Morning, sir."

"Okay, young man," says Lieutenant Paul, and the chief nods minutely, gently, tilting his head toward the DCA, letting me know to pay attention. "Now. You were involved in an incident two nights ago, in the basement."

"What—oh."

My face flushes, and I begin to explain: "One of the new people—newer, I should say—" I've only been on the force for sixteen months myself, "—one of the newer people brought in a suspect for preventive detention under Title XVI. A vagrant. A homeless individual, that is."

"Right," says Paul, and I see that she's got an incident report in front of her, and I'm not liking this at all. I'm sweating now, literally sweating in the cold office.

"And he was, the officer I mean, he was being verbally abusive to the suspect, in a way I felt was inappropriate and contrary to department guidelines."

"And you took it open yourself to intervene. To, let's see," and she looks down at her desk again, flips over the onion-skin pink paper of the report, "to recite the relevant statute in an aggressive and threatening manner."

"I'm not sure that I would characterize it that way." I glance at the chief, but he's looking at Lieutenant Paul, her show.

"It's just, I happened to know the gentleman—sorry, the, I should say, the suspect. Duane Shepherd, Caucasian male, age fifty-five." Paul's gaze, unwavering but distant, disinterested, is flustering me, as is the quiet presence of the chief. "Mr. Shepherd was my scout leader when I was a kid. And he used to work as an electric-crew foreman, in Penacook, but I gather he's had a hard time. With the recession."

"Officially," says Paul quietly, "I believe it is a depression."

"Yes, ma'am."

Lieutenant Paul looks down at the incident report again. She looks exhausted.

This conversation is taking place in early December, deep in the cold months of uncertainty. On September 17 the asteroid went into conjunction, got too close to the Sun to be observed, too close for new readings to be taken. So the odds, which had been inching steadily upward since April—three percent chance of impact, ten percent chance, fifteen—were stalled, late fall and early winter, at fifty-three percent. The world economy went from bad to worse, much worse. On October 12 the president saw fit to sign the first round of IPSS legislation, authorizing an influx of federal money to state and local law-enforcement agencies. In Concord, this meant all these young kids, younger than me, some recent high-school dropouts, all of them rushed through a sort of quasi-police-academy boot camp. Privately, McConnell and I call them the Brush Cuts, because they all seemed to have that same haircut, the same baby faces and cold eyes and swagger.

The thing with Mr. Shepherd was not, in truth, my first run-in with my new colleagues.

The chief clears his throat, and Paul leans back, happy to let him take over. "Son, listen. There is not a person in this building who does not want you here. We were proud to welcome you to the patrol division, and were it not for the present unusual circumstances—"

"Sir, I was first in my class at the academy," I say, aware that I am talking loudly and that I have interrupted Chief Ordler, but I can't stop, I keep going. "I have a perfect attendance record, zero violations, zero citizen complaints pre- and post-Maia."

"Henry," says the chief gently.

"I am trusted implicitly, I believe, by Watch Command."

"Young man," says Lieutenant Paul sharply, and holds up her hand. "I think you misunderstand the situation."

"Ma'am?"

"You're not being fired, Palace. You're being promoted."

Chief Ordler steps forward into a slant of sunlight from the small window. "We think that, given the circumstances and your particular talents, you'd be better off in a seat upstairs."

I gape at him. I scramble for and then recover the power of

speech. "But department regulation says that an officer must put in two years and six months on patrol before becoming eligible for service in the detective unit."

"We're going to waive that requirement," Paul explains, folding up the incident report and dropping it in the trash. "I think we'll also not bother with reclassifying your 401(k), just for the time being."

This is a joke, but I don't laugh; it's all I can do to stay upright. I'm trying to get oriented, trying to form words, thinking *new times* and thinking *a seat upstairs* and thinking *this is not how it happens, in the dream.*

"Okay, Henry," says Chief Ordler mildly. "That's the end of the meeting."

* * *

I learn later on that it's Detective Harvey Telson whose spot I'm filling, Telson having taken an early retirement, gone "Bucket List" like many others were doing by this point, by December, heading off to do the things they've always wanted to do: speed around in race cars, experiment with long-suppressed romantic or sexual inclinations, track down the old bully and punch him in the face. Detective Telson, as it turns out, always wanted to race yachts. America's Cup kind of stuff. A lucky break for me.

Twenty-six days after the meeting in her office, two days after the asteroid emerged from conjunction with the Sun, Lieutenant Paul quit the force and moved to Las Vegas to be with her grown children.

I don't have the dream anymore, the one where Ordler lays my hand on the Bible and makes me a detective. There's another dream that I've been having a lot instead.

* * *

Like Dotseth says, the cellular phones are getting dicey. You dial, you wait, sometimes you get through and sometimes not. A lot of people are convinced that Maia is bending Earth's gravitational field, our magnets or ions, or something, but of course the asteroid, still 450 million kilometers away, is having no more effect on cellphone service than on the weather. Officer Wilentz, our tech guy, he explained it to me once: cellular service is chopped up into sectors—cells—and basically the sectors are dropping out, the cells are dying, one by one. The telecom companies are losing service people because they can't pay them, because no one is paying their bill; they're losing their executives to the Bucket List; they're losing telephone poles to unrepaired storm damage, and they're losing long stretches of wire to vandals and thieves. So the cells are dying. As for all the other stuff, the smartphone stuff, the apps and the gizmos, forget it.

One of the five major carriers announced last week that it's begun winding down its business, describing this fact in a newspaper advertisement as an act of generosity, a "gift of time" to the company's 355,000 employees and their families, and warning customers to expect total suspension of service within the next two months. Three days ago, Culverson's *New York Times* had the Department of Commerce predicting total collapse of telephony by late spring, with the administration supposedly crafting a plan to nationalize the industry.

"Meaning," McGully noted, chortling, "total collapse by early spring."

Sometimes, when I notice that I have a strong signal, I'll make a call real quick, so as not to waste it.

"Oh, man. Man oh man, what in hell do *you* want?"

"Good afternoon, Mr. France. This is Detective Henry Palace, from the Concord Police Department."

"I know who it is, okay? I know who it is."

Victor France sounds riled, agitated; he always sounds like that. I'm sitting in the Impala outside Rollins Park now, a couple blocks from where Peter Zell used to live.

"Come on, Mr. France. Take it easy, now."

"I don't want to take it easy, okay? I hate your guts. I hate it when you call me, okay?" I hold the phone an inch or two away from my ear as France's scattershot snarl pours from the earpiece. "I'm trying to live my life here, man. Is that such an awful and terrible thing, just to live my life?"

I can picture him, the thug resplendent: loops of chain drooping from black jeans, skull-and-crossbones pinky ring, scrawny wrists and forearms crawling with several species of tattoo snakes. The rat-eyed face twisted with melodramatic outrage, having to answer the phone, take orders from a stuck-up egghead policeman like myself. But look, I mean, that's what you get for being a drug dealer, and moreover for getting caught, at this juncture in American history. Victor may not know by heart the full text of the Impact Preparation Security and Stabilization Act, but he's got the gist.

"I don't need much help today, Mr. France. A little research project, is all."

France blows out one last exasperated "oh man oh man," and then he comes around, just like I knew he would. "All right, okay. All right, what is it?"

"You know a little bit about cars, don't you?"

"Yeah. Sure. I mean, what, Detective, what, you calling me to fill your tires?"

"No, thank you. The last few weeks, people have started converting their cars to vegetable-oil engines."

"No shit. You seen gas prices lately?" He clears his throat noisily, spits.

"I'm trying to find out who did one such conversion. It's a midsize red pickup, a Ford. American flag painted on the side. You think you can handle that?"

"Maybe. And what if I can't?"

I don't answer. I don't have to. France knows the answer.

One of the most striking effects of the asteroid, from a law-enforcement perspective, has been the resulting spike in drug use and drug-related crime, with skyrocketing demand for every category of narcotic, for opiates, for Ecstasy, for methamphetamine, for cocaine in all its varieties. In small towns, in docile suburbs, farming communities, everywhere—even midsize cities like Concord, which had never experienced serious narcotics crime in the past. The federal government, after some tacking back and forth in the summer and fall, late last year resolved on a firm and uncompromising law-and-order stance. The IPSS Act incorporated provisions stripping the right of habeas corpus and other due-process protections from anyone accused of importing, processing, growing, or distributing controlled substances of all kinds.

These measures were deemed necessary "in the interest of controlling violence, promoting stability, and encouraging productive economic activity in the time remaining before impact."

Personally, I do know the full text of the legislation.

The car is off and the wipers are still, and I'm watching as gray blobs of snow build up in uneven slopes on the windshield.

"All right, man, all right," he says. "I'll figure out who juiced the truck. Give me a week."

"I wish I could, Victor. I'll call you tomorrow."

"Tomorrow?" He heaves an extravagant sigh. "Asshole."

The irony is, pot is the one exception. The use of marijuana has been decriminalized, in a so-far-unsuccessful effort to dampen demand for the harder and more societally destabilizing drugs. And the amount of marijuana I found on Victor France's person was five grams, small enough that it could easily have been for his personal use, except that the way I discovered it was that he tried to sell it to me as I was walking home from the Somerset Diner on a Saturday afternoon. Whether to make an arrest, under those ambiguous circumstances, is at the discretion of the officer, and I have decided in France's case not to exercise that discretion—conditionally.

I could lock Victor France up for six months on Title VI, and he knows it, and so at last he emits a long, agitated noise, a sigh filled with gravel.

Six months is hard time, when it's all the time you've got left.

"You know, a lot of cops are quitting," says France. "Moving to Jamaica and so forth. Did you ever think about that, Palace?"

"I'll talk to you tomorrow."

I hang up and put the phone in the glove box and start the car.

No one is really sure—even those of us who have read the eight-hundred-page law from beginning to end, scored it and underlined it, done our best to keep current with the various amendments and codicils—not a hundred percent sure what the "Preparation" parts of IPSS are supposed to be, exactly. McGully likes to say that sometime around late September they'll start handing out umbrellas.

* * *

"Yeah?"

"Oh—I'm sorry. Is this—is this Belknap and Rose?"

"Yeah."

"I have a request for you."

"Don't get your hopes up. Not a lot left in here. We been looted twice, and our wholesalers are basically AWOL. Want to come in and see what's left, I'm here most days."

"No, excuse me, my name is Detective Henry Palace, with the Concord Police Department. Do you have copies of your register receipts from the last three months?"

"What?"

"If you do, I wonder if I could come down there and see them. I'm looking for the purchaser of one house-label belt, in black, size XXL."

"Is this a joke?

"No, sir."

"I mean, are you joking?"

"No, sir."

"All right, buddy."

"I'm investigating a suspicious death, and the information might be material."

"*Alllll* right, buddy."

"Hello?"

* * *

Peter Zell's townhouse, 14 Matthew Street Extension, is a new building, cheap construction, with just four small rooms: living room and kitchen on the first floor, bedroom and bathroom upstairs. I linger on the threshold, recalling the relevant text from *Criminal Investigation* advising me to work slowly, divide the house into a grid, take each quadrant in its turn. Then the thought of the Farley and Leonard—my reflexive reliance on it—reminds me of Naomi Eddes: *it sounds like you're quoting from a textbook or something.* I shake that off, run a hand over my mustache, and step inside.

"Okay, Mr. Zell," I say to the empty house. "Let's have a look."

The first quadrant gives me precious little to work with. A thin beige carpet, an old coffee table with ring-shaped stains. A small but serviceable flat-screen TV, wires snaking up from a DVD player, a vase of chrysanthemums that turn out, on close inspection, to be made of fabric and wire.

Most of Zell's bookshelf space is given over to his professional interests: math, advanced math, ratios and probabilities, a thick history of actuarial accounting, binders from the Bureau of Labor Statistics and the National Institutes of Health. Then he's got one shelf where all the personal stuff sits, as if quarantined, all the nerdy sci-fi and fantasy stuff, *Battlestar Galactica: The Complete Series*, vintage D&D rulebooks, a book on the mythological and philosophical underpinnings of *Star Wars*. A small armada of spaceship miniatures is suspended from wires in the doorway to the kitchen, and I duck to avoid them.

In the pantry are nine boxes of cereal, carefully alphabetized: Alpha-Bits, Cap'n Crunch, Cheerios, and so on. There is one empty slot in the neat row, like a missing tooth between the Frosted Flakes and the Golden Grahams, and my mind automatically fills in the missing box: Fruity Pebbles. A stray candy-pink grain confirms my hypothesis.

"I like you, Peter Zell," I say, carefully closing the pantry door. "You, I like."

Also in the kitchen, in an otherwise empty drawer beside the sink, is a pad of plain white paper, with writing on the top sheet that says, *Dear Sophia*.

My heart catches on a beat, and I breathe and I pick up the pad, flip it over, rifle through the pages, but that's all there is, one sheet of paper with the two words, *Dear Sophia*. The handwriting is precise, careful, and you can tell, you can feel that this was not a casual note Zell was writing, but an important document, or was meant to be.

I tell myself to remain calm, because it could after all be nothing, though my mind is blazing with it, thinking that whether it's the start of an aborted suicide note or not, it is definitely *something*.

I tuck the pad into the pocket of my blazer, walk up the stairs, thinking, who is Sophia?

The bedroom is like the living room, sterile and unornamented, the bed haphazardly made. A single framed print hangs over the bed, a signed still from the original *Planet of the Apes* film. In the closet hang three suits, all in dull shades of brown, and two threadbare brown belts. In a small, chipped-wood night table beside the bed, in the second drawer down, is a shoebox, wrapped tightly in duct tape, with the number 12.375 written on the outside in the same precise handwriting.

"Twelve point three seven five," I murmur. And then, "What is this?"

I tuck the shoebox box under my arm and stand up, take a look at the one photograph in the room: it's a small print in a cheap frame, a school picture of a boy, maybe ten or eleven years old, thin yellow flyaway hair, gawky grin. I tug it from the frame and flip it over, find careful handwriting on the back. *Kyle, February 10.* Last year. Before.

I use the CB to raise Trish McConnell.

"Hey," I say, "it's me. Were you able to locate the victim's family?"

"Yes, indeed."

Zell's mother is dead, as it turns out, buried here in Concord, up at Blossom Hill. The father is living at Pleasant View Retirement, suffering the opening phases of dementia. The person to whom Mc-Connell delivered the bad news is Peter's older sister, who works as a midwife at a private clinic near Concord Hospital. Married, one child, a son. Her name is Sophia.

* * *

On my way out, I stop again on the threshold of Peter Zell's house, awkwardly carrying the shoebox and the photograph and the white notepad, feeling the weight of the case and balancing it against an ancient memory: a policeman standing in the doorway of my childhood home on Rockland Road, hatless and somber, calling, "Anybody home?" into the morning darkness.

Me standing at the top of the stairs, in a Red Sox jersey, or it might have been a pajama top, thinking my sister is probably still asleep, hoping so anyway. I've already got a pretty good idea what the policeman's there to say.

* * *

"Let me guess, Detective," says Denny Dotseth, "We've got another 10-54S."

"Not a new one, actually. I wanted to touch base with you about Peter Zell."

I'm easing the Impala down Broadway, hands at ten and two. There's a New Hampshire state trooper parked at Broadway and Stone, engine on, the blue lights slowly rotating on the roof, a machine gun clutched in his hand. I nod slightly, raise two fingers off the wheel, and he nods back.

"Who's Peter Zell?" says Dotseth.

"The man from this morning, sir."

"Oh, right. Hey, you hear they named the big day? When we'll know where she comes down, I mean. April 9."

"Yep. I heard."

Dotseth, like McGully, likes to keep up-to-date on every unfolding detail of our global catastrophe. At the last suicide scene, not Zell's but the one before that, he talked excitedly for ten minutes about the war on the Horn of Africa, the Ethiopian army swarming into Eritrea to avenge ancient grievances in the time remaining.

"I thought it made sense to present you with what I've learned so far," I say. "I know your impression from this morning, but I think this might be a homicide, I really do."

Dotseth murmurs, "Is that a fact?" and I take that as a go-ahead, give him my sense of the case thus far: The incident at Merrimack Life and Fire, on Halloween. The red pickup truck, burning vegetable oil, that took the victim away the night he died. My hunch on the belt from Belknap and Rose.

All of this the assistant AG receives with a toneless "interesting," and then he sighs and says, "What about a note?"

"Uh, no. No note, sir."

I decide not to tell him about *Dear Sophia*, because I feel fairly certain that whatever that is, it is *not* an aborted suicide note—but Dotseth will think it was, he'll say, "There you go, young man, you're barking up the wrong tree." Which he pretty clearly thinks I'm doing anyway.

"You got some straws to grasp at there," is what he says. "You're not going to refer this case to Fenton, are you?"

"I am, actually. I already did. Why?"

There's a pause, and then a low chuckle. "Oh, no reason."

"What?"

"Hey, listen, kid. If you really think you can build a case, of course I'll take a look. But don't forget the context. People are killing themselves right and left, you know? For someone like the fella you're describing, someone without a lot of friends, with no real support system, there's a powerful social incentive to join the herd."

I keep my mouth shut, keep driving, but this line of reasoning I do not like. *He did it because everyone else is doing it?* It's like Dotseth is accusing the victim of something: cowardice, perhaps, or mere faddishness, some color of weakness. Which, if in fact Peter Zell *was* murdered, murdered and dragged into a McDonald's and left in that bathroom like meat, only adds insult to injury.

"I'll tell you what," says Dotseth genially. "We'll call it an attempted murder."

"Sorry, sir?"

"It's a suicide, but you're attempting to make it a murder. Have a great day, Detective."

* * *

Driving down School Street there's an old-time-style ice-cream parlor on the south side of the road, right where you pass the YMCA, and today it looks like they're doing a pretty brisk business, snow or no snow, dairy prices or no dairy prices. There's a nice-looking young couple, early thirties maybe, they've just stepped outside with their colorful cones. The woman gives me a small tentative friendly-policeman wave, and I wave back, but the man looks at me dead-eyed and unsmiling.

People in the main are simply muddling along. Go to work, sit at your desk, hope the company is still around come Monday. Go to the store, push the cart, hope there's some food on the shelves today. Meet your sweetheart at lunch hour for ice cream. Okay, sure, some people have chosen to kill themselves, and some people have chosen to go Bucket List, some people are scrambling around for drugs or "wandering around with their dicks out," as McGully likes to say.

But a lot of the Bucket Listers have returned, disappointed, and a lot of newly minted criminals and wild pleasure-seekers have found themselves in jail, waiting in terrified solitude for October.

So, yeah, there are differences in behavior, but they are on the margins. The main difference, from a law-enforcement perspective, is more atmospheric, harder to define. I would characterize the mood, here in town, as that of the child who isn't in trouble yet, but knows he's going to be. He's up in his room, waiting, "Just wait till your father gets home." He's sullen and snappish, he's on edge. Confused, sad, trembling against the knowledge of what's coming next, and right on the edge of violence, not angry but anxious in a way that can easily shade into anger.

That's Concord. I can't speak to the mood in the rest of the world, but that's pretty much it around here.

*   *   *

I'm back at my desk on School Street, back in Adult Crimes, and I'm carefully cutting away the duct tape that holds the lid of the shoebox, and for the second time since I met her I hear the voice of Naomi Eddes—standing there with her arms crossed, staring at me, *so what are you looking for, anyway?*

"This," I say, when I have the lid off the box and I'm staring inside. "This is what I'm looking for."

Peter Zell's shoebox contains hundreds of newspaper articles, magazine pages, and items printed from the Internet, all relating to Maia and its impending impact with Earth. I lift the first of the articles off the top of the stack. It's from April 2 of last year, an Associated Press squib about the Palomar Observatory at Caltech and the unusual but almost certainly harmless object the scientists there had spotted, which had been added to the Potentially Hazardous Asteroid list at the Minor Planet Center. The author concludes the article by dryly noting that "whatever its size or composition, this mysterious new object's odds of impacting Earth are estimated at 0.000047 percent, meaning there is a one in 2,128,000 chance." Zell, I note, has carefully circled both numbers.

The next item in the shoebox is a Thomson Reuters piece from two days later, headlined "Newly Discovered Space Object Largest in Decades," but the article itself is rather mundane, a single paragraph, no quotes. It estimates the size of the object—in those early days still being referred to by its astronomical designation of $2011GV_1$—as "among the largest spotted by astronomers in some decades, possibly as large as three kilometers in diameter." Zell has circled that estimate, too, faintly, in pencil.

I keep reading, fascinated by this grim time capsule, reliving the recent past from Peter Zell's perspective. In each article, he has circled or underlined numbers: the steadily increasing estimates of Maia's size, its angle in the sky, its right ascension and declination, its odds of impact as they inch higher, week by week, month by month. He's put neat boxes around each dollar amount and percentage of stock-value loss in an early-July *Financial Times* survey of the desperate emergency actions of the Fed, the European Central Bank, and the International Monetary Fund. He has, too, articles on the political side: legislative wrangling, emergency laws, bureaucratic shuffles at the Justice Department, the refunding of the FDIC.

I am picturing Zell, late at night, every night, at his cheap kitchen table, eating cereal, his glasses resting at his elbow, marking up these clippings and printouts with his mechanical pencil, considering every unfolding detail of the calamity.

I pluck out a *Scientific American* piece dated September 3, asking in big bold letters, "How Could We Not Have Known?" The short answer, which I already know, which everyone knows by now, is that 2011GV$_1$'s highly unusual elliptical orbit brings it close enough to be visible from Earth only once every seventy-five years, and seventy-five years ago we weren't looking, we had no program in place to spot and track Near-Earth Asteroids. Zell has circled "75" each time it appears; he's circled 1 in 265 million, the now-moot odds of such an object existing; he's circled 6.5 kilometers, which by then had been determined to be Maia's true diameter.

The rest of the *Scientific American* article gets complicated: astrophysics, perihelions and aphelions, orbital averaging and values of elongation. My head is spinning reading all of this, my eyes hurt, but Zell has clearly read every word, thickly annotated every page of it, made dizzying calculations in the margins, with arrows leading to and from the circled statistics and amounts and astronomical values.

Carefully I place the cover back on the box, look out the window.

I place my long flat palms on the top of the box, stare again at the number on the side of the box, written firmly, in black marker: 12.375.

I'm feeling it again—something—I don't know what. But something.

* * *

"May I speak to Sophia Littlejohn? This is Detective Henry Palace of the Concord Police Department."

There's a pause, and then a woman's voice, polite but unsettled.

"This is she. But I think you folks have got your wires crossed. I already spoke to someone. This is—you're calling about my brother, right? They called earlier today. My husband and I both spoke to the officer."

"Yes, ma'am. I know."

I'm on the landline, at headquarters. I'm judging Sophia Littlejohn, picturing her, painting myself a picture from what I know, and from the tone of her voice: alert, professional, compassionate. "Officer McConnell gave you the unfortunate news. And I'm really sorry to be bothering you again. As I said, I'm a detective, and I just have a few questions."

As I'm talking I'm becoming aware of an unpleasant gagging noise; over there on the other side of the room is McGully, his black Boston Bruins scarf twisted up over his head into a comedy noose, going "erk-erk." I turn away, hunch over my chair, holding the receiver close to my ear.

"I appreciate your sympathy, Detective," Zell's sister is saying. "But I honestly don't know what else I can tell you. Peter killed himself. It's awful. We weren't that close."

First Gompers. Then Naomi Eddes. And now the guy's own sister. Peter Zell certainly had a lot of people in his life with whom he wasn't that close.

"Ma'am, I need to ask if there's any reason your brother would have been writing you a letter. A note of some kind, addressed to you?"

On the other end of the phone, a long silence. "No," says Sophia Littlejohn finally. "No. I have no idea."

I let that hang there for a moment, listen to her breathe, and then I say, "Are you sure you don't know?"

"Yes. I am. I'm sure. Officer, I'm sorry, I don't really have time to talk right now."

I'm leaning all the way forward in my chair. The radiator makes a metallic chugging noise from its corner. "What about tomorrow?"

"Tomorrow?"

"Yes. I'm sorry, but it really is very important that we speak."

"Okay," she says, after another pause. "Sure. Can you come to my home in the morning?"

"I can."

"Very early? Seven forty-five?"

"Anytime is fine. Seven forty-five is fine. Thank you."

There's a pause, and I look at the phone, wondering if she's hung up, or if the landlines are now having trouble, too. McGully tousles my hair on his way out, bowling bag swinging from his other hand.

"I loved him," says Sophia Littlejohn suddenly, hushed but forceful. "He was my little brother. I loved him so much."

"I'm sure you did, ma'am."

I get the address, and I hang up, and I sit for a second staring out the window, where the slush and sleet just keep on coming down.

"Hey. Hey, Palace?"

Detective Andreas is slumped in his chair on the far side of the room, tucked away in darkness. I hadn't even known he was in the room.

"How you doing, Henry?" His voice is toneless, empty.

"Fine. How about you?" I'm thinking about that glistening pause, that lingering moment, wishing I could have been inside Sophia Littlejohn's head as she cycled through all the reasons her brother might have had for writing *Dear Sophia* on a piece of paper.

"I'm fine," Andreas says. "I'm fine."

He looks at me, smiles tightly, and I think the conversation is over, but it's not. "I gotta say, man," Andreas murmurs, shaking his head, looking over at me. "I don't know how you do it."

"How I do what?"

But he's just looking at me, not saying anything else, and from where I'm sitting across the room it looks like there are tears in his eyes, big pools of standing water. I look away, back out the window, just no idea what to say to the guy. No idea whatsoever.

4.

A loud and terrible noise is filling my room, a shrieking and violent eruption of sound rushing into the darkness, and I'm sitting up and I'm screaming. It's here, I'm not ready, my heart is exploding in my chest because it's here, it's early, it's happening now.

But it's just my phone. The shrieking, the horrendous noise, it's just the landline. I'm sweating, my hand clutched to my chest, shivering on my thin mattress on the floor that I call a bed.

It's just my stupid phone.

"Yeah. Hello?"

"Hank? What are you doing?"

"What am I doing?" I look at the clock. It's 4:45 a.m. "I'm sleeping. I was dreaming."

"I'm sorry. I'm sorry. But I need your help, I really do, Henny."

I breathe deeply, sweat cooling on my forehead, my shock and confusion rapidly fading into irritation. Of course. My sister is the only person who would be calling me at five o'clock in the morning, and she's also the only person who still calls me Henny, a miserable childhood nickname. It sounds like a vaudeville comedian or a small addled bird.

"Where are you, Nico?" I ask, my voice gruff with sleep. "Are you okay?"

"I'm at home. I'm flipping out." Home means the house where we grew up, where Nico still lives, our grandfather's renovated redbrick farmhouse, on one and a half rolling acres on Little Pond Road. I'm cycling through the litany of reasons my sister would be calling with such urgency at this ungodly hour. Rent money. A ride. Plane ticket, groceries. Last time, her bicycle had been "stolen," loaned to a friend of a friend at a party and never returned.

"So, what's going on?"

"It's Derek. He didn't come home last night."

I hang up, throw the phone on the ground, and try to fall back asleep.

* * *

What I'd been dreaming about was my high-school sweetheart, Alison Koechner.

In the dream, Alison and I are strolling with linked arms through the lovely downtown area of Portland, Maine, gazing through the window of a used-book store. And Alison's leaning gently on my arm, her wild bouquet of orchid-red curls tickling into my neck. We're eating ice cream, laughing at a private joke, deciding what movie to see.

It's the kind of dream that's hard to get back into, even if you can fall back asleep, and I can't.

* * *

At seven-forty it is bright and clear and cold and I am winding my way through Pill Hill, the upscale West Concord neighborhood that wraps around the hospital, where its surgeons and administrators and attending physicians live in tasteful colonials. These days a lot of these homes are patrolled by private-duty security guards, gun bulges under their winter coats, as if all of a sudden this is a Third World capital. There's no guard, though, at 14 Thayer Pond Road, just a wide lawn blanketed with snow so perfect and vivid in its new-fallen whiteness I almost feel bad tromping across it in my Timberlands to get to the front door.

But Sophia Littlejohn is not at home. She had to rush out early to perform an emergency delivery at Concord Hospital, a turn of events for which her husband is profusely apologetic. He meets me on the stoop wearing khaki slacks and a turtleneck, a gentle man with a trim golden beard carrying a mug of fragrant tea, explaining how Sophia often has irregular hours, especially now that most of the other midwives in her practice have quit.

"Not her, though. She's determined to do right by her patients, right up to the end. And believe it or not, there are plenty of new patients. My name is Erik, by the way. Would you care to come inside anyway?"

He looks slightly surprised when I say yes, says, "Oh, okay . . . great," steps back into the living room, and gestures me inside. The thing is, I've been up and dressed for two hours, waiting to learn more about Peter Zell, and his brother-in-law is bound to know something. Littlejohn leads me inside, takes my coat and hangs it on a hook.

"Can I offer you a cup of tea?"

"No, thanks. I won't take but a few minutes of your time."

"Well, good, because that's about what I have available," he says, and tips me a friendly little wink, makes sure I know his diffidence is playful. "I need to walk our son to school and myself to the hospital for nine o'clock."

He gestures me into an armchair and sits down himself, crossing his legs, relaxing. He has a broad gracious face, a wide and friendly mouth. There's something powerful but unthreatening about the man, like he's a friendly cartoon lion, the genial overseer of his pride.

"These must be difficult times to be a policeman."

"Yes, sir. You work at the hospital?"

"Yes. I've been there about nine years. I'm the director of Spiritual Services."

"Oh. And what is that, exactly?"

"Ah." Littlejohn leans forward, laces his fingers, clearly pleased with the question. "Anyone who walks through the doors of a hospital has needs beyond the strictly physical. I'm referring to the patients, of course, but also family members, friends, and, yes, even the doctors and nurses themselves." All this he presents in a smooth, confident disquisition, rapid and unfaltering. "It is my job to minister to such needs, however they might manifest themselves. I am, as you can imagine, rather busy these days."

His warm smile is unwavering, but I can hear the echoes in the single word, *busy*, see it in the big expressive eyes: the exhaustion, the long nights and wearying hours, trying to offer comfort to the perplexed and the terrified and the ill.

From the corner of my eye I'm catching flashes of my interrupted dream, pretty Alison Koechner as if she were sitting next to me, gazing out the window at the snow-frosted dogwoods and black tupelo.

"But—" Littlejohn clears his throat abruptly, looking significantly at my blue book and pen, which I have out and balanced on my lap. "You're here to ask about Peter."

"Yes, sir."

Before I can pose a specific question, Littlejohn sets in, speaking in the same tone, rapid and composed. He tells me how his wife and her brother had grown up here, in West Concord, not far from where we're sitting. Their mother is dead of cancer, twelve years ago, and the father is at Pleasant View Retirement with a host of physical problems, plus the early stages of dementia—very sad, very sad, but God's plans are for God alone to divine.

Peter and Sophia, he explains, have never been terribly close, not even as children. She was tomboyish, outgoing; he was nervous, inward, shy. Now that they both had careers, and Sophia her family, they socialized only rarely.

"We reached out to him once or twice, of course, when all this began, but without much success. He was in rather a bad place."

I look up, raise one finger to pause Littlejohn's onrushing tide of narrative.

"What do you mean, 'a bad place'?"

He takes a deep breath, as if weighing whether it's fair to say what he's about to, and I lean forward, pen poised above my book.

"Well, look. I have to tell you that he was extremely disturbed."

I tilt my head. "He was depressed, or disturbed?"

"What did I say?"

"You said disturbed."

"I meant depressed," says Littlejohn. "Would you excuse me a quick second?"

He rises before I can answer and walks to the far side of the room, allowing me a view into a bright and well-loved kitchen: a row of hanging pots, a gleaming refrigerator adorned with alphabet magnets, report cards, and school pictures.

Littlejohn is at the foot of the stairs, gathering together a navy blue backpack and a pair of child-size hockey skates from where they're slung over the banister. "Are we brushing teeth up there, Kyle?" he shouts. "We're at T-minus nine minutes, here."

A hollered "okay, dad" echoes down the steps, followed by the rattle of footsteps, a faucet going on, a door slamming open. The framed picture on Zell's dresser, the clumsily smiling lad. The Concord School District, I know, has remained open. A feature had run in the *Monitor*: the dedicated staff, learning for the sake of learning. Even in the newspaper pictures, you could see that the classrooms were half full. A quarter, even.

Littlejohn settles back in his chair, runs a hand through his hair. He's got the skates cradled in his lap. "Kid can play. He's ten years old, skates like Messier, no kidding. He'll play in the NHL one day, make me a millionaire." He smiles softly. "Alternate universe. Where were we?"

"You were describing your brother-in-law's mental state."

"Right, right. I'm thinking of our little summer party. We had a barbecue, you know, hot dogs, beer. The whole drill. And Peter, he was never the most social person, the most outgoing, but it seemed clear that he was sinking into a depression. There but not there, if you can see what I mean."

Littlejohn takes a deep breath, looks around the room, as if he's afraid of the eavesdropping ghost of Peter Zell. "You know, to tell you the truth, after that, we weren't crazy having him around Kyle. All of this, it's hard enough—on the boy—" His voice breaks, he clears his throat. "Excuse me."

I nod, writing, my mind moving quickly.

So what do we have, then? We have a man who, at work, appears to be basically disaffected, quiet, head down, registering no reaction to the coming calamity except for that one shocking outburst on Halloween. Then it turns out that he's squirreled away a massive and comprehensive trove of information on the asteroid, that he's privately obsessed with what he's shrugging off in public.

And now it seems that, at least according to his brother-in-law, outside the office he was not only affected but overwhelmed; distraught. The kind of man who would, after all, be inclined to take his own life.

Oh, Peter, I think. *What is your story, friend?*

"And this mood, this depression, it hadn't improved lately?"

"Oh, no. Heavens, no. To the contrary. It was much worse since, you know, since January. Since the final determination."

The final determination. Meaning the Tolkin interview. Tuesday, January 3. A *CBS News Special Report*. Garnered 1.6 billion viewers worldwide. I wait in silence for a moment, listening to Kyle's energetic footsteps overhead. Then I decide, what the heck, and I take out the small white pad of paper from my breast pocket and hand it to Erik Littlejohn. "What can you tell me about this?"

I watch while he reads it. *Dear Sophia.*

"Where did this come from?"

"Is that Peter Zell's handwriting, as far as you know?"

"Sure. I mean, I think so. As I said—"

"You didn't know him that well."

"Right."

"He was going to write something to your wife, before he died, and he changed his mind. Do you know what that might have been?"

"Well, a suicide note, presumably. An unfinished suicide note." He looks up, looks in my eyes. "What else would it be?"

"I don't know," I say, standing up, tucking away my little book. "Thanks very much for your time. And if you would just let Sophia know I'll be calling again to set up a time to talk."

Erik stands also, his brow furrowing. "You still need to speak to her?"

"I do."

"All right, sure." He nods, sighs. "This is a trial for her. All of it. But of course I'll let her know."

I get in the Impala but don't go anywhere, not yet. I sit outside the house for about a minute, until I see Littlejohn shepherding Kyle out and across the lawn, thick with unbroken snow like vanilla buttercream frosting. A goofy ten-year-old, tromping in oversized winter boots, pointy elbows jutting out from the pushed-up sleeves of his windbreaker.

At Zell's apartment, I saw the picture and I remember thinking he was an average-looking, even homely child. But now I'm revising that assessment, seeing him as his father sees him: a princeling, dancing in morning light as he marches across the snow.

* * *

I'm driving away and I'm thinking about the Tolkin interview, imagining Peter Zell on that night.

It's January 3, it's a Tuesday, and he's home from work, settled in his sterile gray living room, staring at the screen of his small TV.

On January 2, the asteroid $2011GV_1$, known as Maia, had at last emerged from conjunction with the Sun, was again observable from Earth, was at last sufficiently close and bright for the scientists to see it clearly, to gather new sets of data, to *know*. Observations were pouring in, being compiled and processed at one collection center, the NASA Jet Propulsion Lab, in Pasadena, California. What had been, since September, a fifty-fifty chance was about to be resolved— either one hundred percent, or zero.

So there's Peter Zell on his living room sofa with his latest accumulation of asteroid-related articles spread out in front of him, all the scientific discourse and anxious analysis finally boiling down to predictions and prayers, to *yes or no*.

CBS had won the bidding war for broadcast rights. The world was ending, maybe, but if it wasn't, they'd feast on the ratings coup for years. There was an elaborate preshow centered on the head engineer at JPL, Leonard Tolkin, the man overseeing that final burst of number crunching. "I'll be the one," he had promised David Letterman three weeks earlier, his smile twitching, "to give the good news." Pale, bespectacled, in a white lab coat, a central-casting government astronomer.

There's a countdown clock on the lower-right corner of the screen accompanying cheesy B-roll, tracking shots of Tolkin walking the hallways of the institute, scrawling columns of math on a dry-erase board, huddling with his subordinates around computer screens.

And there's short, paunchy, lonely Peter Zell in his apartment, watching in silence, surrounded by his articles, glasses perched on his nose, hands flat on his knees.

The program goes live, featuring the newsman Scott Pelley, square chinned and grave, gray hair and solemn made-for-television face. Pelley watches, on behalf of the world, as Tolkin emerges from the decisive meeting with a stack of manila folders clutched under one arm, peels off his horn-rimmed spectacles, and begins to sob.

Now, driving slowly in the direction of the Somerset Diner, I'm trying to capture the memory of someone else's feelings, trying to decide exactly what Peter Zell was experiencing in that moment. Pelley leans forward, all empathy, asks the magically stupid question that all the world needed to hear:

"So, then, Doctor. What are our options?"

Dr. Leo Tolkin trembling, almost laughing. "Options? There are no options."

And then Tolkin just keeps talking, babbling really, about how sorry he is, on behalf of the world astronomical community, how this event never could have been predicted, how they had studied every realistic scenario—small object, short lead time; large object, long lead time—but this, this never could have been imagined, an object with such a near perihelion, with such an epically long elliptical period, such a staggeringly large object—the odds of such an object's existence so vanishingly low as to be statistically equivalent to impossible. And Scott Pelley is staring at him, and all over the world people are sinking into grief or hysteria.

Because all at once there was no more ambiguity, no more doubt. All at once it was just a matter of time. Odds of impact one hundred percent. October 3. No options.

Many people remained glued to their televisions after the program ended, watching pundits and professors of astronomy and political figures stammering and weeping and contradicting one another on the various cable stations; waiting for the president's promised address to the nation, which ultimately did not materialize until noon the next day. Many people ran to the phones to try to reach loved ones, though all the circuits were jammed and would remain that way for the week that followed. Other people went out into the streets, bitter January weather notwithstanding, to commiserate with neighbors or strangers, or to engage in small acts of vandalism or petty mischief—a trend that would continue and culminate, in the Concord area at least, with a small wave of rioting on Presidents' Day.

I, personally, turned off the TV and went to work. I was in my fourth week as a detective, I had an arson case I was working on, and I had a strong suspicion, ultimately proved true, that the next day would be a busy and stressful one at police headquarters.

The question, though, is what about Peter Zell? What did he do, when the show was over? Whom did he call?

A summary review of the bare facts suggests that, behind his attempts to keep up a brave face, Zell had been despondent all along about the possibility of Earth's imminent destruction. And with the confirmation of that fact, it's not hard to imagine that on the night of January 3, seeing the bad news on television, he had been pitched past despondence and into a brutal depression. He had staggered around for eleven weeks in a haze of dread and then, two nights ago, had hung himself with a belt.

So why am I driving around Concord, trying to figure out who killed him?

I'm in the parking lot of the Somerset Diner, nestled at the three-way intersection of Clinton, South, and Downing. I'm contemplating the snow in the parking lot, churned up by the morning influx of pedestrians and bicyclists. I'm comparing this rutted, brown-and-white mess to the unbroken blanket of snow on the front lawn of the Littlejohns' house. If Sophia had really been called out for an emergency delivery this morning, she had left by catapult, or teleportation machine.

* * *

The walls of the Somerset, where you first come in, are lined with photographs of presidential candidates shaking hands with Bob Galicki, the former owner, now deceased. There's a picture of sallow Dick Nixon, one of stiff and unconvincing John Kerry, hand stiffly protruding like a broken piece of fence. Here's John McCain with his skull-face grin. John F. Kennedy, impossibly young, impossibly handsome, doomed.

The music from the stereo in the kitchen is Bob Dylan, something from *Street Legal*, which means Maurice is cooking, which augurs well for the quality of my lunch.

"Sit anywhere, honey," says Ruth-Ann, rushing past with a carafe of coffee. Her hands are withered but strong, steady around the thick black handle of the carafe. When I used to come here in high school, we would joke about Ruth-Ann's ancientness, whether she'd been hired for this gig or if they'd built the place around her. That was ten years ago.

I drink my coffee and ignore the menu, surreptitiously inspecting the faces of my fellow diners, weighing the relative melancholy in each of their eyes, the shell-shocked expressions. An old couple murmuring to each other, bent over their soup bowls. A girl, nineteen maybe, with an enervated stare, joggling a pallid baby on her knee. A fat businessman glaring angrily at the menu, a cigar clenched in the corner of his mouth.

Everybody is smoking, actually, dull gray tendrils curling up under every light fixture. It's like how it used to be in here, before they outlawed smoking in places of public accommodation, a law I strongly supported, as the only nonsmoker among my group of misfit high-school sophomores. The regulation is still on the books, but it's widely flouted, and CPD policy at this point is to look the other way.

I fiddle with my cutlery and sip my coffee and think.

Yes, Mr. Dotseth, it is true a lot of people are depressed, and a lot of those people have chosen to take their own lives. But I cannot, as a responsible police detective, accept this piece of context as evidence that Peter Zell was a 10-54S. If the coming destruction of the planet was enough to make people kill themselves, this restaurant would be empty. Concord would be a ghost town. There'd be no one left for Maia to kill, because we'd all be dead already.

"Three-egg omelet?"

"Whole wheat toast," I say, and then add, "Ruth-Ann, I got a question for you."

"I have an answer." She has not written down my order, but I've been ordering the same thing since I was eleven. "You go first."

"What do you make of all this hanger-town business? The suicides, I mean. Would you ever—"

Ruth-Ann growls, disgusted.

"You kidding? I'm Catholic, honey. No. Absolutely not."

See, I don't think I would either. My omelet arrives and I eat it slowly, staring into space, wishing it weren't so smoky in here.

5.

The expansion of Concord Hospital was announced with much fanfare eighteen months ago: a public–private partnership to add a new long-term-care wing and make wide-ranging improvements to pediatrics, to obstetrics/gynecology, and to the ICU. They broke ground last February, made steady progress through the spring, and then financing dried up and construction slowed and then stopped entirely by the end of July, leaving a maze of half-built hallways, towers of skeletal scaffolding, lots of awkward temporary arrangements made permanent, everybody walking in circles and giving one another wrong directions.

"The morgue?" says a white-haired volunteer in a cheerful red beret, consulting a handheld map. "Let's see . . . the morgue, the morgue, the morgue. Oh. Here." A pair of doctors rushes past, clutching clipboards, while the volunteer gestures at her map, which I can see is covered with scrawled emendations and exclamation points. "What you need is Elevator B, and Elevator B is . . . oh, dear."

My hands are twitching at my sides. One thing you don't want to do, when you're meeting Dr. Alice Fenton, is be late.

"Oh. That way."

"Thank you, ma'am."

Elevator B, according to the sign written in black permanent marker and taped above the buttons, goes either up—to oncology, to special surgery, to the pharmacy—or down, to the chapel, the custodial department, and the morgue. I step off, checking my watch, and hustle down the hallway past an office suite, past a supply closet, past a small black door with a white Christian cross on it, thinking, *oncology*—thinking, *you know what would really be awful right about now? Having cancer.*

But then I push open the thick metal doors of the morgue, and there's Peter Zell, his body laid out on the table in the center of the room, spot-lit dramatically by the arching bank of hundred-watt autopsy lights. And standing beside him, waiting for me, is the chief medical examiner of the state of New Hampshire. I stick out a hand in greeting. "Good morning, Dr. Fenton. Afternoon, sorry. Hello."

"Tell me about your corpse."

"Yes, ma'am," I say, letting my proffered hand float dumbly back to my side, and then I just stand there like an idiot, speechless, because Fenton is here, in front of me, standing in the stark white light of the morgue, one hand resting on the front end of her sleek silver cart like a captain at the tiller. She stares out from behind her famous perfect-circle glasses, waiting with an expression I've heard repeatedly described by other detectives, owlish and expectant and intense.

"Detective?"

"Yes," I say, again. "Okay." I get my act together and give Fenton what I've got.

I tell her about the crime scene, about the expensive belt, the absence of the victim's cell phone, the absence of a suicide note. As I speak, my eyes are flicking back and forth from Fenton to the items on her cart, the tools of the pathologist's trade: the bone saw, the chisel and the scissors, rows of vials for the collection of various precious fluids. Scalpels of a dozen different widths and keennesses, arrayed on clean white fabric.

Dr. Fenton remains silent and still through my recitation, and when at last I shut up she continues to stare, her lips pursed and her brow minutely furrowed.

"Okay, then," she says at last. "So, what the hell are we doing here?"

"Ma'am?"

Fenton's hair is steely gray and cut short, bangs running in a precise line across her forehead.

"I thought this was a suspicious death," she says, her eyes narrowing to two flashing points. "What I'm hearing from you does not comprise evidence of a suspicious death."

"Well, yes, no," I stammer. "Not evidence, per se."

"Not evidence, per se?" she echoes, in a tone that somehow makes me keenly aware of the basement's unusually low ceiling, the fact that I'm standing slightly stooped so as not to bang my forehead on the bank of overhead lights, whereas Dr. Fenton, at five foot three, stands fully upright, her spine military-straight, glaring at me from behind the glasses.

"Per Title LXII statute 630 of the criminal code of New Hampshire, as revised in January by the general court sitting in combined session," Fenton says, and I'm nodding, vigorously nodding to show her that I know all this, I've studied the binders, federal, state, and local, but she keeps going, "the OCME will not perform autopsies when it can be reasonably ascertained at the scene that the death was the result of suicide."

"Right," I say, muttering "yes" and "of course," until I can respond. "And it was my determination, ma'am, that there may have been some question of foul play."

"There were signs of struggle at the scene?"

"No."

"Signs of forced entry?

"No."

"Missing valuables?"

"Well, the, uh, he didn't have a phone. I think I mentioned that."

"Who are you again?"

"We haven't met, officially. My name is Detective Henry Palace. I'm new."

"Detective Palace," says Fenton, pulling on her gloves with a series of fierce movements, "my daughter has twelve piano recitals this season, and I am, at this very moment, missing one of them. Do you know how many piano recitals she will have next season?"

I don't know what to say to that. I really don't. So I just stand there for a minute, the tall and stupid man in the brightly lit room full of corpses.

"Okey-dokey then," says Alice Fenton with menacing cheer, turning to her cart of equipment. "This better be a goddamn murder."

She takes up her blade and I stare at the floor, feeling distinctly that what I'm supposed to do, here, is stand very quietly until she is through—but it's hard to do that, it really is, and as she begins the meticulous stepwise progression of her work, I look up and inch forward and watch her do it. And it is a glorious thing to watch, the cold and beautiful precision of the autopsy, Fenton in motion, a master moving meticulously through the steps of her craft.

The perseverance in this world, despite it all, of things done right.

Carefully Dr. Fenton cuts free the black leather belt and slips it off Zell's neck, measures the width of the band and the length from end to end. With brass calipers she takes the dimensions of the bruising beneath the eye, and the bruise from the belt buckle, digging up beneath the chin, yellowish and dry like a patch of sere terrain running up on either side toward his ears, an angry ragged *V*. And she's pausing, moment to moment, to take pictures of everything: the belt while it's still on the neck, the belt alone, the neck alone.

And then she cuts away the clothes, rinses off the insurance man's pallid body with a damp cloth, her gloved fingers moving rapidly over his midsection and his arms.

"What are you looking for?" I venture, and Fenton ignores me; I fall silent.

With a scalpel she tucks into the chest, and I take another step forward, now I'm standing beside her under the bright halo of the mortuary light, peering wide-eyed as she makes a deep Y-shaped incision, peels back the skin and the flesh beneath. I'm leaning way over the body, pushing my luck, as Fenton draws the dead man's blood, piercing a vein near the center of the heart, filling three vials in quick succession. And I realize at some point during all this that I'm barely breathing, that as I'm watching her go point by point through this process, weighing the organs and recording their weights, lifting the brain from the skull and turning it in her hands, I'm waiting for her impassive expression to sharpen, waiting for her to gasp or mutter "hmm" or turn to me in astonishment.

To have found whatever it is that will prove that Zell was killed, and not by his own hand.

Instead, at last, Dr. Fenton puts down her scalpel and flatly says, "Suicide."

I stare at her. "Are you sure?"

Fenton doesn't answer. She's moving rapidly back over to her cart, opening a box containing a thick roll of plastic bags, and peeling the top one off.

"Wait, ma'am. I'm sorry," I say. "What about that?"

"What about what?" I can feel myself growing desperate, a heat building in my cheeks, a squeak sneaking into my voice, like a child's voice. "That? Is that bruising? Above his ankle?"

"I saw that, yes," Fenton says coolly.

"Where did it come from?"

"We shall never know." She doesn't stop bustling, doesn't look at me, her flat voice glazed with sarcasm. "But we do know he didn't die from a bruise to the calf."

"But aren't there are other things we *do* know? Just in terms of determining the cause of death?" I'm saying this and I'm fully conscious of how ridiculous it is to be challenging Alice Fenton, but this can't be right. I scour my memory, flipping frantically in my mind through the pages of the relevant textbooks. "What about the blood? Do we perform a toxicity screening?"

"We would if we'd found anything to indicate it. Needle marks, muscles atrophied in suggestive patterns."

"But we can't just do it?"

Fenton laughs dryly, shaking open the plastic bag. "Detective, are you familiar with the state police forensic lab? On Hazen Drive?"

"I've never been there."

"Well, it is the only forensic laboratory in the state, and right now there is a new person running the show over there, and he is an idiot. He is an assistant to an assistant who is now chief toxicologist, since the real chief toxicologist left town in November to go study life drawing in Provence."

"Oh."

"Yes. Oh." Fenton's lip curls up with evident distaste. "Apparently it's what she's always wanted to do. It's a mess over there. Orders getting left on the table. It's a mess."

"Oh," I say again, and I turn to what remains of Peter Zell, the chest cavity yawning open on the table. I'm looking at him, at it, and I'm thinking how sad it is, because however he died, whether he killed himself or not, he's dead. I'm thinking the dumb and obvious thought that here was a person, and now he's gone and he's never coming back.

When I look up again, Fenton is standing beside me, and her voice has changed a little, and she's pointing, directing my gaze to Zell's neck.

"Look," she says. "What do you see?"

"Nothing," I say, confused. The skin is peeled back, revealing the soft tissue and muscle, the yellow-white of the bone beneath. "I don't see anything."

"Exactly. If someone had snuck up behind this man with a rope, or strangled him with bare hands, or even with this extremely expensive belt you've become fixated on, the neck would be a mess.

There would be tissue abrasion, there would be pools of blood from internal hemorrhaging."

"Okay," I say. I nod. Fenton turns away, back to her cart.

"He died by asphyxiation, Detective," she says. "He leaned forward, on purpose, into the knot of the ligature, his airway was sealed, and he died."

She zips the corpse of my insurance man back into the body bag from whence it came and slides the body back into its designated slot in the refrigerated wall. I'm watching all this mutely, stupidly, wishing I had more to say. I don't want her to leave.

"What about you, Dr. Fenton?"

"Excuse me?" She stops at the door, looks back.

"Why haven't you left, gone off to do whatever it is you've always wanted to do?"

Fenton tilts her head, looks at me like she's not exactly sure she understands the question. "This *is* what I've always wanted to do."

"Right. Okay."

The heavy gray door swings closed behind her, I rub my knuckles into my eyes, thinking, *what next?* Thinking, *what now?*

I stand there alone for a second, alone with Fenton's rolling cart, alone with the bodies in their cold lockers. Then I take one of the vials of Zell's blood off the cart, slip it into the inside pocket of my blazer, and go.

* * *

I find my way out of Concord Hospital, weaving my way through the unfinished corridors, and then, because it's already been a long and difficult day, because I am frustrated and exhausted and confused, and wanting to do nothing but figure out what I'm going to do next, my sister is waiting for me at my car.

Nico Palace in her ski hat and winter coat is seated cross-legged on the sloping front hood of the Impala, undoubtedly leaving a deep dent, because she knows I will hate that, and tapping ash from her American Spirit cigarette directly onto the windshield. I trudge toward her through the snow-crusted emptiness of the hospital parking lot, and Nico greets me with one hand raised, palm up, like an Indian squaw, smoking her cigarette, waiting.

"Come on, Hank," she says, before I can say a word. "I left you, like, seventeen messages."

"How'd you know where I was?"

"Why'd you hang up on me this morning?"

"How'd you know where I was?"

This is how we talk. I pull the sleeve of my jacket up over my hand and use it to brush ash off the car down into the snow.

"I called the station," says Nico. "McGully told me where I could find you."

"He shouldn't have done that," I say. "I'm working."

"I need your help. Seriously."

"Well, I'm seriously working. Would you climb down off the vehicle, please?"

Instead she casts out her legs and settles back on the windshield like she's spreading out on a beach chair. She's wearing the thick army-issue winter coat that was our grandfather's, and I can see where the brass buttons are etching little trails into the paint job of the department's Impala.

I wish Detective McGully hadn't told her where to find me.

"I don't mean to be a pain in the ass, but I'm freaking out, and what's the point of having a brother who's a cop if he won't help you?"

"Indeed," I say, and look at my watch. The snow has started again, very lightly, stray slow drifting flakes.

"Derek didn't come home last night. I know you're going to be like, okay, they had another fight, he disappeared. But that's the thing, Hen: we didn't fight this time. No argument, nothing. We made dinner. He said he had to go out. Said he wanted to take a walk. So I said sure. I cleaned up the kitchen, smoked a joint, and went to bed."

I scowl. My sister, I believe, loves the fact that she can smoke pot now, that her policeman brother can no longer lecture her sternly about it. For Nico, I think, this is a silver lining. She takes a last drag and pitches the butt into the snow. I crouch down and pick up the doused stub of cigarette between two fingers and hold it in the air. "I thought you cared about the environment."

"Not so much, anymore," she says.

Nico swivels back to a sitting position, wrapping the thick collar of the coat around her. My sister could be so beautiful if she just took care of herself—combed her hair, got some sleep every once in a while. She's like a picture of our mother that someone crumpled up and tried to smooth out again.

"So then it's midnight, and he's not back. I called him, no answer."

"So he went to a bar," I offer.

"I called all the bars."

"All of them?"

"*Yes*, Hen."

There are a lot more bars than there used to be. A year ago you had Penuche's, the Green Martini, and that was pretty much as far as it went. Now there are lots of places, some licensed, some pirated, some just basement apartments where someone has got a bathtub full of beer, a cash register, and an iPod set on shuffle.

"So he went to a friend's house."

"I called them. I called everyone. He's gone."

"He's not gone," I say, and what I'm not saying is the truth, which is that if Derek really had pulled a runner on her, it would be the best thing to happen to my sister in a long time. They had gotten married on January 8, that first Sunday after the Tolkin interview. That particular Sunday had set the record, apparently, for the most weddings on a single day, a record unlikely ever to be beaten, unless it's on October 2.

"Are you going to help me or not?"

"I told you, I can't. Not today. I'm on a case."

"God, Henry," she says, her studied insouciance abruptly gone, and she's hopping off the car and jabbing me in the chest with a forefinger. "I quit my job as soon as we knew this shit was really happening. I mean, why waste time at work?

"You worked three days a week at a farmers' market. I solve murders."

"Oh, excuse me. I'm sorry. My husband is missing."

"He's not really your husband."

"Henry."

"He'll be back, Nico. You know he will."

"Really? What makes you so sure?" She stamps her foot, eyes blazing, not waiting for an answer. "And what are you working on that's so important?"

I figure, what the heck, and I tell her about the Zell case, explain how I've just come from the morgue, that I'm developing leads, trying to impress upon her the seriousness of an ongoing police investigation.

"So wait. A hanger?" she says, sullen, peevish. She's only twenty-one years old, my sister. She's just a kid.

"Maybe."

"You just said the guy hung himself at the McDonald's."

"I said it *appeared* that way."

"And that's why you're too busy to take ten minutes to find my husband? Because some jerk-off killed himself at the *McDonald's*? In the goddamn bathroom?"

"Nico, come on."

"What?"

I hate it when my sister uses foul language. I'm old-fashioned. She's my sister.

"I'm sorry. But a man has died, and it's my job to find out how and why."

"Yeah, well, *I'm* sorry. Because a man is missing, and it's my man, and I happen to love him, okay?"

There's a hitch in her voice all of a sudden, and I know that's it, that's game over. She's crying, and I'll do whatever she wants.

"Oh, come on, Nico. Don't do that." It's too late, she's sobbing, open mouthed, violently pushing tears from her eyes with the back of her hands. "Don't do that."

"It's just, all of this." She gestures, a vague and woeful gesture encompassing all of the sky. "I can't be alone, Henry. Not now."

A bitter wind courses across the parking lot, flicking drifting snow upward into our eyes.

"I know," I say. "I know."

And then I'm gingerly stepping forward, gathering my little sister in my arms. The family joke was that she got the math genes and I got all the height. My chin is a good six inches up from the top of her head, her sobs burying themselves somewhere in my sternum.

"All right, kid. All right."

She backs out of my awkward embrace, stifles a final moan, and lights herself a fresh American Spirit, shading a gold-plated lighter against the wind as she sucks the thing to life. The lighter, like the coat, like the brand of cigarettes, was my grandfather's.

"So you'll find him?" she asks.

"I'll do my best, Nico. Okay? That's all I can do." I pluck the cigarette from the corner of her mouth and toss it under the car.

* * *

"Good afternoon. I'd like to speak to Sophia Littlejohn, if I could."

I've got a nice strong signal, out here in the parking lot.

"She's with a patient just now. May I ask who's calling?"

"Uh, sure. No—it's just—a friend of mine's wife is a patient of . . . gee, what do you even call a midwife? Doctor Littlejohn, is that what I would—?"

"No, sir. Just the name. Ms. Littlejohn."

"Okay, well, my friend's wife is a patient of . . . of Ms. Littlejohn, and I understood that she had gone into labor. Like, early this morning?"

"This morning?"

"Yeah. Late last night, early this morning? My friend left me a message, early this morning, and I could've sworn that's what he said. But it was garbled, his phone was all staticky, and—hello?"

"Yes, I'm here. There may be a mistake. I don't think Sophia was delivering. You said this morning?"

"I did."

"I'm sorry. What was your name?"

"Never mind. It's not a big deal. Never mind."

*　*　*

At headquarters I walk briskly past a trio of Brush Cuts in the break room, hanging around in a circle by the Coke machine, laughing like frat boys. I don't recognize any of them, and they don't recognize me. No one among them, I warrant, could quote from Farley and Leonard, not to mention the New Hampshire Criminal Code, not to mention the United States Constitution.

In Adult Crimes, I lay out what I've got for Detective Culverson: tell him about the house, the *Dear Sophia* note, Dr. Fenton's conclusions. He listens patiently, his fingers steepled together, and then he doesn't say anything for a long time.

"Well, you know, Henry," he begins slowly, and that's plenty, I don't want to hear the rest.

"I get what it looks like," I say. "I do."

"Hey. Listen. It's not my case." Culverson inclines his head slightly backward. "If you feel like you've got to solve it, you've got to solve it."

"I do, Detective. I really do."

"Okay, then."

I sit there for a second, and then I go back to my desk and pick up the landline and initiate my search for stupid Derek Skeve. First I repeat the calls that Nico has already made: the bars and the hospitals. I reach the men's prison and the new, auxiliary men's prison, I reach the Merrimack County sheriff's office, I reach admitting departments at Concord Hospital and New Hampshire Hospital and every other hospital I know of in three counties. But no one's got him, no one matching that description.

Outside, there's a thick clutch of God people clustered in the plaza, thrusting their pamphlets at passersby, hollering in gospel cadences about how prayer is all we've got left, prayer is our only salvation. I nod noncommittally and I keep on moving.

* * *

And now I'm lying in my bed and I'm not sleeping because it's Wednesday night, and it was Tuesday morning that I first looked into the dead eyes of Peter Zell, which means he was killed sometime on Monday night, and so maybe it's *almost* forty-eight hours since he got killed, or maybe the forty-eight hours have already passed. Either way, my window is sliding closed and I am nowhere near identifying and apprehending his murderer.

So I'm lying in my bed and I'm staring at the ceiling with my fists clenching and unclenching at my sides, and then I get up and open the blinds, and I look out the window, into the cloud-fogged blackness, past the handful of visible stars.

"You know what you can do?" I say softly, raising one finger and pointing it at the sky. "You can go fuck yourself."

PART TWO

....

Non-Negligible
Probabilities

....

Thursday, March 22

Right ascension 19 05 26.5
Declination -34 18 33
Elongation 79.4
Delta 3.146 AU

1.

"Wake up, sweetheart. Wakey-wakey-wakey."

"Hello?"

Last night, before going to bed, I unplugged the phone from the wall but left my cell phone on and set to vibrate, so tonight's pleasant dream of Alison Koechner has been interrupted not by the alarm-bell clamor of the landline, Maia shrieking into the windows and setting the world on fire, but by a gentle shivering rattle on the night table, a sensation that has inserted itself into my dream as the purr of a cat at ease in Alison's gentle lap.

And now Victor France is cooing at me. "Open your eyes, sweetheart. Crack open those big moody peepers, Mustache McGee."

I crack open my big moody peepers. Outside is darkness. France's voice is whispery and grotesque and insistent. I blink awake and catch one final sidewise glimpse of Alison, radiant in the auburn front room of our wooden house on Casco Bay.

"I'm so sorry to wake you, Palace. Oh, wait, I'm not sorry at all." France's voice dissolves into a queer little giggle. He's high on something, that's for sure; maybe marijuana, maybe something else. High as a satellite, my father used to say. "No, definitely not sorry."

I yawn again, crack my neck, and check the clock: 3:47 a.m.

"I don't know how you've been sleeping, Detective, but I have not been sleeping too well, me, personally. Every time I'm about to crash out I think to myself, now, Vic, baby, that's just dead hours. That's just golden hours right down the tubes." I'm sitting upright, feeling around on my night table for the light switch, grabbing my blue book and my pen, thinking, *he's got something for me*. He wouldn't be calling except that he's got something for me. "I'm keeping track, at my house, can you believe that? I've got this big poster with every day that's left, and every day I check one off."

Behind France's ragged monologue is the rapid-fire thump and robotic piano of electronic music, a large crowd hooting and chanting. Victor is partying in a warehouse somewhere, probably out on Sheep Davis Road, way east of the city proper.

"It's like an Advent calendar, you know what I mean, my man?" He slips into a horror-movie narrator's basso profondo. "An Advent calendar . . . of *doom*."

He cackles, coughs, cackles again. It's definitely not marijuana. Ecstasy is what I'm now thinking, though I shudder to think how France would have funded a purchase of Ecstasy, the prices for synthetics being as high as they are.

"Do you have information for me, Victor?"

"Ha! Palace!" Cackle, cough. "That's one of the things I like about you. You do not mess around."

"So do you have something for me?"

"Oh, my goodness gracious." He laughs, pauses, and I can picture him, twitching, skinny arms tensing, the teasing grin. In the silence the bass-and-drum behind him pipes through, tinny and distant. "Yeah," he says finally. "I do. I found it, about your pickup truck. I actually got it yesterday, but I waited. I waited until I was sure it would wake you up, and do you know why?"

"Because you hate me."

"Yes!" he hollers and cackles. "I hate you! You got a pen, beautiful?"

The red pickup truck with the flag on the side was converted to a waste-oil engine, according to Victor France, by a Croatian mechanic named Djemic, who runs a small shop near the burned-out Nissan dealership on Manchester Street. I don't know the place he's talking about, but it will be easy to find.

"Thank you, sir." I'm wide awake now, writing quickly, this is great, holy moly, and I'm feeling a surge of excitement and a wild rush of kindness toward Victor France. "Thanks, man," I say. "This is great. Thank you so much. Go back to your party."

"Wait, wait, wait. Now, you listen to me."

"Yes?" My heart is shivering in my chest; I can see the outlines of the next phase of my investigation, each piece of information properly following forward from the last. "What?"

"I just wanna say . . . I wanna say something." Victor's voice has lost its ragged overlay of addled giddiness, he's drawn down very quiet. I can see him, clear as though he's standing before me, hunched forward over the warehouse pay phone, jabbing a finger in the air. "I just wanna say, this is it, man."

"Okay," I say. "This is it." I mean it, too. He's given me what I asked for, and more, and I'm ready to cut him loose. Let him dance in his warehouse till the world burns down.

"Do you—" His voice catches, thick with suppressed tears, and now the tough guy is gone, he's a little boy pleading his way out of punishment. "Do you promise?"

"I do, Victor," I say. "I promise."

"Okay," he says. "'Cause also, I know whose truck it is."

* * *

I know what the dream is about, by the way. I'm not an idiot. There is little novelty in the detective who cannot solve himself.

The dream that I've been having, about my high-school sweetheart, is not really about my high-school sweetheart, when you get right down to it. It's not a dream about Alison Koechner and our lost love and the precious little three-bedroom house in Maine we might have built together, had things gone a different way. I am not dreaming of white picket fences and Sunday crosswords and warm tea.

There's no asteroid in the dream. In the dream, life continues. Simple life, happy and white-picket lined or otherwise. Mere life. Goes on.

When I'm dreaming of Alison Koechner, what I'm dreaming of is not dying.

Okay? See? I get it.

* * *

"I just wanted to go over a few things with you, Mr. Dotseth, just to let you know—this case, this hanger, it's got legs. It really does."

"Mom? Is that you? "

"What? No—it's Detective Palace."

A pause, a low chuckle. "I know who it is, son. I'm having a little fun."

"Oh. Of course."

I hear newspaper pages flipping, I can practically smell the bitter steam rising off of Denny Dotseth's cup of coffee. "Hey, did you hear about what's happening in Jerusalem?"

"No."

"Boy, oh boy. Do you want to?"

"No, sir, not right now. Hey, so, this case, Mr. Dotseth."

"I'm sorry, remind me what case we're talking about?"

Sip of coffee, crinkle of newspaper page, he's teasing me, me at my kitchen table drumming long fingers over a page of my blue book. On which page, as of four o'clock this morning, is written the name and home address of the last person to see my insurance man alive.

"The Zell case, sir. The hanger from yesterday morning."

"Oh, right. The attempted murder. It's a suicide, but you're attempting—"

"Yes, sir. Listen, though: I've got a strong lead on the vehicle."

"What vehicle is that, kiddo?"

My fingers, drumming faster, rat-a-tat-tat. *C'mon, Dotseth.*

"The vehicle I mentioned when we spoke yesterday, sir. The red pickup truck with the vegetable-oil engine. In which the victim was last seen."

Another long pause, Dotseth trying to drive me insane.

"Hello? Denny?"

"So, okay, so you have a lead on the vehicle."

"Yes. And you said to keep you apprised if there was any real chance it's more than a hanger."

"Did I?"

"Yeah. And I think there is, sir, I think there is a real chance. I'm going to swing over there this morning, talk to the guy, and if it looks like anything, I'll come back to you and we can get a warrant, right?" I trail off. "Mr. Dotseth?"

He clears his throat. "Detective Palace? Who's your detective-sergeant these days?"

"Sir?"

I wait, my hand still poised over my notebook, my fingers curling over the address: 77 Bow Bog Road. It's just south of us, in Bow, the first suburb over the city line.

"Down in Adult Crimes. Who is supervising the division?"

"Uh, no one, I guess. Chief Ordler, technically. Sergeant Stassen went Bucket List at the end of November, I think, before I even moved upstairs. A replacement appointment is pending."

"Right," says Dotseth. "Okay. Pending. Respectfully, buddy: you want to follow the case, follow the damn case."

2.

"Petey's not dead."

"He is."

"Just hung out with him. Couple days ago. Tuesday night, I think."

"No, sir, you didn't."

"Think I did."

"Actually, sir, it was Monday."

I'm at the bottom of a metal extension ladder that's leaned against the side of a house, a squat frame house with a sharp shingle roof. My hands are cupped together, my head is tilted back, and I'm calling up through a light drift of snow. J. T. Toussaint, an unemployed construction worker and quarryman, a giant of a man, is up on the ladder, heavy tan work boots planted on the topmost metal rung, a considerable stomach balanced against the overhanging gutters of his roof. I can't yet clearly see his face, just the lower-right quadrant of it, turned down toward me, framed inside the hood of a blue sweatshirt.

"You picked him up from his place of employment on Monday evening."

Toussaint makes a noise for "oh yeah?" but elided into one thick uncertain utterance: "Ohuh?"

"Yes, sir. In your red pickup truck, with the American flag on the side. That's your truck right there?"

I point to the driveway, and Toussaint nods, shifts his weight against the rain spout. The base of the ladder trembles a little.

"On Tuesday morning he was found dead."

"Oh," he says, up on the roof. "Damn. A hanger?"

"That's how it looks. Will you come down off the ladder, please?"

It's an ugly block of a house, wooden and dilapidated and uneven, like the torso of a soapbox racer left forgotten in the dirt. In the front yard is a single ancient oak tree, crooked branches reaching for the sky as if under arrest; around the side there's a doghouse and a row of thick, untended thorn bushes along the property line. As Toussaint descends, the ladder's metal legs jerk back and forth alarmingly, and then he's standing there in his hooded sweatshirt and his heavy workingman's boots, a caulking gun dangling loosely from one thick fist, looking me up and down, both of us breathing cold puffs of condensation.

It's true what everyone has been saying, he's a big man, but he's big and solid, the sturdily formed weight of someone who used to play football. There's a steel in his bigness, and he looks like he could run and jump if he had to. Throw a tackle if he had to. Toussaint's head is like a brick of granite: jutting oblong jaw, broad forehead, the flesh hard and mottled, as if irregularly eroded.

"My name is Detective Henry Palace," I say. "I'm a policeman."

"No kidding," he says, and then he takes a big sudden lunging step toward me, yelps twice sharply and claps his hands, and I jerk backward, startled, fumble for my shoulder holster.

But it's just a dog, he's calling his dog. Toussaint squats and it scampers over, a scruffy thing with patchy curls of white fur, some kind of poodle or something.

"Hey, Houdini," he says, opens his arm. "Hey, boy."

Houdini rubs his small face along Toussaint's meaty palm, and I'm trying to get it together, take a deep breath, and the big man looks up at me from his crouch, amused, and he can tell, I know he can—he can see right through me.

* * *

The house is ugly and dull inside, with dingy walls of yellowing plaster, every ornamentation strictly functional: a clock, a calendar, a bottle opener bolted to the doorframe of the kitchen. The small fireplace is filled with garbage, empty bottles of imported beer—expensive stuff when even the cheap brands are price controlled by ATF at $21.99 for a six-pack, ranging a lot higher on the black market. As we walk past, a bottle of Rolling Rock slips free from the pile and rattles across the hardwood of the living room.

"So," I say, pulling out a blue book and a pen. "How do you know Peter Zell?"

Toussaint lights a cigarette and slowly inhales before answering. "From grammar school."

"Grammar school?"

"Broken Ground. Right up the street, here. Curtisville Road." He tosses his caulking gun into a toolbox, kicks the toolbox under the beat-up sofa. "Sit if you want, man."

"No, thanks."

Toussaint doesn't sit either. He lumbers past me into the kitchen, cigarette exhaust swirling up around his head like dragon-smoke.

There's a scale model of the New Hampshire state house on the mantel above the fireplace, six inches high and fastidiously detailed: the white stone facade, the gilded dome, the tiny imperious eagle jutting from the top.

"Like that?" says Toussaint when he comes back in, holding a Heineken by the neck, and I set the model down abruptly. "My old man made that."

"He's an artist?"

"He's dead," he says, and flips open the dome, revealing the inside to be an ashtray. "But yeah, an artist. Among other things."

He taps his ash into the inverted dome of the state house and looks at me and waits.

"So," I say. "Grammar school."

"Yeah."

According to Toussaint, he and Peter Zell had been best friends from the second grade through the sixth. Both were unpopular, Toussaint a poor kid, a free-breakfast kid, wearing the same dime-store clothes every day; Zell well-off but painfully awkward, sensitive, a born victim. So they formed a bond, two little weirdos, played ping-pong in the Zells' finished basement, rode their bikes up and down the hills around the hospital, played Dungeons & Dragons in this very house, right where we're sitting now. Summertime, they'd ride the couple miles to the quarry on State Street, past the jail, strip down to their underpants and dive in, splash around, dunk each other's heads under the cold fresh water.

"You know," Toussaint concludes, smiling, enjoying his beer. "Kid stuff."

I nod, writing, intrigued by the mental picture of my insurance man as a child: the pasty adolescent body and the thick glasses, clothes carefully folded at the lip of the swimming hole, the young version of the obsessive, timid actuary he was destined to become.

J. T. and Peter, as was perhaps inevitable, drifted apart. Puberty hit and Toussaint got tough, got cool, started shoplifting Metallica CDs from Pitchfork Records and sneaking beers and smoking Marlboro Reds, while Zell remained locked in the stiff and permanent contours of his character, rigid and anxious and geeky. By middle school they would nod to each other in the hallway, and then Toussaint dropped out and Peter graduated and went to college and then twenty years passed without a word between them.

I write it all down. Toussaint finishes his beer and tosses the empty into the pile in the fireplace. There are small gaps in the joinings of the house's wooden sides, or there must be, because in the pauses in our conversation there's a howling whistle, the wind whipping around out there, intensified as it tries to slide in through the cracks.

"Then he calls me up, man. Jack-blue sky. Says, let's have lunch."

I click my pen open and closed three times.

"Why?"

"Don't know."

"When?"

"Don't know. July? No. It was right after I got shit-canned. June.

Says he's been thinking about me, since all this bullcrap got started."

He extends one forefinger and aims it out the window, up at the sky. *All this bullcrap*. My phone rings, and I glance down at it. Nico. I thumb it off.

"And so, what exactly did you and Mr. Zell do together, the two of you?"

"Same stuff, man."

"You played Dungeons & Dragons?"

He looks at me, snorts, shifts in his chair. "Okay, man. Different stuff. We drank beers. We drove around. Did some shooting."

I pause, the wind whipping. Toussaint lights another butt, guesses what I'm going to say next. "Three Winchester rifles, officer. In a cabinet. Unloaded. They're mine and I can prove they're mine."

"Locked up tight, I hope."

Gun theft is a problem. People are stealing them and hoarding them, and other people are stealing them to sell, for astronomical sums, to the first kind of people.

"Nobody's going to take my fucking guns," he says quickly, harshly, and levels a hard look at me, like I was considering it.

I move on. I ask Toussaint about Monday night, the last night of Peter Zell's life, and he shrugs.

"Picked him up after work."

"What time?

"I don't know," he says, and I can feel it, he's liking me less and less, he's ready for me to go, and maybe this man killed Peter and maybe he didn't, but there is no avoiding the impression that he could pound me to death if he wanted to, just like that, three or four blows, like a caveman destroying a deer. "After-work time."

Toussaint says they cruised around for a bit, then went to see the new episode of *Distant Pale Glimmers*, the science-fiction serial, at the Red River. They had some beers, they watched the movie, and then they split up, Peter saying he wanted to walk home.

"Did you see anyone at the theater?"

"Just the people who work there and stuff."

He sucks the last life out of his second cigarette, crushes out the butt in the state house. Houdini pads over unevenly, darting pink tongue finding the last bites of biscuit at the corners of his mouth, and rubs his thin head against the broad expanse of his master's leg.

"I'm gonna have to shoot this dog," Toussaint says, suddenly, absently, matter-of-fact, and stands up. "At the end, I mean."

"What?"

"He's a little scaredy cat, this one." Toussaint is looking down at the dog, his head tilted, as if evaluating, trying to imagine how it's going to feel. "Can't think of him dying like that, fire or cold or drowning. Probably I'm gonna go ahead and shoot him."

I'm ready to get out of here. I'm ready to go.

"Last thing, Mr. Toussaint. Did you happen to notice the bruising? Under Mr. Zell's right eye?"

"He said he fell down some stairs."

"Did you believe him?"

He chuckles, scratches the dog's thin head. "If it were anyone else, I wouldn't. I'd figure he whistled at the wrong dude's girlfriend. But Pete, who knows? I bet he fell down some stairs."

"Right," I say, thinking, *I bet he didn't.*

Toussaint cradles Houdini's head in his hands, and they're gazing at each other, and I can see into the future to the terrible and agonized moment, the raised .270, the trusting animal, the blast, the end.

He looks away from his dog, back up at me, and the spell is broken.

"Anything else? Mr. Policeman?"

* * *

One of my father's favorite jokes was when people asked him what he did for a living, he would say he was a philosopher king. He would make this claim with perfect seriousness, and the thing about Temple Palace was that he wouldn't let go of it. Inevitably, he would get that blank look from whoever had asked—the barber, say, or someone at a cocktail party, or one of my friends' parents, and there I am looking at the ground in rank embarrassment—and he'd just say, "What?" opening his palms, imploring, "What? I'm *serious.*"

What he really did was teach English literature, Chaucer and Shakespeare and Donne, down at St. Anselm's. At home he was always coming out with quotes and allusions, murmuring literary lessons from the side of his mouth, responding to the random events and mundane conversations of our household with dollops of abstract commentary.

The substance of most of these asides I have long since forgotten, but one stays with me.

I'd come home whimpering, tearful, because this kid Burt Phipps had shoved me off a swing. My mother, Peg, pretty and practical and efficient, wrapped three pieces of ice in a sandwich bag and held them to my injury, while my father leaned against the green linoleum counter, wondering why this Burt character would do such a thing.

And I, sniffling, go, "Well, because he's a jerk."

"Ah, but no!" pronounces my father, holding his glasses up to the kitchen light, polishing them with a dinner napkin. "One thing we can learn from Shakespeare, Hen, is that every action has a motive."

I'm looking at him, holding this drooping sandwich bag full of ice to my bruised forehead.

"Do you see it, son? Anybody does anything, I don't care what it is, there's a reason for it. No action comes divorced from motive, neither in art nor in life."

"For heaven's sake, dear," says my mother, squatting before me, peering into my pupils to eliminate the possibility of concussion. "A bully is a bully."

"Ah, yes," Father says, pats me on the head, wanders out of the kitchen. "But, wherefore doth he *become* a bully?"

My mother rolls her eyes at him and kisses me on my wounded head, gets up. Nico's in the corner, age five, building a multistory palace of Legos, lowering into place the carefully cantilevered roof.

Professor Temple Palace did not live to see the advent of our present unfortunate circumstance; neither, unfortunately, did my mother.

In a little more than six months, according to the most reliable scientific predictions, at least half the planet's population will die in a series of interlocking cataclysms. A one hundred teraton explosion, roughly equaling the blast force of a thousand Hiroshimas, will scorch a massive crater into the ground, touching off a series of Richter-defying earthquakes, sending towering tsunamis ricocheting across the oceans.

And then will come the ash cloud, the darkness, the twenty-degree dip in global temperatures. No crops, no cattle, no light. The slow cold fate of those who remain.

Answer this, in your blue books, Professor Palace: what effect does it have on motive, all this information, *all this unbearable imminence*?

Consider J. T. Toussaint, a laid-off quarryman with no previous criminal history.

No verifiable alibi for the time of death. He was at home, he says, reading.

Under normal circumstances, then, we would next turn our attention to the question of motive. We would wonder about those hours they spent together, that final evening: they went to *Distant Pale Glimmers*, they got loaded on movie-theater beer. They fought over a woman, perhaps, or some silly old half-remembered elementary-school insult, and tempers flared.

The first problem with such a hypothesis is that's just not how Peter Zell got killed. A murder resulting from a long night of drinking, a murder about a woman or a pissing contest, is a murder committed with a bat, or a knife, or a .270 Winchester rifle. Here instead we have a man who is strangled, his body moved, a suicide scene deliberately and carefully constructed.

But the second and much larger problem is that the very idea of motive must be reexamined in the context of the looming catastrophe.

Because people are doing all sorts of things, for motives that can be difficult or impossible to divine clearly. In recent months the world has seen episodes of cannibalism, of ecstatic orgies; outpourings of charity and good works; attempted socialist revolutions and attempted religious revolutions; mass psychoses including the second coming of Jesus; of the return of Mohammed's son-in-law Ali, the Commander of the Faithful; of the constellation Orion with sword and belt, climbing down from the sky.

People are building rocket ships, people are building tree houses, people are taking multiple wives, people are shooting indiscriminately in public places, people are setting fire to themselves, people are studying to be doctors while doctors quit work and build huts in the desert and sit in them and pray.

None of these things, so far as I know, has happened in Concord. Still, the conscientious detective is obliged to examine the question of motive in a new light, to place it within the matrix of our present unusual circumstance. The end of the world changes everything, from a law-enforcement perspective.

* * *

I'm at Albin Road just past Blevens when the car catches a patch of bad ice and heaves itself violently to the right, and I try to jerk it back to the left and nothing happens. The steering wheel spins uselessly under my hands, I'm rolling it this way and that, and I can hear the snow chains ricocheting against the rims with a series of vicious clangs.

"Come on, come on," I say, but it's like the wheel has lost communication with the steering column, spinning and spinning, and meanwhile the whole car is hurtling to the right, a giant hockey puck that someone whaled at, sliding furiously toward the ditch at the side of the road.

"Come on," I say again, "come on," my stomach lurching. I'm

pumping the brake, nothing is happening, and now the back of the car is rolling up and pulling even with the front, the nose of the Impala nearly perpendicular to the roadway, and I feel the back wheels lift up while the front goes sailing forward, bounces over the ditch and into the wide sturdy trunk of an evergreen, and my head slams back against the headrest.

And then all is still. The silence sudden and complete. My breath. A winter bird sounding, way off somewhere. A small defeated hiss from the engine.

Slowly, I become aware of a clicking noise and it takes me a second to discover that the sound is my teeth, chattering. My hands are trembling, too, and my knees are clacking like marionette legs.

My collision with the tree shook loose a lot of snow, and some of it is still drifting down, a gentle powdery false storm, a dusting of accumulation on the cracked windshield.

I shift, breathe, pat myself down like I'm frisking a suspect, but I'm fine. I'm fine.

The front of the car is bent in, just one big dent, dead center, like a giant reeled back and kicked it once, hard.

My snow chains have come off. All four of them. They lay splayed out in crazy directions like fishermen's nets, in jumbled heaps around the tires.

"Holy moly," I say aloud.

I don't think he killed him. Toussaint. I gather up the snow chains and lay them in the trunk in a loose pile.

I don't think he's the killer. I don't think it's right.

* * *

There are a total of five staircases at police headquarters but only two that go down to the basement. One is a set of rough concrete steps that descends from the garage, so when the units pull in with cuffed suspects in the backseat, they can be led right down to processing, to the part of the basement with the mug-shot camera and the fingerprint ink and the regular holding cell and the drunk tank. The drunk tank is always full these days. To access the other part of the basement you use the front northwest stairwell: you wave your ID badge at the keypad, wait for the door to click open, and go down to the cramped domain of Officer Frank Wilentz.

"Why, Detective Sky-high," says Wilentz, and he throws me a friendly mock-salute. "You look a little pale."

"I hit a tree. I'm fine."

"How's the tree?"

"Can you run a name for me?"

"Do you like my hat?"

"Wilentz, come on."

The administrative technician of the CPD records unit works in a four-foot-square caged-off pen, a former evidence enclosure, at a desk littered with comic books and bags of candy. A row of hooks along the chain mesh of his cage is hung with major-league ball caps, one of which, a bright red souvenir Phillies cap, sits on Wilentz's head at a rakish angle.

"Answer me, Palace."

"I like your hat very much, Officer Wilentz."

"You're just saying that."

"So, I need you to run a name for me."

"I got one hat for every team in the league. D'ja know that?"

"I think you've mentioned it, yes."

The problem is that at this point Wilentz has the only consistently functional high-speed Internet connection in the building; for all I know, it's the only consistently functional high-speed Internet connection in the county. Something to do with the CPD being allowed one machine that connects with some kind of gold-plated Department of Justice law-enforcement router. It just means that if I want to connect to the FBI's servers to perform a nationwide criminal-background check, I first need to admire Frank's hat collection.

"I used to be collecting these bastards to give 'em to my children one day, but since now it seems clear that I shall not be having any children, I'm just enjoying 'em myself." His deadpan gives way to a big, gap-toothed grin. "I'm a glass-half-full kind of guy, myself. Did you need something?"

"Yep. I need you to run a name for me."

"Oh, right, you said that."

Wilentz types in the name and the address on Bow Bog, checks off boxes on a DOJ login screen, and I'm standing at his desk, watching while he types, tapping my own fingers thoughtfully on the side of his cage.

"Wilentz?"

"Yes?"

"Would you ever kill yourself?"

"No," he says immediately, still typing, clicking on a link. "But I will confess that I have considered it. The Romans, you know, they thought it was, like, the bravest thing you could do. In the face of tyranny. Cicero. Seneca. All those guys." He slowly draws a finger across his neck, slash.

"We're not facing tyranny, though."

"Ah, but we are. Fascist in the sky, baby." He turns away from the computer and selects a miniature Kit Kat from his pile. "But I won't do it. And you know why not?"

"Why?"

"Because . . . I . . ." He turns back, hits a final key. ". . . am a coward."

It's hard to tell, with Wilentz, if he's kidding, but I think he's not, and anyway I turn my attention to what's happening on the monitor, long columns of data marching up the screen.

"Well, my friend," says Officer Wilentz, unwrapping his candy. "What you got here is a gosh-darn Boy Scout."

"What?"

Mr. J. T. Toussaint, as it turns out, has never committed a crime, or at least has never been caught for one.

Never has he been arrested by the Concord force, pre- or post-Maia, nor by the state of New Hampshire, nor by any other state, county, or local official. He's never done federal time, he's got no FBI or Justice Department file. Nothing international, nothing military. Once, it looks like, he parked a motorcycle illegally in a small town called Waterville Valley, up in the White Mountains, and earned himself a parking ticket, which he promptly paid.

"So, nothing?" I say, and Wilentz nods.

"Nothing. Oh, unless he popped someone in Louisiana. New Orleans is cut off from the grid." Wilentz stands, stretches, adds the crumpled candy wrapper to the pile on the desk. "Kind of thinking of going down there, myself. Wild times down there. All kinda sex stuff going on, I hear."

I head back up the stairs with a one-page printout of J. T. Toussaint's criminal history, or lack thereof. If he's the kind of guy who goes around killing people and stringing them up in fast-food-restaurant bathrooms, he only recently elected to become so.

* * *

Upstairs, at my desk, I get back on the landline and try Sophia Littlejohn again, and I am again treated to the bland peppy tones of the Concord Midwifery receptionist. No, Ms. Littlejohn is out; no, she doesn't know where; no, she doesn't know when she'll be back.

"Could you tell her to call Detective Palace, at the Concord PD?" I say, and then I add, impulsively, "Tell her I'm her friend. Tell her I want to help."

The receptionist pauses for a moment and then says, "Ooookay," drawing out that first syllable like she doesn't really know what I'm talking about. I can't blame her, because I don't entirely know what I'm talking about, either. I take the tissue I've been holding up to my head and throw it in the garbage. I'm feeling restless and dissatisfied, staring at J. T. Toussaint's clean record, thinking about the whole house, the dog, the roof, the lawn. The other thing is, I have a fairly clear memory of carefully latching my snow chains yesterday morning, checking their slack, as is my habit, once a week.

"Hey, Palace, come over here and look at this."

It's Andreas, at his computer. "Are you watching this on dial-up?"

"No," he says. "This is on my hard drive. I downloaded it the last time we were online."

"Oh," I say, "All right, well . . ." But it's too late, I've walked across the room to his desk and now I'm standing beside him, and he's got one hand clutched at my elbow, the other hand pointed at the screen.

"Look," says Detective Andreas, breathing rapidly. "Look at this with me."

"Andreas, come on. I'm working on a case."

"I know, but look, Hank."

"I've seen it before."

Everyone has seen it. A few days after Tolkin, after the CBS special, the final determination, the Jet Propulsion Laboratory at NASA released a short video to promote public understanding of what's going on. It's a simple Java animation, in which crude pixelated avatars of the relevant celestial bodies wing their way around the Sun: Earth, Venus, Mars, and, of course, the star of the show, good old $2011GV_1$. The planets and the infamous minor planetoid, all cruising around the Sun at their varying speeds in their varying ellipses, clicking forward, frame by frame, each instant on screen representing two weeks of real time.

"Just wait a second," says Andreas, loosening his grip but not letting go, leaning forward even farther on his desk. His cheeks are flushed. He's staring at the screen with an awestruck expression, wide-eyed, like a kid gazing into the aquarium glass.

I stand there behind him, watching in spite of myself, watching Maia make her wicked way around the Sun. The video is eerily entrancing, like an art film, an installation in a gallery: bright colors, repetitive motion, simple action, irresistible. In the outer reaches of its orbit, $2011GV_1$ moves slowly, methodically, just sort of chugging along in the sky, much slower on its track than Earth on hers. But then, in the last few seconds, Maia speeds up, like the second hand of a clock suddenly swooping from four to six. In proper obedience to Kepler's Second Law, the asteroid gobbles up the last few million miles of space in the last two months, catches up with the unsuspecting Earth, and then . . . *bam!*

The video freezes on the last frame, dated October 3, the day of impact. *Bam!* In spite of myself, my stomach lurches at the sight of it, and I turn away.

"Great," I mutter. "Thanks for sharing." Like I told the guy, I've seen it before.

"Wait, wait."

Andreas drags the scroll bar back, to a few seconds before impact, moment number 2:39.14, then lets it play again; the planets jerk forward two frames, and then he pauses it again. "There? You see it?"

"See what?"

He rewinds it again, plays it again. I'm thinking about Peter Zell, thinking about him watching this—surely he saw the video, probably dozens of times, and maybe he took it apart, frame by frame, as Andreas is doing. The detective lets go of my arm, pushes his face all the way forward, until his nose is almost brushing against the cold plastic of the monitor.

"Right there: the asteroid joggles only slightly to the left. If you read Borstner—have you read Borstner?"

"No."

"Oh, Hank." He looks around at me, like I'm the crazy one, then he turns back to the screen. "He's a blogger, or he was, now he's got this newsletter. A friend of mine out in Phoenix, he called me last night, gave me the whole rundown, told me to watch the video again, to stop it right . . ." He clicks Pause, 2:39.14. "Right there. Look. Okay? See?" He plays it again, pauses it again, plays it again. "What Borstner points out, here, if you compare this video, I mean."

"Andreas."

"If you compare it with other asteroid-path projections, there are anomalies."

"Detective Andreas, no one doctored the film."

"No, no, not the film. Of course no one doctored the *film*." He cranes his head around again, squints at me, and I catch a quick whiff of something on his breath, vodka, maybe, and I step back. "Not the film, Palace, the *ephemeris*."

"Andreas." I'm fighting a powerful urge, at this point, simply to yank his computer free from the wall and throw it across the room.

I have a murder to solve for God's sake. A man is dead.

"See—there—see," he's saying. "See where she almost strays, but then sort of veers back? If you compare it to Apophis or to 1979 XB. If you—see—Borstner's theory is that an error was made, a fundamental early error in the, the, calculus, you know, the math of the thing. And just starting with the discovery itself, which, you must know, was totally unprecedented. A seventy-five-year orbit, that's off the charts, right?" He's talking quicker and quicker, his words spilling out, slipping over one another. "And Borstner has tried to contact JPL, he's tried to contact the DOD, explain to them what, what's, you know—and he's just been rebuffed. He's been ignored, Palace. Totally ignored!"

"Detective Andreas," I say firmly, and instead of smashing his computer I just lean forward next to him, wrinkling my nose at his stink of stale liquor and sweaty desperation, and turn off the monitor.

He lifts his head to me, eyes wide. "Palace?"

"Andreas, are you working on any interesting cases?"

He blinks, baffled. The word *cases* is from a foreign language he used to know, a long time ago.

"Cases?"

"Yeah. Cases."

We stare at each other, the radiator making its indistinct gurglings from the corner, and then Culverson comes in.

"Why, Detective Palace." He's standing in the doorway, three-piece suit, Windsor knot, a warm grin. "Just the man I was looking for."

I'm glad to turn away from Andreas, and he from me; he fumbles for the button to turn his monitor on again. Culverson is waving me over with a small slip of yellow paper. "You doing okay, son?"

"Yeah. I ran into a tree. What's up?"

"I found that kid."

"What kid?"

"The kid you were looking for."

As it turns out, Culverson was paying attention from his side of the room when I was on the phone yesterday, spinning my wheels in search of my sister's village idiot of a husband. So, Culverson, he goes ahead and makes some calls of his own, God bless him, and because he's a much better investigator than I will ever be, he cracked it.

"Detective," I say. "I don't know what to say."

"Forget about it," he says, still grinning. "You know me, I like a challenge. And also, before you thank me too much, take a look at what I found out."

He slides the little piece of paper into my palm, and I read it and groan. We stand there for a second, Culverson grinning wickedly, Andreas in his corner watching his movie and wringing his sweaty hands together.

"Good luck, Detective Palace," says Culverson, patting me on the shoulder. "Have fun."

* * *

He's wrong.

Andreas, I mean.

Along with this Borstner, the blogger or pamphleteer or whatever he is: the jackass in Arizona getting people's hopes up.

There are many such characters, and they're all wrong, and it's irritating to me because Andreas has responsibilities, he has a job to do; the public is relying on him, just as they are on me.

Still, at some point, a few hours later, before I call it a day, I stop at his desk to watch the Jet Propulsion Lab video again. I lean forward, hunch forward really, and squint. There's no swerve, no stop-start flicker in the animation that might credibly suggest an error in the underlying data. Maia does not jog or bobble on its course, it's clear forward motion all the way. It just comes, on and on, unerring, as it's been coming since long before I was born.

I can't purport to understand the science, but I know that there are a lot of people who do. There are many observatories, Arecibo and Goldstone and the rest of them, there are a million or more amateur astronomers tracking the thing across the sky.

Peter Zell, he did understand the science, he studied it, he sat in his small apartment silently absorbing the technical details of what is happening, making his notes, underlining details.

I restart the video, watch the asteroid swing around one more time, speed up furiously in the homestretch, and then ... *bam!*

3.

"Roll through, please."

The soldier's chin is perfectly square, his eyes are sharp and cheerless, his face is cold and impassive beneath a wide black helmet, the minuteman logo of the National Guard emblazoned across the brim. He motions me forward with the tip of his firearm, which appears to be an M-16 semiautomatic. I roll through. This morning I reattached the snow chains, triple-checking the cable connects, drawing tight the slack. Thom Halburton, the department mechanic, said the car'll drive just fine even with the dent, and so far it seems like he's right.

I'm not even a half mile from downtown Concord, I can still see the spire of the state house in one direction and the Outback Steakhouse billboard in the other, but it's a different world. Barbed-wire fences, one-story windowless brick buildings, a blacktop service road marked with white arrows and yellow arrows and stone pylons. Guard towers, green directional signs riddled with cryptic acronyms. More soldiers. More machine guns.

The IPSS Act is known to contain a raft of so-called black titles, classified sections generally assumed to relate to the various branches of the armed services. The exact content of those black titles is unknown—except, presumably, to its drafters, a joint House and Senate armed forces committee; to the military commanders and high-level officers of the affected branches; and to various relevant members of the executive branch.

But everyone knows, or at least everyone in law enforcement is fairly certain, that the organization of the United States military has been extensively revamped, its powers and resources expanded—all of which makes this the last place I would choose to be, on a gray and windy Friday morning when I'm hip-deep in a murder investigation: navigating my Chevrolet Impala through the headquarters of the New Hampshire National Guard.

Thanks, Nico. I owe you one.

I climb out of the Impala at the brig, a squat and windowless concrete building with a small forest of antennae bristling along the flat lines of its roof, at 10:43. Thanks to Culverson, and Culverson's contacts, I've got five minutes, beginning at exactly 10:45 a.m.

A severe and charmless female reserve officer in green camouflage pants stares at my badge in silence for thirty seconds before nodding once and ushering me down a short hallway to a massive metal door with a small square Plexiglas window in its dead center.

"Thanks," I say, and she grunts and heads back down the hallway.

I peer in the window, and there he is: Derek Skeve, sitting in the middle of the floor of his cell, cross-legged, breathing slowly and elaborately.

He's meditating. For the love of God.

I make a fist and knock on the little window.

"Skeve. Hey." Knock, knock. "Derek."

I wait a second. I tap again.

"Hey." Louder, sharper: "Derek."

Skeve, eyes still closed, raises one finger of one hand, like a doctor's receptionist busy on the phone. Rage boils in my cheeks, this is it, I'm ready to go home. Surely it's better to let this self-involved doofus sit in military prison aligning his chakras until Maia gets here. I'll turn around, say "thanks anyway" to the charmer at the door, call Nico and give her the bad news, and get back to work finding Peter Zell's killer.

But I know Nico, and I know myself. I can tell her whatever I feel like, I'll just end up driving back out here tomorrow.

So I bang on the window again, and at last the prisoner unfolds himself and stands. Skeve is in a tan jumpsuit with NHNG stenciled across the front, an incongruous complement to his long, matted ropes of hair, those ridiculous Caucasian dreadlocks that make him look like a bike messenger—which in fact he has been, among many other short-lived quasi-professions. Several days' growth of fuzz coat his cheeks and chin.

"Henry," he says, smiling beatifically. "How are you, brother?"

"What's going on, Derek?"

Skeve shrugs absently, as if the question doesn't really concern him.

"I am as you find me. A guest of the military-industrial complex."

He looks around at the cell: smooth concrete walls, a thin and utilitarian bunk bed bolted to one corner, a small metal toilet to the other.

I lean forward, filling the small window with my face. "Can you expand on that, please?"

"Sure. I mean, what can I tell you? I've been arrested by the military police."

"Yes, Derek. I see that. For what?"

"I think the charge is operating an all-terrain vehicle on federal land."

"That's the charge? Or you think that's the charge?"

"I believe that I think that is the charge." He smirks, and I would smack him if it were physically possible, I really would.

I step away from the window, take a deep calming breath, and look at my watch. 10:48.

"Well, Derek. Were you, in fact, operating an ATV on the base for some reason?"

"I don't remember."

He doesn't remember. I stare at him, standing there, still smirking. It's such a fine line with some people, whether they're playing dumb or being dumb.

"I'm not a policeman right now, Derek. I'm your friend." I stop myself, start again. "I'm Nico's friend. I'm her brother, and I love her. And she loves you, and so I'm here to help you. So start at the beginning, and tell me exactly what happened."

"Oh, Hank," he says, like he pities me. Like my entreaties are something childish, something he thinks is cute. "I seriously wish that I could."

"You wish?"

This is madness. It's madness.

"When are you being arraigned?"

"I don't know."

"Do you have a lawyer?"

"I don't know."

"What do you mean, you don't know?" I check my watch. Thirty seconds left, and I can hear the heavy footfalls of the reservist from the desk, making her way back to collect me. One thing about the military, they like their schedules.

"Derek, I came all the way down here to help you."

"I know, and that's really decent of you. But, you know, I didn't ask you to do that."

"Yes, but Nico *did* ask me. Because she cares about you."

"I know. Isn't she an amazing person?"

"All right sir."

It's the guard. I talk quickly into the hole in the door. "Derek, there is nothing I can do for you unless you can tell me what's going on."

Derek's smug grin widens for a moment, the eyes misting with kindness, and then he walks slowly over to the bed and sprawls out, his hands folded behind his head.

"I totally hear what you're saying, Henry. But it's a secret."

That's it. Time's up.

*   *   *

I was twelve years old and Nico was only six when we moved from the house on Rockland to the farmhouse on Little Pond Road, halfway to Penacook. Nathanael Palace, my grandfather, only recently retired from forty years in banking, had a wide range of interests: model trains, shooting, building stone walls. Already by prepubescence a bookish and private person, I was uninterested to varying degrees in all these activities but was forced by Grandfather to take part. Nico, a lonesome and anxious child, was avidly interested in all of them and rigorously ignored. He once got a set of World War II–era model airplanes, and we sat in the basement, the three of us, and Grandfather harangued me for an hour, refusing to let me quit until I'd successfully attached both wings to the body, while mechanically minded Nico sat in the corner, clutching a handful of tiny gunmetal gray airplane parts, waiting for her turn: at first excited, then restlessly, and finally in tears.

That was springtime, I think, not that long after we moved in with him. The years have been like that, for her and me, a lot of ups and downs.

"So, you'll go back."

"No."

"Why not? Can't Culverson get you another appointment? Maybe Monday."

"Nico."

"Henry."

"*Nico.*" I'm leaning forward, sort of hollering into the phone, which is on speaker on the passenger seat. We've got a terrible line, cell to cell, all kinds of stops and starts, which isn't helping. "Listen to me."

But she's not going to listen.

"I'm sure you just misunderstood him or something. He can be weird."

"That is true."

I'm parked in the abandoned lot next to what remains of the Capitol Shopping Center, a several-block stretch just east of Main Street along the banks of the Merrimack. The Presidents' Day riots burned away the last remaining shops here, and now there are just a few scattered tents full of drunks and homeless people. This is where Mr. Shepherd, my scout leader, was living when the Brush Cuts ran him in on vagrancy.

"Nico, are you okay? Are you eating?"

"I'm fine. You know what I bet?" She's not fine. Her voice is raspy, haggard, like she's been doing nothing but smoking since Derek's disappearance. "I bet he just didn't want to say anything in front of the guards."

"Nope," I say. "No, Nico." Exasperating. I tell her how easy it was for me to get in there, how few guards are watching over Derek Skeve.

"Really?"

"There's one woman. A reservist. They don't care about some kid who went joyriding on a military base."

"So why can't you get him out?"

"Because I don't have a magic wand."

Nico's denial of reality, as maddening as her husband's dull obstinacy, is a long-standing aspect of her character. My sister was a mystic from an early age, a firm believer in fairies and miracles, and her starry little spirit demanded magic. In the immediate aftermath of our becoming orphans, she could not and would not accept that it was all real, and I'd gotten so mad, I'd stormed away, and then I'd reeled back around, shouting. "They're both *dead*! Period. End of story. Dead, dead, d-dead-d-dead! Okay? No ambiguity!"

This was at Father's wake, the house full of friends and well-meaning strangers. Nico had stared back at me, tiny rose lips pursed, the word *ambiguity* vastly above her six-year-old pay grade, the severity of my tone nevertheless unmistakable. The assembled mourners staring at the sad little pair of us.

And now, the present, new times, Nico's powers of disbelief unwavering. I try to change the subject.

"Nico, you're good at math. Does the number 12.375 mean anything?"

"What do you mean, does it mean anything?"

"I don't know, is it, like, pi or something, where—"

"No, Henry, it's not," she says quickly, coughs. "So what are we going to do next?"

"Nico, come on. Are you not listening to me? It's military, which is on a totally different set of rules. I wouldn't even know how to try to get him out of there."

One of the homeless guys stumbles out of his tent, and I give him a small two-fingered wave; his name is Charles Taylor, and we went to high school together.

"This thing is going to fall out of the sky," says Nico, "it's going to fall on our heads. I don't want to be sitting here by myself when it happens."

"It is not falling on our heads."

"What?"

"Everybody says that, and it's just—it's just arrogant, is what it is." I'm so tired of this, all of it, and I should stop talking, but I can't. "Two objects are moving through space on separate but overlapping orbits, and this one time, we'll both be at the same place at the same time. It's not 'falling on our heads,' okay? It's not 'coming for us.' It just *is*. Do you understand?"

It suddenly seems incredibly, weirdly, quiet, and I realize I must have been yelling. "Nico? I'm sorry. Nico?"

But then she's back, her voice small and flat. "I just miss him, is all."

"I know that."

"Forget it."

"Wait."

"Don't worry about me. Go solve your case."

She hangs up, and I sit there in the car, my chest trembling as if struck.

Bam!

*   *   *

It's a science-fiction serial, is what it is, *Distant Pale Glimmers,* one new half-hour episode coming out every week, running like gangbusters since Christmastime. Here in Concord it's showing at the Red River, the indie house. Apparently it's about an intergalactic battleship called the *John Adams,* piloted by a General Amelie Chenoweth, who is portrayed by a bombshell named Kristin Dallas, who also writes and directs. The *John Adams* charts the distant reaches of the universe circa 2145. Of course the subtext, as subtle as a blow to the head, is that somehow, someone makes it, survives, prospers, the human race resurgent among the stars.

I went with Nico and Derek once, a few weeks ago, the first Monday in March. I didn't care for it much, personally.

I wonder if Peter was there, that same night? Maybe alone,

maybe with J. T. Toussaint.

I bet he was.

* * *

"Detective Culverson?"

"Yeah?"

"How reliable are the snow chains on the Impalas?"

"How reliable are they? What do you mean?"

"The chains. On the cars. They're good, right? They stay on, for the most part?"

Culverson shrugs, engrossed in the newspaper. "I guess."

I'm in my chair, at my desk, blue books arranged in a neat rectangle in front of me, trying to forget about my sister, move on with my life. A case to investigate. A man is dead.

"They're fucking tremendous," calls McGully from his desk, and his pronouncement is punctuated by the slam of his front chair legs hitting the floor as he leans forward. He's got a pastrami sandwich from the Works, he's got a napkin for a bib, spread out like a picnic blanket over his stomach. "They won't come off for shit, not unless you latch 'em wrong. What happened? You spin out?"

"I did. Yesterday afternoon. Hit a tree."

McGully bites his sandwich. Culverson mutters "Jesus," but not about the accident, about something in the newspaper. Andreas's desk is empty. Our window unit is clanking, burping out drifts of heat. Outside, on the sill, a slowly deepening shelf of new snow.

"It's a tricky little latch on those bastards, and you really gotta keep the slack out." McGully grins, mustard on his chin. "Don't beat yourself up."

"Yep. But, you know, I've been doing them a while. I did a winter on patrol."

"Yeah, but were you servicing your own vehicle last winter?"

"No."

Culverson, meanwhile, sets down his newspaper and looks out the window. I get up and start pacing. "Someone could have uncoupled them pretty easily, right? If they wanted to."

McGully snorts, swallows a big bite of sandwich. "In the garage, here?"

"No, out in the field. While I was parked somewhere."

"You mean—" he stares at me, lowers his voice, mock-serious, "somebody who's trying to murder you?"

"Well—I mean—sure."

"By unlatching your snow chains?" McGully brays laughter, hunks of pastrami erupting from his maw and bouncing off the napkin, onto the desk. "I'm sorry, kid, are you in a spy movie?"

"No."

"Are you the president?"

"No."

People have been trying to assassinate the president, that's one of the deranged features of the national scene, the last three months— that's the joke there.

I look at Culverson, but he's still up in his head somewhere, eyes fixed on the drifting snow.

"Well, then, no offense, kid," says McGully, "but I don't think anybody's trying to murder you. Nobody cares about you."

"Right."

"Nothing against you. Nobody cares about anything."

Culverson stands abruptly, drops his newspaper in the garbage.

"What's up your ass?" says McGully, craning his head around.

"The Pakistanis. They want to nuke it."

"Nuke what?"

"Maia. They made some kind of a proclamation. They cannot leave the survival of their proud and sovereign people in the hands of the Western imperialist et cetera et cetera et cetera."

"The Pakistanis, huh?" says McGully. "No kidding? I thought Iran were the pricks to worry about on this thing."

"No, see, the Iranians have uranium, but no missile. They can't fire it."

"Pakistanis can fire it?"

"They have missiles."

I'm thinking about my snow chains, feeling the lurch of the road spinning out from under me, remembering the shudder and the thud of impact.

Culverson's shaking his head. "So the State Department is saying, basically, you try to nuke it, we'll nuke you first."

"Good times," says McGully.

"I have a pretty clear memory of checking the chain latches," I say, and they both look over at me. "Monday morning, first thing."

"Jesus, Palace."

"But, so, wait. Let's just imagine I am a murderer. Let's imagine there's a detective who's working the case, and he's, he's"—I pause, conscious of coloring a little—"he's closing in on me. So I want this detective dead."

"Yes," says McGully, and I think for a second he's being serious, but then he sets down his sandwich, rises slowly with a solemn expression. "Or maybe it was a *ghost*."

"Okay, McGully."

"No, I'm serious." He comes over. His breath smells like pickles. "It's the ghost of this hanger, and he's so annoyed that you're trying to pretend he got murdered, he's trying to scare you into dropping the investigation."

"Okay, McGully, okay. I don't think it was a ghost."

Culverson has pulled the *Times* out of the trash, he's reading the story again.

"Yeah, you're right," says McGully, going back to his desk and the remainder of his lunch. "You probably forgot to latch the chains."

* * *

Another of my father's favorite jokes was the one he rolled out whenever people asked why we lived up in Concord, considering that he worked at St. Anselm's, half an hour away, outside Manchester. He would reel back, astonished, and just say, "Because it's *Concord*!" as if it that were explanation enough, like it's London or Paris.

This was to become a favorite joke between Nico and me, in our years of surly teenage discontent, which for Nico have never really ended. Why couldn't we find a place to eat a decent steak after nine p.m.? Why did every other city in New England get a Starbucks before we did?

Because it's Concord!

But the real reason my parents stayed was for my mother's work. She was the department secretary for the Concord police, planted behind the bullet-proof glass in the front lobby, handling visitors, calmly accepting complaints from drunks and vagrants and sex of-fenders, ordering a cake shaped like a semiautomatic pistol for every retiring detective.

Her salary was maybe half of my father's income, but she'd held that job before she even met Temple Palace, and she married him only on the express condition that they would remain in Concord.

He was trying to be funny when he said "because it's Con-cord!" but really, he didn't care where he lived. He loved my mother a whole heck of a lot, was the explanation, and he just wanted to be where she was.

* * *

It's Friday, late, coming up on midnight. The stars are gleaming dully through a gray wreath of clouds. I'm sitting on my back porch, looking out on the undeveloped acreage, former farmland, that abuts my row of townhouses.

I'm sitting here telling myself I was honest with Nico, and there's nothing else I can do.

But she's right, unfortunately. I love her, and I don't want her to die alone.

Technically, I don't want her to die at all, but there's not much I can do about that.

It's way past business hours, but I go inside and pick up the landline and dial the number anyway. Someone will answer. It's never been the sort of office that shuts down for nights and weekends, and I'm sure that in the asteroid era the schedule has only gotten busier.

"Hello?" says a voice, quiet and male.

"Yeah, good evening." Tilting my head back, taking a deep breath. "I need to speak to Alison Koechner."

* * *

On Saturday morning I go for a jog, five miles along an eccentric route of my own invention: up to White Park, over to Main Street, and then home along Rockingham, sweat trickling down my forehead, mingling with the dusting of snow. My leg drags a little from the car accident, and there's a tightness in my chest, but it feels good to be running, to be outdoors.

Okay. I could have forgotten to latch one of the chains on the tires, sure, I could see that. I'm hurrying, I'm anxious. Maybe I neglected to latch one. But all four?

I get home and turn on my cell phone and find that I have two service bars, and that I've missed a call from Sophia Littlejohn.

"Oh, *no*," I mutter, pressing the button to play the voicemail. Forty-five minutes I'd been out, an hour maybe, and it was the first time I had turned off my phone in a week, the first time since I laid eyes on Peter Zell's body in the bathroom of the pirate McDonald's.

"I'm sorry it's taken me so long to get back to you," says Ms. Littlejohn on the message, her voice neutral and steady. I'm cradling the phone under my neck, flipping open a blue book, clicking open a pen. "But the thing is, I really don't know what to tell you."

And then she just starts talking, a four-minute message that does nothing but recapitulate what her husband told me at their house on Wednesday morning. She and her brother had never been close. He had reacted terribly to the asteroid, become withdrawn, detached, more so than ever. She is obviously disappointed that he chose to kill himself, but not surprised.

"And so, Detective," she says, "I thank you for your diligence, for your concern." She stops, and there's a few seconds of silence, I think the message is over, but then there's a murmuring, supportive whisper behind her—handsome husband Erik—and she says, "He was not a happy man, Officer. I wanted you to know that I cared for him. He was a sad man, and then he killed himself. Please don't call me again."

Beep. End of message.

I sit drumming my fingers on the warped tile of my kitchen counter, the warm sweat of my exertion drying and turning cold on my forehead. In her message, Sophia Littlejohn hadn't mentioned the aborted suicide note, if that's what it was—*Dear Sophia.* But I had told her husband about it, and it's a safe bet that he told her.

I call her back on the landline. At home, and then on her cell, and then at work, and then at home again.

Maybe she's not answering because she doesn't recognize the number, so I try all the numbers again on my cell phone, except halfway through the second call I lose all my bars, no signal, dead plastic, and I throw the stupid thing across the room.

* * *

You can't see it in people's eyes, not in this weather: winter hats pulled down low, faces turned down to the sleet-covered sidewalk. But you read it in their gaits, in that low weary shuffle. You can see the ones who aren't going to make it. There's a suicide. There's one. This guy's not going to make it. That woman, the one with face front, chin up high. She'll hold up, do her best, pray to someone or something, right up until the end.

On the wall of the former office building, the graffiti: LIES LIES IT'S ALL LIES.

I'm walking over to the Somerset for a bachelor's solitary Saturday night dinner, and I go out of my way to pass the McDonald's on Main Street. I eye the empty parking lot, the stream of pedestrians going in, coming out with their paper bags, steaming from the tops. There's an overflowing black Dumpster along the side of the building, partially concealing the side entrance. I stand for a second, and I imagine that I'm a killer. I've got my car—it's a WVO engine, or I've put together a half tank somehow.

I've got a body in the trunk.

I wait patiently for midnight to roll around, midnight or one. Well past the dinner rush but before the tide of late-night postbar customers starts to wash in. The restaurant is mostly empty.

Casually, looking around the dimly lit lot, I pop the trunk and pull out my friend; lean him against my body and walk with him, three-legged, like a couple of drunks supporting ourselves, past the barrier of the Dumpster and in that side entrance, right down the little hall to the men's john. Slide closed the lock. Take off my belt . . .

When I get to the Somerset, Ruth-Ann nods hello and fills up

my coffee. Dylan is playing from the kitchen, Maurice loudly singing
along to "Hazel." I push the menu aside, surround myself with blue
books. Listing and relisting the facts I've got thus far.

Peter Zell died five days ago.

He worked in insurance.

He loved math.

He was obsessed with the oncoming asteroid, collected information and tracked it in the sky, learning everything he could. He
kept this information in a box marked "12.375," for reasons I have yet
to understand.

His face. He died with bruises on his face, below his right eye.

He was not close with his family.

He appeared to have had only one friend, a man named J. T.
Toussaint, whom he'd loved as a child and then decided, for reasons
of his own, to make contact with again.

I sit in front of my dinner for an hour, reading and rereading my
notes, muttering to myself, waving away the slow-moving cigarette
clouds that drift over from neighboring tables. At some point Maurice wanders out of the kitchen, white apron, hands on his hips, and
looks down at my plate with stern disapproval.

"What's the problem, Henry?" he says. "There a ladybug in
your eggs or something?"

"Just not hungry, I guess. No offense."

"Well, you know, hate to waste the food," says Maurice, a high-
pitched giggle sneaking into his voice, and I look up, sensing a punch
line coming. "But it's not the end of the world!"

Maurice dies laughing, stumbles back into the kitchen.

I pull out my wallet, slowly count out three tens for the check and an even thousand for a tip. The Somerset has to abide by the price controls or get shut down, so I always try to make it right on the table.

Then I gather up my blue books and shove them in the inside pocket of my blazer.

Basically, I know nothing.

4.

"Hey, Palace?"

"Yeah?" I blink, clear my throat, sniff. "Who's this?"

My eyes find the clock. 5:42. Sunday morning. It's like the world has decided I'm better off on Victor France's plan, up and at 'em no time to waste. *The Advent calendar . . . of doom.*

"It's Trish McConnell, Detective Palace. I'm sorry to wake you."

"That's all right." I yawn, stretch my limbs. I haven't spoken to Officer McConnell in days. "What's up?"

"It's just—like I said, I'm really sorry to bother you. But I've got your victim's phone."

In ten minutes she's at my house—small town, no traffic—and we're sitting at my ramshackle kitchen table, which wobbles every time one of us picks up or puts down our mug of coffee.

"I couldn't shake the scene of the crime," says McConnell, in uniform from cap to shoes, the thin gray stripe running down the leg of her blue pants. Her expression is intent, fixed, a woman with a story to tell. "Couldn't stop thinking about it."

"Yeah," I say quietly. "Me, neither."

"Everything about it seemed off somehow, you know what I mean?"

"I do."

"Especially the absence of a phone. Everyone's got a phone. All the time. Even now. Right?"

"Right." Except Denny Dotseth's wife.

"*So.*" McConnell pauses, holds up one finger for dramatic effect, a sly smile starting to tug at the corners of her mouth. "I'm halfway through my shift two nights ago, overnight on Sector 7, and it comes to me. Somebody boosted the guy's phone."

I nod sagely, trying to give the impression that I've considered this possibility and discarded it for some higher-level, detective-grade reason, all the while kicking myself, because I'd pretty much forgotten about the phone angle entirely. "You think the killer took the phone?"

"No, Hank. Detective." McConnell's tight pony tail flicks back and forth as she shakes her head. "His wallet was still on him, you said. Wallet and keys. If someone killed him for gain, they'd take everything, right?"

"So maybe he got killed for the phone itself," I say. "Something on there? A number. A photograph. Some piece of information."

"I don't think so."

I rise to take our mugs over to the counter, the table teetering in my wake.

"So I'm thinking, it's not the murderer, it's someone at the scene," says McConnell. "Someone at that McDonald's snatched the phone from the dead man's pocket."

"Serious crime. Stealing from a corpse."

"Yes." she says. "But you gotta do a risk analysis."

I glance up from the counter, where I'm emptying the Mr. Coffee carafe into our mugs. "Excuse me?"

"Let's say I'm a regular citizen. I'm not homeless or broke, because here I am at a restaurant on a weekday morning."

"Okay."

"I've got a job, but it's a scrub job. If I can pawn a cell phone to a metal bug, someone collecting cadmium, that's a serious payday. Enough to keep me going for a month or two, maybe even get me out of work for the end of it. So that's a reward, a significant-percent chance of a significant reward."

"Sure, sure." I like the way she's doing this.

"So I'm standing there at the McDonald's, cops are on the way," says McConnell. "I figure I've got a ten percent chance of getting caught."

"With cops descending on the scene? Twenty-five percent chance."

"One of them is Michelson. Eighteen percent."

"Fourteen."

She's laughing, I'm laughing too, but I'm thinking about my father, and Shakespeare, and J. T. Toussaint: motive reconsidered in the matrix of new times. "But if you get caught, that's no arraignment, no habeas, that equals one hundred percent chance of dying in jail."

"Well, I'm young," she says, still in character. "I'm cocky. I decide I like my odds."

"All right, I'll bite," I say, stirring milk into my coffee. "Who took the phone?"

"It was that kid. The kid at the counter."

I remember him immediately, the kid she's talking about: greasy mullet, flipped-up visor, the acne scars, looking back and forth between hated boss and hated cops. The smirk just screaming, *I got one over on all you bastards, didn't I?*

"Son of a gun," I say. "Son of a gun."

McConnell is beaming. She joined the force in February of last year, so she'd gotten—what?—four months active duty before someone took an axe handle and bashed in the face of the world.

"I radio in to Watch Command I'm leaving my sector—you know, nobody cares all that much—and I head right over to that McDonald's. I walk in the door, and as soon as that kid sees my face he takes off running. Hurdles the counter, he's out the door, across the lot, out in the snow, and I'm like, not today, friend. Not today."

I laugh. "Not today."

"So I draw my sidearm and I give chase."

"You do not."

"I do."

This is terrific. Officer McConnell is maybe five foot one, 105 pounds, twenty-eight years old, a single mother of two. Now she's on her feet, gesturing, pacing around my kitchen.

"He books it into that little playground there. I mean the guy is zooming like the Road Runner, skidding through the gravel and the slush and everything. I'm yelling, 'Police, police! Stop, motherfucker!'"

"You do not yell, 'Stop, motherfucker.'"

"I do. Because you know, Palace, this is it. This is the last chance

I get to run after a perp yelling, 'Stop, motherfucker.'"

McConnell has the kid in cuffs and she leans on him hard, right there in the churned-up snow of the West Street playground, and he spills. He'd pawned the phone to a blue-haired lady named Beverly Markel, who runs a junk shop out of a boarded-up bail bondsman's next to the county courthouse. Markel is a goldbug, stockpiling coins and bullion, but she has a sideline in pawnbroking. McConnell works the lead: Beverly had sold the phone already, to a fat loon named Konrad, who was collecting lithium-ion cell phone batteries to communicate with the aliens who he thinks are on the way from the Andromeda galaxy to load the human race onto a flotilla of rescue ships. McConnell paid Konrad a visit, and after he was made to understand that she was a visitor not from outer space but from the police department, he grudgingly handed over the phone—still, miraculously, intact.

I reward this dramatic conclusion with a long, low appreciative whistle and a round of applause, while McConnell produces her prize and slides it on the table between us: a slim black smartphone, slick and gleaming. It's the same make and model as my own, and for a brief, disorienting instant I think it *is* mine, that somehow Peter Zell died in possession of Detective Henry Palace's cellular telephone.

"Well, Officer McConnell." I scoop up the phone and feel its cool flat weight in my palm. It's like holding one of Zell's organs, a kidney, a lobe of the brain. "That is one solid piece of police work."

She looks down at her hands, then back up at me, and that's it, our business is concluded. We sit there in easy morning silence, two human beings framed by the single window of a small white kitchen, the sun struggling to make itself known outside through the dampening gray of the low-hanging clouds. I've got a pretty decent view out here, especially first thing in the morning: a nice little copse of winter pine, the farmland beyond, deer tracks dancing across the snow.

"You'll make a great detective one day, Officer McConnell."

"Oh, I know," she says, flash of a smile, drains her coffee. "I know I will."

* * *

Turning on the phone I am greeted by a home-screen picture of Kyle Littlejohn, Peter Zell's nephew, in action on the ice, giant hockey mask covering his face, elbows jutted out to either side.

Kid must be terrified, I think, and I close my eyes to the thought, blink it away. *Stay on target. Stay focused.*

My first observation is that, within the three-month period covered by the list of "recent calls," there have been two calls placed to the number listed as Sophia Littlejohn's. One was last Sunday at 9:45 a.m., and it was twelve seconds long: just long enough for him to have gotten her voicemail or, say, for her to have answered, recognized his voice, and hung up. The second call, thirteen seconds, was on Monday, the day of his death, at 11:30 a.m.

I've got my blue book out and I'm writing down these observations and reflections, the pencil scritching rapidly, in the background the burbling of my second pot of coffee.

My second observation is that there have been seven conversations within that same three-month period, with the contact listed as "JTT." Most were on Mondays, in the afternoon, perhaps making arrangements to go see that night's *Distant Pale Glimmers.* The final call, incoming, lasting a minute and forty seconds, this past Monday at 1:15.

Interesting—interesting—very interesting. Thank you again, Officer McConnell.

It's my third observation that really gets my heart pumping, that's got me sitting here at the table with the phone in my hand, ignoring the eager beeping of the coffeemaker, staring at the screen, my mind rolling and gunning. Because there's a number with no name assigned to it, to which Peter Zell had placed a twenty-two-second telephone call at ten o'clock on the night of his death.

And a forty-two-second call at exactly ten o'clock the night before that.

I scroll through the list again, my fingers dancing across the screen, faster and faster. Every night, the same number. Ten o'clock. Outgoing call. Call less than a minute long. Every single night.

Peter Zell's phone is getting service in my house, two bars, the same as me. I call the mystery number and it is picked up after two rings.

"Hello?"

The voice answers as if from within a haze, whispering, confused—which is totally understandable. You don't get calls every day from a dead man's cell phone.

But I recognize her right away.

"Ms. Eddes? It's Detective Henry Palace, from the Concord Police Department. I'm afraid we're going to need to chat again."

* * *

She's early, but I'm even earlier, and Ms. Eddes sees me waiting and comes right over. I half rise, the ghost of my father in the small ritual gesture of politeness, and she slides into her side of the booth. And then, before I am fully back in my seat, I tell her I appreciate her coming, and she's got to tell me everything she knows about Peter Zell and the circumstances surrounding his death.

"My goodness, Detective," she says mildly, lifting up the thick glossy menu. "You don't mess around."

"No, ma'am."

And I give it to her again, my whole tough-guy deadpan speech about how she's got to tell me everything she knows. She lied to me before, left things out, and I'm trying to make it clear that such omissions will not be tolerated. Naomi Eddes looks back at me with raised eyebrows. She's wearing dark red lipstick, her eyes are dark and wide. The white curve of her scalp.

"And what if I don't?" she says, looking down at her menu, untroubled. "If I don't tell you everything, I mean."

"The thing is, you're a material witness, Ms. Eddes." I practiced this speech several times this morning, hoping I wouldn't have to deliver it. "Given the information I now have, I mean the fact that your number is all over the victim's phone . . ."

I should have practiced more; this sort of tough-as-nails posturing is a lot easier with Victor France. "And given that you chose, last time we spoke, to keep that information to yourself. The fact is, I have cause to take you in."

"Take me in?"

"Have you held. Under state statutes. Federal, also. Revised New Hampshire criminal code, section—" I pluck a sugar packet from the caddy in the center of the table. "I'd have to look up the section."

"Okay." She nods solemnly. "Understood." She smiles, and I exhale, but she's not done. "Held for how long?"

"For the . . ." I look down, look away. I give the bad news to the sugar packet. "Held for the rest of it."

"So, in other words, if I don't start spilling everything right this second," she says, "then you'll throw me in a deep, dark dungeon and leave me there until Maia makes landfall and all the world is consumed in darkness. Is that it, Detective Palace?"

I nod without speaking, look up and find her smiling still.

"Well, Detective, I do not think you would do that."

"Why not?"

"Because I think you have a little bit of a crush on me."

I don't know what to say to that, I really don't, but my hands are really doing a number on the crimped paper border of this sugar packet. Ruth-Ann comes over, fills my coffee, and takes Ms. Eddes's order for an unsweetened iced tea. Ruth-Ann scowls at the little mound of sugar I've left on her table and heads back to the kitchen.

"Ms. Eddes, on Monday morning you told me you weren't that close to Peter Zell. It turns out this is not true."

She purses her lips, exhales.

"Can we start with something else, please?" she says. "Aren't you wondering why I'm bald?"

"No." I turn a page in my blue book and begin to recite. "'Detective Palace: You're Mr. Gompers's executive assistant?' 'Ms. Eddes: Please. Secretary.'"

"You wrote all that down?" She's unwrapping her cutlery bundle, idly playing with her fork.

"'Detective Palace: Did you know the victim well?' 'Ms. Eddes: To be totally honest, I'm not sure I would have noticed him not being here. Like I said, we weren't that close.'"

I set down my book and lean forward across the table, lift the cutlery from her hands like a gentle parent. "If you weren't that close, why did he call you every night, Ms. Eddes?"

She takes her fork back. "Why don't you need to ask me why I'm bald? Do you think I have cancer?"

"No, ma'am." I scratch my mustache. "I think, based on the length and curve of your eyelashes, that you have very long, thick hair. I think you decided that, with the world ending, it was no longer worth the time and trouble to deal with it. Style it and comb it and all that woman-type stuff."

She looks at me, rubs a palm across her scalp. "That's very clever, Detective Palace."

"Thanks." I nod. "Tell me about Peter Zell."

"Let's order first."

"Ms. Eddes."

She raises her hands, palms up, imploring. "Please?"

"All right. We'll order first."

Because I know, now, that she's going to talk. Whatever she's holding back, she's going to give it to me, I can feel it, it's only a matter of time, and I'm starting to get this kind of powerful nervousness, a sweet humming anticipation against my ribs, like when you're on a date and you know that there will be a goodnight kiss—maybe more than a kiss—and it's just a matter of time.

Eddes orders the BLT, and Ruth-Ann says, "Good choice, dear."

I get the three-egg omelet with whole wheat toast, and Ruth-Ann notes dryly that there are other kinds of food besides eggs.

"So," I say. "We've ordered."

"One more minute. Let's talk about you. Who's your favorite singer?"

"Bob Dylan."

"Favorite book?"

I take a sip of coffee. "Right now I'm reading Gibbon. *The Decline and Fall of the Roman Empire.*"

"Yeah," says Eddes. "But what's your favorite?"

"*The Watchmen.* It's a graphic novel, from the eighties."

"I know what it is."

"Why did Peter Zell call you every night at exactly ten p.m.?"

"To make sure his watch was working."

"Ms. Eddes."

"He was a morphine addict."

"What?"

I'm staring at the side of her face, she's turned to look out the window, and I'm flabbergasted. It's like she just said that Peter Zell was an Indian chief or a general in the Soviet army.

"A morphine addict?"

"Yeah. I think morphine. Some kind of opiate, for sure. But not now—not anymore—I mean, obviously, he's dead now—but I mean—" She pauses, her fluency has deserted her, and she shakes her head, slows down. "For a period, last year, he was addicted to something, and then he quit."

She keeps talking, and I keep listening, writing down every word she says, even as some hungry part of my mind flies off into a corner, huddles with this new information—*a morphine addict, some kind of opiate, for a period*—and begins to chew on it, taste its marrow, decide how it might be digested. Decide if it's true.

"Zell was not inclined to outsize living, as you may have discovered," says Eddes. "No booze. No dope. No cigarettes, even. Nothing."

"Right."

Peter played Dungeons & Dragons. Peter alphabetized his breakfast cereal. He arranged actuarial data into tables, analyzed it.

"And then, last summer, with everything, I guess he felt like making a change." She smiles grimly. "A new lifestyle choice. He's telling me all this later, by the way. I wasn't privy to his decision-making process when he started."

I write down *last summer* and *lifestyle choice*. Questions are bubbling up on my lips, but I force myself to stay silent, sit still, let her keep talking, now that at last she's begun.

"So, you know, apparently this dalliance in illicit substances, it didn't go that well for him. Or, it went really well at first, and then really poorly. As it happens, you know?"

I nod like I do know, but everything I know is from law-enforcement training materials and cop movies. Personally, I'm like Peter: a beer now and again, maybe. No pot, no smokes, no booze. My whole life. The skinny policeman-to-be at sixteen waiting in the restaurant with a paperback copy of *Ender's Game*, his friends in the parking lot pulling hits off a purple ceramic head-shop bong and then sliding, giggling, back into the booth—this very booth. Not sure why. Just never been all that interested.

Our food comes, and Eddes pauses to deconstruct her sandwich, making three small piles on her plate: vegetables over here, bread over there, bacon at the farthest edge of the plate. Inside I'm quivering, thinking about these new pieces of the puzzle that are falling from the sky, trying to grasp them and slide each falling brick into the place where it fits, like in that old video game.

The asteroid. The shoebox.

Morphine.

J. T. Toussaint.

12.375. Twelve point three seven five *what?*

Pay attention, Henry, I tell myself. *Listen. Follow where it goes.* "Sometime in October, Peter stopped using." Eddes is talking with her big eyes shut, her head tilted back.

"Why?"

"I don't know."

"Okay."

"But he was suffering."

"Withdrawing."

"Yeah. And trying to cover it up. And failing."

I'm writing, trying to piece together the timeline on all this. Old Gompers, his voice soaked in gin and stentorian malaise, explaining how Peter had flipped out at work, screamed at the girl. The asteroid costume. Halloween night.

Eddes keeps talking. "Kicking morphine is not easy, is nearly impossible, in fact. So I volunteered to help the guy out. Told him he had to go home for a little bit, and I would help him."

"Okay . . ."

A week? Gompers had said. *Two weeks? I thought he was gone, but then he turned up again, no explanation, and he's been the same as ever.*

"All I did was, I checked in with him on my way to work each day. Lunch, sometimes. Make sure he had everything he needed, bring him a fresh blanket, soup, whatever. He didn't have any family. No friends."

By the week before Thanksgiving, she says, Peter was up and around, shaky on his feet but ready to go back to work, to insurance data.

"And the phone calls every night?"

"Well, nighttime's the hard part, and he was alone. Each night he would call me to check in. So I knew he was okay, and so he knew there was someone waiting to hear his voice."

"Every night?"

"I used to have a dog," she says. "That was a lot more burdensome."

I'm thinking this over, wishing it rang entirely true.

"Why did you say you weren't that close?"

"We weren't. Before last fall, before all of this, we'd never actually spoken."

"So, why go to all this trouble for the guy?

"I had to." She looks down, looks away. "He was suffering."

"Yeah, but that's an awful lot of time and effort. Especially now."

"Well, exactly." Now she stops looking away; she stares at me, her eyes flashing, as if daring me to reject the possibility of such a far-fetched motive as simple human kindness. "Especially now."

"What about the bruises?"

"Below his eye? I don't know. Showed up two weeks ago, said he had fallen down some stairs."

"Did you believe him?"

She shrugs. "Like I said . . ."

"You weren't that close."

"Yeah."

And here I'm feeling this strange and strong impulse to reach across the table, to take her hands in my own, to tell her it's okay, that it's all going to be okay. But I can't do that, can I? It's *not* okay. I can't tell her it's okay, because it's not okay, and because I have one more question.

"Naomi," I say, and her eyes flicker in quick teasing recognition that I've never used her first name before. "What were you doing there that morning?"

The spark dies in her eyes; her face tightens, pales. I wish I hadn't asked. I wish we could just be sitting here, two people, order some dessert.

"He used to talk about it. On the phone, at night, especially around December. He was done with the drugs, I really think he was, but he was still—he was not entirely happy. On the other hand, no one is. Entirely happy. How can we be?"

"Yeah. So, but, he would talk about the McDonald's?"

She nods. "Yeah. He'd say, you know that place? If I was going to kill myself, that would be the place to do it. Just *look* at that place." I don't say anything. From elsewhere in the restaurant, spoons clinking of coffee cups. Other people's melancholy conversation. "Anyway. As soon as he didn't show up for work, I came over to that McDonald's. I knew it. I knew he would be over there."

From Maurice's radio in the kitchen come the opening chords of "Mr. Tambourine Man."

"Hey," says Naomi. "This is Dylan, isn't it? You like this one?"

"No. I only like the seventies Dylan and the post-1990s Dylan."

"That's ridiculous."

I shrug. We listen for a minute. The song plays. She takes a bite of tomato.

"My eyelashes, huh?"

"Yeah."

* * *

It's probably not true.

Almost certainly, this woman is gulling me, misdirecting me for reasons still to be discovered.

From all that I have learned, the idea of Peter Zell having experimented with hard drugs—not to mention having sought out and purchased drugs, given their current scarcity and extreme expense, and the severity of the penalties for such purchases under the post-Maia criminal codes—it all seems like a one-in-a-million chance. On the other hand, isn't it so that even the one-in-a-million chance must be true one time, or there would be no chance at all? Everybody's been saying that. Statisticians on television talk shows, scientists testifying before Congress, everyone trying to explain, everyone desperate for all of this to make some kind of sense. Yes, the odds were extremely unlikely. A statistical unlikelihood approaching zero. But the strong unlikelihood of a given event is moot once that event has nevertheless transpired.

Anyway, I just don't think she was lying. I don't know why. I close my eyes and I can picture her telling me, her big dark eyes are steady and sad, she's casting them down at her hands, her mouth is still and set, and I think for some insane reason that she was telling it straight.

The question of Peter Zell and morphine rotates in a slow el-
lipse in my mind, drifting past the other new fact spinning around up
there: Zell's preoccupation with the McDonald's as a site of suicide.
So what, Detective? So he got murdered, and the murderer left him
to be found, by coincidence, in the very same spot? What are the
odds of *that*?

It's a different kind of snow right now, big fat drops falling
slowly, almost one at a time, each adding its weight to the drifts in the
parking lot.

"You all right, Hank?" says Ruth-Ann, slipping the hundreds
I've left on the table into her apron pocket without looking at them.

"I don't know." I shake my head slowly, look out the window
at the parking lot, lift my cup of coffee for one final sip. "I feel like I
wasn't made for these times."

"I don't know, kid," she says. "I think maybe you're the only
person who was."

* * *

I wake up at four o'clock in the morning, wake from some abstract dream of clocks and hourglasses and gambling wheels, and I
can't fall back asleep, because suddenly I've got it, I've got one piece
of it, I've got *something*.

I get dressed, blazer and slacks, I put on coffee, I slide my
department-issued semiautomatic pistol in its holster.

The words are turning around in my head, in a long slow circle: *what are the odds?*

There's a lot to do when the day begins.

I've got to call Wilentz. I've got to get over to Hazen Drive.

I look at the moon, fat and bright and cold, and wait for day-break.

5.

"Excuse me? Good morning. Hi. I need you to run a sample for me."

"Yeah. Well, that's what we do. Gimme a second, all right."

"I need you to run it right now."

"Didn't I just say, give me a second?"

This is the assistant to the assistant that Fenton warned me about, the individual now running the state lab on Hazen Drive. He's young and disheveled and late for work, and he is looking at me like he's never seen a policeman before in his life. He stumbles toward his desk, gestures vaguely at a row of hard plastic orange chairs, but I decline.

"I need these done right away."

"Dude, dude. *Give* me a damn second."

He's clutching a bag of doughnuts, grease staining its bottom, and he looks bleary eyed and unshaven and hungover.

"Sir?"

"I just walked in the door. It's like ten in the morning."

"It's ten forty-five. I've been waiting since nine."

"Yeah, well, the world's about to end."

"Yes," I say. "I heard."

Tonight it will be one week since Peter Zell was killed, and at last I've got a bite on it. One piece. One idea. My hands tap on the toxicologist's desk while he breathes open-mouthed and settles heavily into his rolling chair, and then I place my sample on his desk. A vial of dark red blood drawn from the heart of Peter Zell, which I removed this morning from the back of my freezer and zipped in the insulated box I use for my lunch.

"Dude, come on. This isn't tagged." The functionary lifts the vial to the pallid halogen light. "There's no sticker on it, no date. This could be chocolate syrup, man."

"It's not."

"Yeah, but, this isn't *procedure*, Officer."

"The world's about to end," I say, and he looks at me, sour.

"It has to have a sticker, and someone's gotta order it. Who ordered it?"

"Fenton," I say.

"Seriously?"

He lowers the vial, narrows his red-rimmed eyes at me. He scratches his head, and a drift of dandruff tumbles onto the desk.

"Yes, sir," I say. "She told me that this place is a mess. That orders are getting lost all the time."

I'm on thin ice. I am aware of that. I can't help it. The guy is looking at me, a little fearfully, it seems like, and I realize that my fists are clenched, and my jaw is tight. I need to know if there was morphine in this blood. I need to know if Naomi Eddes is telling me the truth. I think she was, but I need to know.

"Please, friend," I say quietly. "Please run my blood. Just run it."

* * *

"Brother?" calls a bespectacled middle-aged man with a beard, as I walk from the parking garage across School Street toward head-quarters, turning over possibilities in my head, laying out my time-line. "Have you heard the good news?"

"Yes," I say, smile politely. "I sure have. Thanks."

I need to get inside, tell my colleagues what I've worked out, determine a plan of action. But first I've got to stop in Wilentz's of-fice, get the results of the search I called him for at 8:45 this morn-ing. But the bearded religious man holds his ground, and when I look up I see that they're out in force this morning, a thick flock of the religious, long black coats, smiling in all directions, wielding their tattered pamphlets.

"Be not afraid," says a plain woman who appears before me, her eyes mildly crossed, dots of red lipstick on her smiling teeth. The others are all dressed similarly, three women and two men, all beam-ing rapturously, all holding thin pamphlets in gloved fingers.

"Thanks," I say, no longer smiling. "Thanks so much."

It's not the Jews, the Jews have the hats. It's not Jehovah's Wit-nesses, the Jehovah's Witnesses stand there quietly holding aloft their literature. Whoever it is, I do what I always do, which is look at my feet and try to keep moving.

"Be not afraid," says the first woman again, and the others form behind her in a ragged semicircle, blocking me like a hockey goal. I take a step back, nearly stumble into the street.

"I'm not afraid, actually. Thanks so much, though."

"The truth is not yours to refuse," murmurs the woman, pressing the pamphlet into my hand. I look down at it, just to avoid her God-glazed eyes, and I scan the bold red-outlined text: IT IS SIMPLY TO PRAY, the cover says on the top, and the same along the bottom: IT IS SIMPLY TO PRAY!

"Read it," says another of the ladies, a small, stout African American woman with a lemon-colored scarf and a silver brooch. Everywhere I turn there's a flap of broadcloth, a heavenly smile. I flip open the pamphlet, skim the bullet points.

★ *IF A MAN'S BLINDNESS CAN BE CURED BY THE PRAYERS OF A DOZEN, MANKIND'S CATASTROPHE CAN BE UNDONE BY THE PRAYERS OF A MILLION.*

I don't really accept the premise, but I go ahead and skim it. If enough of us renounce our wickedness and kneel in the loving light of the Lord, the pamphlet insists, then the ball of fire will bend in its path and sail harmlessly over the horizon. It's a nice thought. I just want to get into the office. I fold the pamphlet and push it back toward the first woman, the one with the batty eyes and the lipstick teeth.

"No thanks."

"Keep it," she insists, gentle and firm, while the chorus calls, "Read it!"

"May I ask you, sir," says the African American woman, with the scarf. "Are you a man of faith?

"No. My parents were."

"God bless them. And where are your parents now?"

"Dead," I say. "They were murdered. Excuse me, please."

"Leave him alone, you jackals," says a booming voice, and I look up: my savior, Detective McGully, an open beer bottle in one hand, a cigar clamped in his teeth. "You want to pray to someone, pray to Bruce Willis in *Armageddon*." McGully tosses me a salute, lifts his middle finger and waves it at the true believers.

"Sneer now, sinner, but wickedness shall be punished," says the saint with the lipstick teeth to Officer McGully, backing away, a pamphlet fluttering from her open pocketbook onto the sidewalk. "You shall face the darkness, young man."

"Guess what, sister," says McGully, handing me his Sam Adams and forming his hands into a megaphone. "You, too."

* * *

"It's a percentage."

"What is?"

"The number," I say. "It's 12.375 *percent*."

I'm pacing, and I've got it under my arm like a football, Peter Zell's shoebox, the one overflowing with asteroid information, all the numbers circled and double underlined. I'm laying it out for my colleagues, explaining what I've got, what I *think* I've got. McGully sits with furrowed brow, tipped back in his chair, rolling his empty morning beer bottle between his palms. Culverson is at his desk in a crisp silver suit, sipping coffee from a mug, considering. Andreas, over in his shadowy corner, head down, eyes closed, asleep. Adult Crimes.

"When Maia first showed up, when they first spotted it and

began tracking it, Peter immediately began following the story."

"Peter is your hanger?"

"The victim, yeah."

I take that first AP article, from April 2, the one ending with the odds of impact at one in two million one hundred twenty-eight thousand, and hand it to Culverson.

"And here's another one, a few days later." I pull out another scrap of dog-eared computer paper and begin reading. "'Though the object appears to be massively large, with an estimated diameter upwards of six and a quarter kilometers, Spaceguard astronomers calculate its current chances of colliding with Earth as barely higher than zero—what Dr. Kathy Goldstone, a professor of astrophysics at the University of Arizona, calls only just within the realm of nonnegligible probability.' And Mr. Zell, he's got that number—six and a quarter—that's underlined, too."

I take out another piece of paper, and another. Zell wasn't just keeping track of the numbers on Maia, on its trajectory and projected density and composition. His box also has articles on all the asteroid-related societal changes: new laws, shifting economic landscape, and he's watching those numbers, too, writing on the backs of the papers, scrawling calculations—long columns of data, exclamation points—adding it all into the matrix.

"Son of a gun," says Culverson suddenly.

"Son of a gun what?" says McGully. "What?"

"See—so—" I start, and Culverson finishes, says it smooth and right: "The strong possibility of death by global catastrophe can be seen as mitigating the risk of death from drug-related misadventure."

"Yes," I say. "Right. Yes."

"Yes, *what?*" growls McGully.

"Palace's hanger was doing a risk assessment."

I beam. Culverson nods at me approvingly, and I place the lid back on the box. It's 11:30 now, shift change, and from the break room a couple doors down we can hear the frat-house rumble of the patrol officers, the young Brush Cuts with their nightsticks. They're rattling around, shouting abuse at one another, drinking their skinny little cans of energy drink, strapping on their bulletproofing. Ready to get out there and aim their sidearms at some looters, ready to fill up the drunk tank.

"My theory is, Zell makes a decision, very early on, that if the odds of impact rise above a certain mathematically determined level, he's going to try something dangerous and illegal, an interest that had always been too risky to indulge. Until now."

In early June the odds rise above his threshold, and Zell heads to the house of his old friend J. T. Toussaint, who figures out how to get ahold of something, and together they get high as satellites.

But then—late October—Zell has a bad reaction, or a change of heart, or maybe the drugs run out. He goes into withdrawal.

At this point, McGully raises a hand slowly, sarcastically, like a surly teenager giving his math teacher a hard time.

"Uh, yes, Detective? Excuse me? How does this tragic tale make the guy into a murder victim?"

"Well, I don't know. But that's what I'd like to find out."

"Okay. Great!" He claps, hops off his desk. "So, let's go to this Toussaint fella's house and run the asshole in."

I turn from Culverson to McGully, my heartbeat accelerating a little. "You think so?"

"Hell, yeah, I think so." In fact, he looks delighted at the prospect, and I'm reminded of McConnell, the philosophical question of our era: *How many more times do I get to yell, "Stop, motherfucker"?*

"But I don't have probable cause," I protest, and I turn back toward Culverson, hoping that he'll object to my objection, hoping to hear him say, "Sure you do, son," but he's still quiet in his corner, ruminating.

"Probable cause?" snorts McGully. "Christ, man, you've got it in spades. You've got the guy procuring a controlled substance, distributing it. Automatic go to jail, do not pass Go, IPSS Title IX—right, hotshot? You've got him lying to a police officer. Same deal—Title I-don't-fucking-know, Title Infinity."

"Well, *I think* he's done those things. I don't *know.*" I appeal to Culverson, the adult in the room. "Maybe we can get a warrant? Search the house?"

"A warrant?" McGully throws his hands up, imploring the room, the heavens, the hushed form of Detective Andreas, who has opened his eyes just enough to stare at something he's got on his desk.

"Wait, wait, you know what? He's driving an oil car, right? He's admitted to that, right? To the WVO?

"Yeah. So?"

"So?" McGully is grinning ear to ear, his hands raised high in the touchdown sign. "Three new provisions just tacked onto Title XVIII, in re: natural resources management and scarcity." He hops over to his desk, scoops up the new binder, fat and black with the American flag stickered on the front. "Hot off the press, *mis amigos.* Presuming your man is juicing his French-fry oil with diesel, that vehicle is in flagrant violation."

I shake my head. "I can't arrest him for retroactively violating a newly enacted statute."

"Oh, well, Agent Ness, how high-minded of you." He gives me both middle fingers and sticks out his tongue for good measure.

"You've got another problem, though," says Culverson. I know what he's going to say; I'm ready for it. I'm actually a little excited about it. "You told me yesterday that Toussaint's got a squeaky-clean record. Hardworking guy. Working man. To the extent that Zell has kept up with him at all, to the extent that he's even crossed the guy's mind, why would he go to him for drugs?"

"Excellent question, Detective," I say, beaming. "Look."

I show him the printout I got from Wilentz, on the way up here, the search results on Toussaint's father. Because that's what I was remembering, that's what I found in my notes from yesterday, something about the way J.T. said it, about his old man: *"Was he an artist?"* *"Yes, among other things."* I watch Culverson skim the report. Roger Toussaint; a.k.a. Rooster Toussaint; a.k.a. Marcus Kilroy; a.k.a. Toots Keurig. Possession. Possession with intent to distribute. Possession with intent to distribute. Possession. Violation of a minor. Possession.

So when Peter Zell decided to get ahold of a controlled substance—when the odds of impact made the decision for him—he remembered his old friend, because his old friend's dad was a drug dealer.

Culverson, at last, nodding, rising slowly from his chair. McGully, out of his chair in a flash. My heart, galloping.

"Okay then," Culverson says. "Let's go."

I nod, there's a pause, and then the three of us move to the door at the same time, three policemen swinging into action, patting their shoulder holsters and shrugging on their coats, and there's a rush of anticipation and joy so strong in my gut that it comes all the way around, to a kind of dread. This is a moment I've imagined all my life, three police detectives up and ready for action, feeling the sturdiness of our legs beneath us, feeling the adrenaline begin to flow.

McGully stops for Andreas on the way out the door—"You coming, gorgeous?"—but the last of the Adult Crimes detectives isn't going anywhere. He's frozen in his chair, a half-empty coffee cup at his elbow, his hair a bird's nest, staring at a tattered pamphlet on his desk: IT IS SIMPLY TO PRAY.

"Come on, pally," McGully urges, snatching away the wrinkled pamphlet. "New Guy has got a scumbag for us."

"Come on," says Culverson, and I say it, too. "Come on."

He turns a quarter of an inch, mutters something.

"What?" I say.

"What if they're right?" says Andreas. "The—the—" he gestures to the pamphlet, and I sort of can't take it anymore.

"They're not right." I place a firm hand on his shoulder. "Why don't we not think about this right now."

"Not think about it?" says Andreas, wide-eyed, pathetic. "Not *think* about it?"

With a quick flat chop I knock over the cup of coffee on Andreas's desk, and the cold brown liquid gushes out, rushing over the pamphlet, flooding his ashtray, his paperwork and computer keyboard.

"Hey," he says dumbly, pushing back from the desk, turning all the way around. "Hey."

"You know what I'm doing right now?" I say, watching the

muddy liquid rush toward the edge of the table. "I'm thinking: Oh no! The coffee's going to spill onto the floor! I'm so worried! Let's keep talking about it!"

And then the coffee waterfalls over the side of the desk, splashing on Andreas's shoes and pooling on the ground beneath the desk.

"Oh, look at that," I say. "It happened anyway."

* * *

All is the same as it was.

The doghouse, the thorn bushes and the oak tree, the ladder propped against the lip of the roof. There's the small white dog, Houdini, weaving anxiously around the legs of the ladder, and there's big J. T. Toussaint, up there fixing shingles, bent to his task in the same brown work pants and black boots. He looks up at the sound of the gravel crunch on the driveway, and I catch a flash of impression, a reclusive animal surprised in his lair by the arrival of the hunters.

I'm out of the car first, straightening up and tugging down the hem of my suit coat, one hand shading my eyes against the winter sun, the other hand raised, flat palmed in greeting.

"Good morning, Mr. Toussaint," I call. "I have just a couple more questions for you."

"What?" he says. He comes up from his crouch, finds his balance, and stands full height on the roof, the sun right behind him and all around him, casting him in a weird pale gray halo. The other doors slam behind me, McGully and Culverson stepping out of the vehicle, and Toussaint flinches, retreats a step upward on the roof, stumbles.

He raises his hands to steady himself, and I hear McGully shout, "Gun!" and I turn my head back and say, "What—no," because it's not, "it's just a caulking gun!"

But McGully and Culverson have their weapons raised, service-issue SIG Sauer P229s. "Freeze, asshole," McGully shouts, but Toussaint *can't* freeze, his boots have lost their purchase on the shingled slope, he's scrabbling, hands in motion, eyes wide, McGully still shouting—and I'm shouting, too, "No, no, don't—no," whipping my head back and forth, because I don't want him dead. I want to know the story.

Toussaint turns on his heel, tries to escape toward the spine of the roof; McGully fires his gun, a sliver of brick spits off the side of the chimney, and Toussaint turns and falls off the house and down onto the lawn.

* * *

"Your house smells like dog shit."

"Let's focus on what's material, Detective McGully."

"Okay. It's true, though, isn't it? Stinks in here."

"Detective, come on."

J. T. Toussaint starts to say something, or maybe he's just moaning, and McGully tells him to shut up, and he shuts up. He's on the living-room floor, giant body prone on the dirty carpet, face buried in the rug, bleeding from his forehead where he caught it on the roof on the way down. McGully is sitting on his back, smoking a cigar. Detective Culverson is over by the mantel, I'm pacing, everyone's waiting, it's my show.

"Okay. Let's—let's just chat," I say, and then my body is wracked by a long shiver, shaking off the last of the adrenaline high, the rush of the gunshots, of hurtling forward, charging through the muddy snow.

Calm, Palace. Easy.

"Mr. Toussaint, it seems as if the last time we spoke, you omitted a few details about your relationship with Peter Zell."

"Yeah," says McGully curtly, shifting so that his full weight digs into the small of Toussaint's back. "Asshole."

"Detective?" I murmur, trying to suggest *take it easy* without saying it in front of the suspect. He rolls his eyes at me.

"So we were getting high," says Toussaint. "Okay? We were getting fucked up. Me and Petey, we got high a few times."

"A few times," I say.

"Yeah. Okay?"

I nod, slowly. "And why did you lie to me, J. T.?"

"Why did he *lie* to you?" McGully asks, staring at me. "Because you're a policeman, you dodo."

Culverson makes an amused noise from his place over by the mantel. I wish I were alone with J. T., in a room, just he and I, and he could tell me the story. Just two people talking.

Toussaint looks up at me, his body immobile under McGully's weight. "You come around here, you think the guy got killed."

"I said he was a suicide."

"Yeah, well, that was you lying," he says. "No one is investigating suicides. Not now they're not."

Culverson makes his amused noise again, and I look at him, at his wry face: *it's a good point.* McGully taps out a fat turd of cigar ash on the suspect's rug.

Toussaint ignores them both, keeps his eyes on me, keeps talking. "You come here looking for a killer, and I tell you that Pete and me were taking fucking pain pills, you're going to conclude that I'm the guy who killed him. Right?"

"Not necessarily."

I'm thinking, pills. Popping pills. Small colorful capsules, waxy coating coming off in a sweaty palm. Trying to imagine it, my insurance man, the squalid details of abuse and addiction.

"J. T.," I start.

"It doesn't matter," he says. "I'm dead now either way. I'm done."

"Yup," says McGully mirthfully, and I will him to shut up.

Because I believe Toussaint. I do. There's a part of me that really does believe him. He lied to me for the same reason that Victor France spent his precious hours snooping around Manchester Road to get me the information I needed—because nowadays every charge is serious. Every sentence is a death sentence. If he had explained his real relationship with Peter Zell, he would have gone to prison and not come out. But there's still no reason to assume that he killed him.

"McGully. Let him up."

"What?" says McGully sharply. "Absolutely not."

We both look to Culverson instinctively; we're all the same rank, but he's the grown-up in the room. Culverson nods minutely. McGully glowers, comes up out of his squat like a gorilla rising from the jungle floor, and steps pointedly on Toussaint's fingers on his way to the ratty sofa. Toussaint struggles to his knees, and Culverson murmurs, "That's far enough," so I get down on my knees, too, so I can look into his eyes, and I give my voice a coaxing, sweet gentleness, somewhere in the vocal range of my mother.

"Tell me what else."

Long silence. "He's—" starts McGully, and I hold up one hand, eyes still on the suspect, and McGully shuts up.

"Please, sir," I say softly. "I just want to know the truth, Mr. Toussaint.

"I didn't kill him."

"I know that," and I mean it. In this instant, looking into his eyes, I don't believe that he did kill him. "I just want to know the truth. You said pills. Where did you get the pills?"

"I didn't get them." Toussaint looks at me, bewildered. "Peter brought 'em over."

"What?"

"God's truth," he says, for he can see my skepticism. We're down there on the floor, kneeling across from each other like two religious fanatics, a pair of penitents.

"Dead serious," says Toussaint. "Guy shows up on my doorstep with two pill bottles, MS Contins, sixty milligrams a pill, a hundred pills in each bottle. He says he'd like to ingest the drugs in a safe and effective manner."

"That's what he said?" snorts McGully, settled in the easy chair, his sidearm trained on Toussaint.

"Yes."

"Look at me," I say. "Tell me what happened then."

"I said, sure, but let me split 'em with you." He looks up, looks around, his narrowed eyes flashing with nervousness, defiance, pride. "Well, what the hell was I supposed to do? I worked my whole life— every day, since I got out of high school I worked. For the specific reason that my old man was a piece of shit, and I didn't want to be my old man."

J. T. Toussaint's massive frame is shaking with the force of expressing all this.

"And then, out of the clear blue sky, this bullshit? An asteroid is coming, no one's building anything, the quarry shuts down, and just like that I got no job, no prospects, nothing to do but wait to die. Two days later Peter Zell comes to my house with a handful of opiates? What would *you* do?"

I look at him, his kneeling trembling frame, his giant head cast down at the rug. I look to Culverson, at the mantel, who shakes his head sadly. I become aware of a light high-pitching hum and look over at McGully on the sofa, his gun in his lap, pretending to play a little violin.

"Okay, J. T.," I say. "Then what happened?"

It wasn't hard for J. T. Toussaint to help Peter ingest morphine sulfate in a safe and effective manner, to circumvent the time-release mechanism and measure out the dosage to ration the share and minimize the risk of accidental overdose. He'd watched his father do it a million times with a million different kinds of pills: scrub off the wax, crush the tablet, measure it out, and place it under the tongue. When they were done, Peter got more.

"He never told you where it came from?"

"Nope." A pause—a half-second hesitation—I stare into his eyes. "Really, man. This went on till, like, October. Wherever he was getting the shit, he ran out of it." After October, says Toussaint, they'd still hang out, started going to see *Distant Pale Glimmers* together when that started up, grab a beer now and then after work. I'm thinking about all this, considering the raft of new details, trying to see what might be true.

"And last Monday night?"

"What?"

"What happened on Monday night?"

"Just like I told you, man. We went to the movie, we had a bunch of beer, and I left him there."

"And you're sure?" I say gently, almost tenderly. "Sure that's the whole story?"

Silence. He looks at me, and he's about to say something, I can see his mind working behind the rock-wall hardness of his face, he wants to tell me one thing more.

"McGully," I say. "What's the mandatory on the waste-vehicle violation?"

"Death," says McGully, and Toussaint's eyes go wide, and I shake my head.

"Come on, Detective," I say. "Seriously."

Culverson says, "Discretion."

"Okay," I say, eyes back on Toussaint. "Okay. So, look, we're going to bring you in. We have to. But I'll make it so you do two weeks on the car." I stand up, hands out to him, to pull him up. "A month maybe. Easy time."

And then McGully says, "Or we could shoot him right now."

"McGully—" I turn away from J. T. Toussaint for one second, to Culverson, trying to get him to get McGully to knock it off, and by the time I turn back to J. T. he's in motion, launching himself up like a rocket and ramming his head into my chest, the massive weight of him like a sledge. I'm down, backward, and McGully is up and Culverson is in motion, guns drawn. Toussaint's big hand has got that model of the New Hampshire state house, and now Culverson has his gun out, too, but he's not firing, and McGully isn't either, because Toussaint is on top of me, and he comes right at my eye with that thing, its wicked golden steeple pointed down, and everything goes black.

"Son of a bitch," says McGully. Toussaint lets me go and I hear him thunder toward the door, and I shout, "Don't," blood gushing from my face, my hands up over my eyes. I shout, "Don't shoot!" but it's too late, everybody's shooting, the bullets a series of hot rushes in the corner of my blindness, and I hear Toussaint scream and fall down.

Houdini barking like crazy from the door by the kitchen, howling and woofing in grief and astonishment.

* * *

"Uh, yes, Detective? Excuse me? How does this tragic tale make the guy into a murder victim?"

These are the words ringing bitterly in the hollowed-out corners of my brain, as I'm lying here in the hospital, in pain. McGully's sarcastic question back at headquarters, before we went over there.

J. T. Toussaint is dead. McGully shot him three times, and Culverson shot him once, and he was dead by the time he arrived at Concord Hospital.

My face hurts. I'm in a lot of pain. Maybe Toussaint went after me with the ashtray and tried to bolt because he murdered his friend Peter, but I don't think so.

I think he attacked me simply because he was afraid. There were too many cops in the room, and McGully was cracking wise and I tried to tell him otherwise, but he was afraid that if we took him in for the stupid engine violation, he would rot in prison until October 3. He took a calculated risk, just like Peter did, and he lost.

McGully shot him three times, and Culverson shot him once, and now he's dead.

"A quarter of an inch higher and your eyeball would have exploded," says the doctor, a young woman with a high blonde ponytail and sneakers and the cuffs of her white doctor's coat rolled up.

"Okay," I say.

She secures a thick pad of gauze over my right eyeball with surgical tape.

"It's called an orbital floor fracture," she says, "and it's going to cause some numbing of the cheek."

"Okay," I say.

"As well as mild to severe diplopia."

"Okay."

"Diplopia means double vision."

"Oh."

Through all of this, the question is still rolling around in my head: *How does this tragic tale make the guy into a murder victim?*

Unfortunately, I think I know the answer. I wish I didn't, but I do.

My doctor keeps apologizing, for her lack of experience, for the lightbulbs that have burned out and not been replaced in this emergency room, for the overall shortage of palliative resources. She looks about nine years old, and she has not technically finished her residency. I tell her it's okay, I understand. Her name is Susan Wilton.

"Dr. Wilton," I say while she's drawing the silken thread in and out of my cheek, wincing with each pull, as if she's stitching her own face, not mine. "Dr. Wilton, would you ever kill yourself?"

"No," she says. "Well—maybe. If I knew I was going to be miserable the whole rest of the time. But I'm not. I like my life, you know? If I was someone who was really miserable already—you know?—then it would be like, why sit around and wait for it?"

"Right," I say. "Right." I keep my face steady while Dr. Wilton sews me up.

There's only one mystery left. If Toussaint was telling the truth, and I think he was, and Peter was the one who supplied the pills, where did he get them?

That's the last part of the mystery, and I think I know the solution to that, too.

* * *

Sophia Littlejohn looks uncannily like her brother, even peering through the crack between the door and the doorjamb, staring at me under the chain. She's got the same small chin and large nose and wide forehead, even the same unfashionable style of eyeglasses. Her hair is cut short, too, boyish, sticking out here and there, just like his.

"Yes?" she says. She's staring at me just like I'm staring at her, and I remember that we've never met, and what I must look like: the fat wad of gauze that Dr. Wilton has taped over my eye, the bruise radiating out around it, brown and pink and puffy.

"It's Detective Henry Palace, ma'am, from the Concord Police Department," I say. "I'm afraid that we—" but the door is already closing, and then there's the quiet tinkle of the chain unlatching, and then the door opens again.

"All right," she says, nodding stoically, as though this day has been coming, she knew it was coming. "Okay."

She takes my coat and gestures me into the same overstuffed blue easy chair I sat in during my last visit, and I'm getting out my notebook and she's explaining that her husband isn't home, he's working late, one of them is always working late these days. Erik Littlejohn's semioccasional nondenominational worship service is now happening every night, and so many hospital staff are attending that he closed the little chapel in the basement and took over an auditorium upstairs. Sophia is talking just to talk, that's clear, one last goal-line effort to avoid this conversation, and what I'm thinking is that these are what Peter's eyes must have looked like, when he was alive: careful, analytical, calculating, a little sad.

I smile, I shift in the chair, I let her trail off, and then I can ask my question, which is really more of a declarative statement than a question. "You gave him your prescription pad."

She looks down at the rug, an endless row of small delicate paisleys, then up at me again. "He stole it."

"Ah," I say. "Okay."

I was in the hospital with my injured face, thinking about this question for an hour before the possibility had occurred to me, and I still wasn't sure. I had to ask my friend Dr. Wilton, who had to look it up: can midwives prescribe?

Turns out, they can.

"I should have told you sooner, and I'm sorry," she says quietly.

Outside the French door connecting the living room to the outdoors, I can see Kyle with another kid, both of them in snow suits and boots, goofing around with a telescope in the otherworldly brightness of the backyard floodlights. Last spring, with odds of impact in the single digits, there was a vogue for astronomy, everyone suddenly interested in the names of the planets, their orbits, their distances from one another. Like how, after September 11, everybody learned the provinces of Afghanistan, the difference between Shiite and Sunni. Kyle and his buddy have repurposed the telescope as a sword, are taking turns knighting each other, kneeling, giggling in the early-evening moonlight.

"It was June. Early June," begins Sophia, and I turn back to her. "Peter called me out of the blue, said he'd like to have lunch. I said that sounded nice."

"You ate in your office."

"Yes," she says. "That's right."

They ate and caught up and had a wonderful conversation, brother and sister. Talked about movies they'd seen as kids, about their parents, about growing up.

"Just, you know, stuff. Family stuff."

"Yes, ma'am."

"It all felt really nice. That's probably what hurt me the most, Detective, when I figured it out, what he had really been up to. We were never very close, Peter and I. Him calling me that way, just out of nowhere? I remember thinking, when this craziness is over, maybe we'll be friends. Like brothers and sisters are supposed to be."

She reaches up and dabs a tear from her eye.

"The odds were still really low then. You could still think like that, *when this is all over.*"

I wait patiently. My blue book is open, balanced on my lap.

"Anyway," she says. "I write prescriptions only rarely. Our practice is largely holistic, and any drugs that do come into play, it's during labor and delivery, not by prescription during the course of pregnancy."

So it was many weeks before Sophia Littlejohn realized that one of her prescription pads had gone missing from the stack in the top-right drawer of her office desk. And more weeks before she pieced it together that her timid brother had stolen it during their pleasant reunion lunch. She pauses during this portion of the story, looks up at the ceiling, shakes her head with self-recrimination; and I am picturing Peter the mild-mannered insurance man in his moment of bravado—he's made his fateful decision—Maia having crossed the 12.375 threshold—summoning the nerve, his sister gone momentarily from her office, to the bathroom or on some small errand—nervous, a bead of sweat slipping down from his forehead under his glasses—lifting himself from his chair, sliding open the top drawer of the desk—

Kyle and the friend scream with laughter outside. I keep my eyes on Sophia.

"So then, in October, you figured it out."

"Right," she says, glances up briefly but doesn't bother to wonder how I know. "And I was furious. I mean, Jesus Christ, we're still human beings, aren't we? We can't just behave like human beings until it's over?" There's real anger in her voice. She shakes her head bitterly. "It sounds ridiculous, I know."

"No, ma'am," I say. "Not ridiculous at all."

"I confronted Peter, and he admitted to taking them, and that was that. I haven't—I'm sorry to say, I haven't spoken to him since."

I'm nodding. I was right. Bully for me. Time to go. But I have to know it all. I have to.

"Why didn't you tell me all this before, why didn't you return my calls—"

"Well, it was a . . . I made a practical decision. I just—decided—" she begins, and then Erik Littlejohn says, "Sweetheart," from the doorway.

He's standing on the threshold, has been standing there who knows how long, snow falling gently all around him. "No."

"It's okay."

"No, it's not. Hello, again, Detective." He steps in, snowflakes melting to water on the leather shoulders of his coat. "I told her to lie. And if there are consequences, they should fall on me."

"I don't think there have to be any consequences. I just want to know the truth."

"Okay. Well, the truth is, I saw no reason to tell you about Peter's theft and drug abuse, and I told Sophia that."

"We made the decision together."

"I talked you into it."

Erik Littlejohn shakes his head, looks at me squarely, almost sternly. "I told her there was no sense in telling you."

I rise to look at him, and he looks back, unflinching.

"Why?" I say.

"What's done is done. The incident with Sophia's prescription pad was unrelated to Peter's death, and there was no sense in telling the police about it." He says "the police" like it's this abstract concept, somewhere out there in the world, "the police," as opposed to me, a person, now standing in their living room with an open blue book.

"Telling the police would mean telling the press, telling the public."

"My father," murmurs Sophia, then looks up. "He means telling my father."

Her father? I think back, scratch my mustache, and I recall Officer McConnell's report: father, Martin Zell, in Pleasant View Retirement, the beginnings of dementia. "It was bad enough for him to know that Peter had killed himself. To find out also that his son had become a drug addict?"

"Why put him through that?" says Erik. "At a time like this? I told her not to tell you. It was my decision, and I take full responsibility."

"Okay," I say. "Okay."

I sigh. I'm tired. My eye hurts. Time to go.

"I have one more question. Ms. Littlejohn, you seem so certain that Peter killed himself. Can I ask what it is that makes you so sure?"

"Because," she says softly, "he told me."

"What? When?"

"That same day. When we had lunch in my office. It already started, you know. There was one on the news. In Durham. The elementary school?"

"Yeah." A man who had grown up in Durham, the Seacoast area, he traveled back there to hang himself in the coat closet of his fourth-grade classroom, just so that the teacher, whom he had loathed, would find him.

Sophia presses her fingertips into her eyes. Erik moves behind her, places his hands comfortingly on her shoulders.

"Anyway, Pete—Peter said that if *he* were ever going to do it, it would be at that McDonald's. On Main Street. You know, it seemed like a joke. But I guess—I guess it wasn't, huh?"

"No, ma'am. Guess not."

There you go, Detective McGully. *How does this tragic tale make the guy into a murder victim?* The answer is, it doesn't.

The fancy belt, the pickup truck, none of it matters. When his experiment with controlled substances had turned out to be a disaster—when he was discovered in his one audacious act of theft and betrayal—left with that shame and the lingering painful symptoms of withdrawal—faced with all that, and with the impending end of time—the actuary Peter Zell did another careful calculation, another analysis of risk versus reward, and went ahead and killed himself.

Bam!

"Detective?"

"Yep."

"You're not writing."

Erik Littlejohn looks at me, almost suspiciously, like I'm hiding something.

My head hurts. The room swims; two Sophias, two Eriks. What did Dr. Wilton call it? Diplopia.

"You've stopped writing down what we're saying."

"No. I'm just—" I swallow, stand up. "This case is closed. I'm sorry to have bothered you."

* * *

Five hours, six hours later, I don't know. It's the middle of the night.

Andreas and I are outside, we've both escaped from Penuche's, the basement bar on Phenix Street, from the din and the smoke and

the grim dive-bar haze of it, and we're standing on the grimy spit of
sidewalk, neither of us having wanted to come out for a beer in the
first place. Andreas was literally dragged from his desk by McGully, to
celebrate me solving my case; a case I didn't solve, and which was
never really a case in the first place. Anyway, it's awful down there, the
fresh cigarette smell mingling with the stale, the TVs blaring, people
crammed against the graffiti-marked load-bearing poles that keep
the whole place from collapsing in on itself. Plus some wiseacre has
larded the jukebox with irony: Elvis Costello, "Waiting for the End
of the World," Tom Waits, "The Earth Died Screaming," and of course
that R.E.M. song, playing over and over and over.

It's snowing out here, fat dirty chunks slanting down and ricocheting off the brick walls. I shove my hands into my pockets and
stand with my head tilted back, staring up at the sky with my one
working eye.

"Listen," I say to Andreas.

"Yeah?"

I hesitate. I hate this. Andreas draws a Camel from a pack, I
watch balls of snow lose themselves in his wet mop of hair.

"I'm sorry," I say, when he's got it lit.

"What?"

"About before. Spilling your coffee."

He chuckles woodenly, draws on his smoke.

"Forget it," he says.

"I—"

"Seriously, Henry. Who cares?"

A small crowd of kids comes out of the stairwell that leads up
from the bar, laughing like crazy, dolled up in weird pre-apocalyptic

fashion: a teenage girl in an emerald ball gown and tiara, her boyfriend in full-goth black. Another kid, gender indeterminate, baggy shorts over plaid tights, broad red clown suspenders. Music drifts out from the open door, it sounds like U2, and then fades again as the door closes.

"Newspaper says the Pakistanis want to blow the thing up," says Andreas.

"Yeah, I heard that."

I'm trying to remember what U2's end-of-the-world song is. I turn away from the kids, stare at the road.

"Yeah. They say they've figured it out, they can make it happen. But we're saying we won't let them."

"Oh, yeah?"

"There was a press conference. The secretary of state, secretary of defense. Someone else. They said, if they try, we'll nuke them before they can nuke it. Why would we say that?"

"I don't know." I feel hollow. I'm cold. Andreas is exhausting.

"It just seems *crazy*."

My eye hurts; my cheek. After the Littlejohns, I gave Dotseth a call, and he graciously accepted my apology for wasting his time, made his jokes about not knowing who I was, what case I was talking about.

Andreas starts to say something else, but there's honking to our right, at the top of Phenix, where the road crests and starts to bend down toward Main Street. Loud, boisterous honking from a city bus, picking up steam as it barrels down the street. The kids cheer and holler, wave at the bus, and Detective Andreas and I look at each other. City bus service has been suspended, and there was never a night-owl route on Phenix Street in the first place.

The bus is getting closer, rattling fast, two wheels up on the sidewalk, and I go ahead and draw my service pistol and aim it in the general direction of the broad windshield. It's like a dream, in the dark, a giant city bus, display lights spelling OUT OF SERVICE, sailing down the hill toward us like a ghost ship. Closer now, and we can see the driver, early twenties, Caucasian male, baseball cap backward, scruffy little mustache, eyes wide with adventure and delight. His buddy, black, also early twenties, also in a baseball cap, has the shot-gun-side pneumatic door open and he's leaning out and hollering, "Ya-hoo!" Everybody always wanted to do something, and here come the guys who always wanted to joyride in a city bus.

The teenagers on the curb with us are dying laughing, cheer-ing. Andreas is staring at the headlights, and I'm standing there with my gun out wondering how to play it. Probably do nothing, let them sail by.

"Oh, well," says Andreas.

"Oh, well, what?"

But it's too late. He twists his body, flicks the half-smoked cig-arette back toward the bar, and throws himself in front of the bus.

"No," is all I've got time for, one cold sorrowful syllable. He's timed it, calculated the vectors, bus and man intersecting as they move through space at their varying speeds. *Bam!*

The bus screeches to a halt and time stops, freeze-frame: the girl in the ball gown with her face hidden in the crook of the goth kid's arm—me with my mouth open, gun out, pointed uselessly at the side of the bus—the bus at a deranged angle, back end on the sidewalk, front end jutting into the road. Then Detective Andreas slowly peels off and slips down onto the street, and the bar crowd is streaming out and surrounding me and chattering and hollering. The joyrider and his friend climb down the steps of the bus and stand a few paces back from Andreas's broken body, staring openmouthed.

And then Detective Culverson is at my side, a firm hand on my wrist, gently lowering my gun hand to my side. McGully works his way through the crowd, pushing and shouting, "Cop!" waving his badge around, a Coors in the other hand, cigar in his mouth. He takes a knee in the middle of Phenix Street and lays a finger on Andreas's throat. Culverson and I stand there in the center of the awestruck crowd, cold puffs of air drifting from our mouths, but Andreas's head is all the way around, his neck is snapped. He's dead.

"Well, Palace, what do you think?" says McGully, heaving up to his feet, looking over. "Suicide, or murder?"

PART THREE

....

Wishful Thinking

....

Tuesday, March 27

Right ascension 19 11 43.2
Declination -34 36 47
Elongation 83.0
Delta 3.023 AU

1.

"Good Lord Almighty, Henry Palace, what *happened* to you?"

This seems like an awfully harsh assessment from a former sweet-heart I haven't seen for six years, until I remember what I look like: my face, my eye. I bring my hand up, adjust the thick stiff packet of gauze, smooth my mustache, feel the bristle of stubble along my jaw.

"I've had a rough couple of days," I say.

"Sorry to hear that."

It's six-thirty in the morning, and Andreas is dead, and Zell is dead, and Toussaint is dead, and here I am standing in Cambridge, on a footbridge over the Charles River, making small talk with Alison Koechner. And it's weirdly pleasant out here, it must be over fifty degrees, as if crossing the Massachusetts state line has tripped me over into a southern latitude. All of it, the gentle spring breeze, the morning sun glinting off the bridge, the soothing ripple of the river in spring, it would all be pleasurable in another world, another time. But I close my eyes and what I see is death: Andreas flattened against the grill of a bus; J. T. Toussaint thrown back against the wall, a hole blown open in his chest; Peter Zell in the bathroom.

"It's great to see you, Alison."

"Okay," she says.

"I mean it."

"Let's not get into all that."

The wild tangle of orchid-red hair that I remember has been cut to an adult length and corralled into a bun with a system of small efficient clips. She wears gray pants and a gray blazer and a small gold pin on her lapel: she really does, she looks terrific.

"So," says Alison, and draws from an inside pocket of her blazer a slim letter-size white envelope. "This friend of yours? Mr. Skeve?"

"He's not my friend," I say immediately, raising one finger. "He's Nico's husband."

She raises an eyebrow. "Nico, as in your sister Nico?"

"Asteroid," I say, no need to expound. Impulse marriage. Shotgun wedding. Biggest imaginable shotgun. Alison nods, just says, "Wow." She knew Nico when Nico was twelve years old, already not the kind of a person you imagined settling down. A sneak smoker, a snatcher of beers from the cooler in Grandfather's garage, a succession of bad haircuts and disciplinary problems.

"Okay then. So, your brother-in-law, Skeve? He's a terrorist."

I laugh. "No. Skeve is not any kind of terrorist. He's an idiot."

"The overlapping Venn-diagram section of those two categories, you will find, can be quite large."

I sigh, lean one hip against the rusted green steel of the bridge's guard rail. A shell slides by, cutting through the surface of the river, the crew grunting as they shoot past. I like these kids, getting up at six in the morning to row crew, keeping in shape, sticking with their program. These kids, I like.

"What would you say," Alison asks, "if I told you that the United States government, long ago anticipating this kind of disaster, had prepared an escape plan? Had constructed, in secret, a habitable environment, beyond reach of the asteroid's destructive effects, where humanity's best and brightest could be relocated and made safe to repopulate the species?"

I bring my palm up to my face, rub it against my cheek, which is only now beginning to emerge, from its numbness, into active pain.

"I'd say that's insane. It's Hollywood nonsense."

"And you would be right. But there are those who are not as perspicacious."

"Oh, for God's sake." I'm remembering Derek Skeve lying on the thin mattress in his cell, his spoiled kid's clowning grin. *I wish I could tell you, Henry, but it's a secret.*

Alison opens the white envelope, unfolds three pieces of crisp white paper, and hands them to me, and my impulse is to say, you know what? Forget the whole thing. I have a murder to solve. But I don't. Not today.

Three single-spaced typed pages, no watermark, no agency seal, pocked here and there with thick black lines of redaction. In 2008 there was a tabletop exercise convened by the Directorate of Strategic Planning of the United States Air Force, drawing on the resources and personnel of sixteen discrete agencies of the United States government, including the DHS, the DTRA, and NASA. The exercise imagined an event "above global-catastrophe threshold" in a "short-warning" scenario—in other words, exactly what has now come to pass—and considered every possible response: nuclear counterstrike, slow push–pull, kinetic options. The conclusion was that realistic response options would be limited to civil defense.

I'm yawning, flipping forward. I'm still on the first page. "Alison?"

She rolls her eyes slightly, the small gentle sarcasm so familiar that it squeezes my heart in my chest, and takes back the papers. "There was a dissent, Palace. An astrophysicist from Lawrence Livermore named Dr. Mary Catchman insisted that the government act preemptively and build habitable environments on the moon. When Maia turned up, certain individuals convinced themselves that the DOD had embraced that dissent, and that these safe havens exist."

"Bases?"

"Yes."

"On the Moon?"

"Yes."

I squint into the gray sun, seeing Andreas plastered against the bus, slowly sliding down. IT IS SIMPLY TO PRAY. Secret government escape bases. People's inability to face up to this thing is worse than the thing, it really is.

"So, Derek was tooling around the Guard station on his ATV looking for, what, blueprints? Escape pods? A giant slingshot?"

"Or something."

"Doesn't make him a terrorist."

"I know, but that's the designation. The way the military-justice system works right now, once he's got that tag, there's nothing that can be done."

"Well, I'm no fan of this guy, but Nico loves him. There's nothing—?"

"There's nothing. Nothing." Alison sends a long look out across the river, at the rowers, the ducks, the clouds easing along in parallel with the water line. She is not the first girl I ever kissed, but she remains the one I've kissed the most, in all my life thus far. "I'm sorry. It's not my department."

"What is your department, anyway?"

She doesn't answer; I knew she wouldn't. We've always stayed in touch, the occasional e-mail, phone numbers exchanged every couple of years. I know that she is based in New England, and I know that she works for a federal agency, operating at a level of law enforcement that is orders of magnitude beyond mine. Before we dated, she had wanted to go to veterinary school.

"Any more questions, Palace?"

"No." I glance at the river, then back at her. "Wait. Yes. A friend of mine asked why we won't let the Pakistanis try and nuke the asteroid, if they want to."

Alison laughs once, mirthlessly, and begins tearing the papers into strips. "Tell your friend," she says, tearing the strips into smaller strips, then those into still smaller ones, "that if they hit it—which they won't—but if they do instead of one asteroid, we'll have thousands of smaller but still devastating asteroids. Thousands and thousands of irradiated asteroids."

I don't say anything. With her small efficient fingers, Alison feeds the tiny bits of paper into the Charles, and then she turns to me and smiles.

"Anyway, Detective Palace," she says. "Whatcha working on?"

"Nothing," I say, turn my face away. "Nothing, really."

* * *

But I tell her about the Zell case anyway, I can't help it. We're walking up John F. Kennedy from Memorial Drive to Harvard Square, and I give her the whole story, top to bottom, and then I ask her, from a professional standpoint, what she makes of the case. We've arrived at a kiosk in what used to be a newsstand, now strung with Christmas lights, a squat portable generator humming outside, grumbling and hissing like a miniature tank. The glass of the newsstand is blacked out, and someone has taped two big pieces of cardboard across the front doors, written THE COFFEE DOCTOR on them in big black letters with a Sharpie.

"Well," she says slowly, as I hold open the door for her. "Not having examined the evidence firsthand, it certainly sounds like you reached the correct conclusion. Ninety-five percent chance, this guy was just another hanger."

"Yep," I say.

It's dark inside the converted news kiosk, a couple of bare bulbs and another string of Christmas lights, an old-fashioned cash register and an espresso machine, squat and gleaming, parked like a tank on the black countertop.

"Greetings, humans," says the proprietor, an Asian kid, maybe nineteen, with a porkpie hat and horn-rimmed glasses and a wispy beard. He gives Alison a cheerful salute. "Pleasure, as always."

"Thanks, Coffee Doctor," she says. "Who's in the lead?"

"Let's see."

I look where he's looking, seven paper coffee cups lined up on the far end of the counter, each cup with the name of a continent scrawled on it. He tilts a couple, rattles them, eyeballs the number of beans that have been tossed in each.

"Antarctica. No contest."

"Wishful thinking," says Alison.

"No shit, sister."

"Couple of the usual."

"Your wish, my command," he says, and works fast, lining up two dainty ceramic demitasses, dunking a steamer wand in a stainless-steel jug of milk and flicking it on.

"Best coffee in the world," notes Alison.

"What's the five percent chance?" I ask, as the espresso machine rattles and hisses.

Alison smiles faintly. "I knew you were going to say that."

"I'm just wondering."

"Henry," says Alison, as the kid presents us with our two short cups of coffee. "Can I tell you something? You can follow this case forever, and you can discover all its secrets, you can build this man's timeline all the way back to his birth, and the birth of his father and his father's father. The world is still going to end."

"Yep. Yeah, I know." We've settled in a corner of the ersatz coffee shop now, huddled at an old plastic card table the Coffee Doctor has set up. "But what's the five percent chance, though, in your analysis?"

She sighs, gives it to me again, that small gentle sarcastic eye roll.

"The five percent is this: for this man Toussaint to attack you with the ashtray like that, to try and run for it? With three armed detectives in the room. That's a Hail Mary. That's a desperation play."

"McGully threatened to have him executed."

"In jest."

"He's scared. He doesn't know that."

"Sure, sure." She tilts her head this way and that, considering. "But you're threatening, at the same moment, to arrest him on a minor violation."

"For two weeks. Engine fraud. A token bid."

"Yes," she says. "But even for a token bid, you're going to search the house, right?"

Alison pauses to sip her espresso. I leave mine alone, for now, staring at her. *Oh, Palace*, I'm thinking. *Oh, Palace. Holy moly.* Someone else comes into the cafe, a college-age girl; the Coffee Doctor says, "Greetings, human," fires up his machine, and the girl tosses a bean into the cup marked EUROPE.

"Still, five percent chance," says Alison. "But you know what they say about odds."

"Yep." I sip my espresso, which is, in fact, delicious. "Yep, yep, yep."

* * *

I'm buzzing. I'm feeling it. The coffee, the morning. Five percent chance.

Ninety-three north, fifty-five miles an hour, eight o'clock in the morning, no other cars on the road.

Somewhere between Lowell and Lawrence my phone picks up three bars, and I call Nico, I wake her up, I give her the bad news: Derek got involved with something foolish, and he's not getting out. I go easy on the details. I don't use the word terrorist. I don't tell her about the secret organization, I don't tell her about the Moon. I just tell her what Alison said about the military-justice system right now:

he's got a label that means he's not going anywhere.

I'm sympathetic but clear: this is the way it is, and there's nothing else to be done, and then I brace myself for her tearful or spiteful or furious rebuttal.

Instead she is silent, and I lift the phone, making sure my bars haven't disappeared. "Nico?"

"Yeah. I'm here."

"So—do you understand?"

I'm rolling north, steadily north, over the state line. Welcome to New Hampshire. Live Free or Die.

"Yeah," says Nico, a pause for the slow exhale of cigarette smoke. "I understand."

"Derek will mostly likely spend the rest of the time in that facility."

"*Okay*, Henry," she says, like maybe now I'm rubbing it in. "I get it. How was it, seeing Alison?"

"What?"

"How does she look?"

"Uh, good," I say. "She looks really good."

And then somehow the conversation slips into a different key, and she's telling me how much she always liked Alison, and we're trading stories from old times: growing up, our first days at Grandfather's, then later, sneaking around with dates in the basement. I'm rolling past the scenery, and for a while we're talking like we used to talk, two kids, brother and sister, the real world.

By the time Nico and I get off the phone, I'm almost home, I'm rolling into the southern part of the Concord metro area, and my cellphone signal is still strong, so I go ahead and put through one more call.

"Mr. Dotseth?"

"Hey, kid. I heard about Detective Andreas. Christ."

"I know. I know. Listen, I'm going to take another peek around."

"Peek around where?"

"The house on Bow Bog Road? Where we tried to arrest a suspect yesterday in the hanger case?"

"Yeah, good collar. Except where you shot the guy to death."

"Yes, sir."

"Hey, did you hear about these goofballs in Henniker? Couple of kids riding one of those two-person bikes, trailing a rolling suitcase on a bungee cord. State police pull 'em over, the suitcase is full of *escopetas*—those little Mexican shotguns. We're talking fifty thousand dollars' worth of firearms these kids are biking around with."

"Huh."

"Today's prices, anyway."

"Huh. So, Denny, I'm going to head back to that house now, give it another look."

"Which house is that?"

* * *

The crime-scene taping job that's been done at J. T. Toussaint's ugly little house is clumsy and haphazard. One thin strip of yellow cellophane, run in a series of slack fluttering *U*'s, from porch post to porch post, then to one of the sagging branches of the oak tree, then across the lawn to the flag of the mailbox. Tied loosely at each station, half slipping, wind teased, like it doesn't matter, like it's birthday party decoration.

Supposedly, subsequent to yesterday's gunplay, this house was secured and searched by a team of patrol officers, per procedure, but I have my doubts, based firstly on the lackluster nature of the crime-scene taping, secondly on the fact that, inside, nothing appears to have been moved. All of Toussaint's battered and stained living-room furniture rests exactly where it did yesterday. It's easy to imagine, say, Officer Michelson, enjoying an egg-and-sausage sandwich, strolling through the house's four small rooms, lifting and dropping sofa cushions, peering in the refrigerator, yawning, calling it a day.

Six thick patches of blood form a black and rust red archipelago across the carpeted floor of the living room and the hardwood of the front hallway. My blood, from my eye; Toussaint's, from the cut on his forehead, from the multiple gunshot wounds that killed him.

I step carefully over and around the blood, and then I stand at the center of the living room, turning in a slow circle, mentally dividing the house into quadrants, as Farley and Leonard recommend, and then I launch into a real search. I go through the house inch by inch, crawling on my belly when necessary, awkwardly shoehorning my body all the way under Toussaint's bed. I dig a stepladder out of the cluttered closet and climb up to punch through the flimsy tiles of the ceiling, find nothing in the crawlspace but insulation fiber and ancient secret stockpiles of dust. I go through Toussaint's bedroom closet carefully—looking for what, exactly? A rack of fancy leather belts, with one missing? A blueprint of the men's room of the Main Street McDonald's? I don't know.

Anyway—pants, shirts, overalls. Two pairs of boots. Nothing.

A five percent chance is what Alison reckoned. Five percent.

A small door beside the pantry opens onto a short flight of concrete stairs, no railing, a grim basement, a single lightbulb with a length of twine as a pull-cord. Opposite a massive dead boiler is the lair of the dog: a pillow bed, a collection of chewed-up rubber toys, a food bowl licked clean, another bowl with a quarter-inch puddle of dirty water.

"Poor thing," I say aloud, and then he appears, Houdini, as if conjured, standing at the top of the steps, a tiny scruffy mop-head of a dog, yellow teeth bared, eyes wide, white fur mottled gray.

What am I supposed to do? I find some bacon and I cook it up, and then, while Houdini is eating, I sit at the kitchen table and I imagine Peter Zell sitting across from me, glasses off and set down beside him, eyes intent on his small delicate task, carefully sniffing up the crushed white interiors of a pain pill.

And then there's the loud bang of the front door slamming closed, and when I leap up my chair tips backward and hits the floor, a second bang, and Houdini looks up and barks and I'm running as fast as I can, through the house, flinging open the door and shouting, "Police!"

Nothing, silence, white lawn, gray clouds.

I sprint down to the road, lose and then gain my balance, sliding the last three feet as if on skis. "Police!" again, one way down the road, and then the other, breathing hard. Whoever it was is gone. They were here, in here with me this whole time, or they've slipped in and out again, looking for whatever it was I'm looking for, and now they're gone.

"Shoot," I say quietly. I turn around and stare at the ground, trying to tell the intruder's footprints in the snow and slush from my own. Big snowflakes are tumbling down, one at a time, as if they've agreed in advance to take turns. My heart slowly decelerates.

Houdini is on the doorstep, licking his chops. Wants more food.

Wait, now. I tilt my head, study the house and the tree and the lawn.

"Wait."

If Houdini lives down there with the boiler, what's in the doghouse?

* * *

The answer is simple: it's pills. Pills and a whole lot of other stuff.

Manila mailing envelopes crammed full with pill bottles, each bottle containing several dozen thirty- or sixty-milligram tablets, each tablet stamped with the name of the medication or the manufacturer. Most of the pills are MS Contin, but there are others: Oxycontin, Dilaudid, Lidocaine. Six of the thick mailing envelopes in total, hundreds of pills in each. There's a small carton filled with small white wax papers; a pill crusher, the kind you get at the drug store; in another box, wrapped in a baggie, inside a paper bag from Market Basket, a snub-nose automatic pistol, which in today's environment must be worth several thousand dollars. There are vials of dark-colored liquid and several dozen syringes wrapped individually in crinkly plastic packaging. In another Market Basket bag is cash, fat bricks of hundred-dollar bills.

Two thousand. Three thousand.

I stop counting after five thousand. My hands are trembling, so I can't count it all, but it's a lot.

Then I limp back to the car again for a roll of crime-scene tape, and I wind it all the way around, secure it properly, tight and taut. Houdini trots along with me around the perimeter, and then stands next to me, panting, and I don't invite him into the Impala, but I don't stop him from getting in, either.

* * *

"Stretch. My brother. You're never going to believe this." McGully is at the window, it's slightly cracked, there's a sweet and heavy smell in the room. "So these jokers up in Henniker are on ten-speeds, they're towing a rolling suitcase—"

"I heard."

"Oh," he says. "Ruin it."

"Are you smoking marijuana?"

"A little bit, yeah, I am. It's been a hard week. I shot a guy, re-member? You want?"

"No, thanks."

I tell him about my haul from Toussaint's house, tell him how I've discovered that there's more to the story, much more. He listens with glazed eyes, and occasionally he takes a deep pull from the tiny rolled-up twist of paper, blowing smoke out the crack in the window. Culverson is nowhere to be seen, Andreas's desk is empty, computer monitor turned to face the wall, phone unplugged. It feels like it's been empty for years.

"So the scumbag was lying," is McGully's conclusion. "I could have told you that. He's a drug dealer, he got his buddy hooked, and then his buddy killed himself."

"Well, except it's true that Zell was the one who brought Toussaint drugs in the first place. He stole his sister's prescription pad."

"Oh. Huh." He grins, scratches his chin. "Oh, wait—you know what? Who gives a shit."

"Yep," I say. "Good point."

"Whoa. Is that the fucking dog from the crime scene?"

"Maybe . . ." I say, and McGully says, "Maybe what?" and now I'm pacing vigorously, the dog is pacing, too, in my footsteps. "Maybe what happens is, Peter brings Toussaint pills in June. They hang out, they get high, and then after Peter gets caught and quits, J.T. keeps it going. Maybe at some point he started selling the overflow, and now he's gotten used to the cash, he's put a customer base together. So he finds himself a new source."

"Yes!" says McGully exuberantly, and pounds his fist on the table. "Probably the same person who tried to murder you with your snow chains."

I look at him and he's clearly making fun of me. I sit back down in my chair.

No use telling McGully about the slamming front door back at the house on Bow Bog Road, because he will say I'm imagining things, or that it was a ghost, and I know that I am not, and it was not. Someone tried to stop me from finding those drugs, and it wasn't J.T. Toussaint, because Toussaint is lying dead in the morgue in the basement of Concord Hospital.

Houdini sniffs around under Andreas's desk, settles in for a nap. My cell phone rings.

"Hello? Detective Palace?"

It's Naomi Eddes, and she sounds nervous, and at the sound of her voice I feel nervous, too, like a kid.

"Yep. This is me. Hi."

I can feel McGully looking at me, so I stand up from my desk, step over to the window.

"What's up?"

"I just—" The phone crackles for a second, and my heart leaps in terror against the possibility that I've lost the connection.

"Ms. Eddes?"

"I'm here. I just—I thought of something that might be help-ful to you, in your case."

2.

"Good evening," she says, and I say, "Good evening," and then we spend a second or two looking at each other. Naomi Eddes is in a bright red dress with black buttons running down the center of it. I look terrible, I'm sure. I'm wishing now I had stopped to change from my day-at-the-office, my gray jacket and blue tie, to something more appropriate for dinner with a lady. Truth is, all my jackets are gray, all my ties are blue.

Eddes lives in a neighborhood in Concord Heights, south of Airport Road, a new development where all the streets are named for fruits, and where the asteroid recession took hold halfway through construction. She's on Pineapple, and everything from Kiwi moving westward is half finished: bare wooden frames like dug-up dinosaur bones, half-tiled roofs, vandalized interiors, never-used kitchens stripped for copper and brass.

"You can't come in," she says, and steps out onto the front stoop, her peacoat draped over her arm, tugging a hat down over her bald head. It's a kind of hat I've never seen before, a kind of girl-style trilby hat. "Place is a mess. Where are we going?"

"You said—" she's walking to my car, I follow her, slipping a little on a patch of black ice on the driveway, "—you said you might have information relevant to my case. To Peter's death."

"I do," she says. "I mean, I think I do. Not information. Just, like, an idea. What happened to your face?"

"Long story."

"Does it hurt?"

"No."

"That's good."

It's true, my wounded eye has been fine all day, but as I'm saying the word *no* an intense pulse of pain seizes the right side of my face, radiating outward from the eyehole, as if the injury is punishing me for lying. I blink the good eye, endure a wave of nausea, and find Naomi standing at the shotgun door in an old-fashioned way, waiting for me to open it for her, and I do, and by the time I come around to my side and slide in, she's reaching for the dashboard computer with fascination, almost but not quite touching the screen.

"So, what is your idea?"

"How does this work?"

"It's just a computer. You can keep track of where every other member of the force is, at any given time."

"What does WC stand for?"

"Watch Commander. What's the idea you had, about the case?"

"It's probably nothing."

"Okay."

She's looking out the window, or at her own ghostly reflection in the window glass. "Why don't we talk about it at dinner?"

Eddes vetoes the Somerset Diner out of hand, and basically what's left are the bars and the pirated fast-food joints and the Panera. I've heard of a fine-dining place still open in Boston where the owners have bribed their way out of price controls, where you can get the whole white-tablecloth experience, but from what people say, it would cost all the money I've got left.

Naomi and I end up at Mr. Chow's, looking at each other over a pot of steaming jasmine tea across a grease-stained linoleum table.

"So how's it going?"

"What?"

"Sorry, how would you say it, in cop language?" A small teasing smile. "What is the status of the case?"

"Well, we did, actually, apprehend a suspect."

"You did? And how did that go?"

"Fine."

I could tell her more, but I don't. The suspect attacked me with a scale model of the New Hampshire state house. The suspect was a drug dealer, and either was supplying or was supplied by the victim. The suspect is dead. Ms. Eddes seems satisfied not to know, and anyway our food comes quickly, a massive lazy Susan laden with dumplings, soups, and cashew chicken. The words *Chow! Chow!* flash in pink neon on the window just past our table.

"What was your idea about the case?"

"You know what?"

"What?"

I knew she was going to do this. Put it off, delay, elide. I feel oddly as if I know her so well.

"Let's have an hour."

"An hour?"

"Henry, please, I really . . ."

She looks at me with clear-eyed sincerity, her face washed of all her teasing swagger. I like it intensely, that clear-eyed face, her pale cheeks, the symmetry of her shaved head. "I know I called because I said I had something to tell you. But to tell you the truth, I was also thinking how much I would love to just, you know, just eat dinner with a human being."

"Sure."

"You know? Have a normal conversation. Eat dinner without talking about death."

"Sure," I say again.

"To the extent that this activity is still possible, I would like to try it."

"Sure.

She lifts her wrist, slim and pale, undoes the little silver buckle of her watch, and places it on the table between us. "One hour of normalcy. Deal?"

I reach out and let my hand rest for one moment, over hers.

"Deal."

* * *

And so we do, we sit there and we eat what is really pretty mediocre Chinese food and we speak about normal things.

We talk about the world we grew up in, the strange old world from before, about music and movies and television shows from ten and fifteen years ago, 'N Sync and *Beverly Hills, 90210* and *The Real World* and *Titanic*.

Naomi Eddes, at it turns out, was born and raised in a suburb called Gaithersburg, in Maryland, what she calls America's Least Remarkable State. Then she went to community college for a couple of semesters, dropped out to be the lead singer in a "terrible but well-meaning" punk-rock band, and then, when she figured out what she really wanted to do, she moved to New York City to finish her bachelor's and get a master's degree. I like hearing her talk when she gets going, there's music in it.

"What was it? What you really wanted to do?

"Poetry." She sips her tea. "I wanted to write poems, and not just in my little journal in my room. I wanted to write good poems, and publish them. Still do, in fact."

"No kidding."

"Yes, sir. So, I got into school, went to New York, I waited tables, I saved my pennies. Ate ramen noodles. All the things you do. And I know what you're thinking.

"What's that?"

"All this, and now she works in insurance."

"Nope. Not what I'm thinking at all."

What I'm actually thinking, as I organize a tangle of thick noodles onto my chopsticks, is that this is the sort of person I've always admired: the person with a difficult goal who takes the necessary steps to achieve it. I mean, sure, it's easy to do what you've always wanted to do, *now*.

The little hand on Naomi's watch makes its way around to the hour, and slips past it, and the lazy Susan gets empty, stray noodles and empty soy-sauce packets littering our plates like shed snakeskins, and now I'm telling her my whole story: my father the professor, my mother who worked at the police station, the whole bit, how they were killed when I was twelve years old.

"They were both killed?" asks Naomi.

"Yeah. Yep. Yeah."

She puts down her chopsticks, and I think, *oh hell*.

I don't know why I told the story. I lift the teapot, dribble out the dregs, Naomi is silent, and I cast about the room for our waitress, motioning with my hands at the empty pot.

You tell a story like that, about your parents being killed, and people end up looking at you really closely, right in the eyes, advertising their empathy, when really what they're doing is trying to peer into your soul, see what kind of marks and stains have been left on there. So I haven't mentioned it to a new person in years—don't mention it as a rule—I am not a fan of people having opinions about the whole thing—not a fan, generally, of people having opinions about me at all.

Naomi Eddes, however, to her credit, when she speaks she just says, "Whoa." There is no glimmer of scandalized fascination in her eyes, no attempt at "understanding." Just that breathy and honest little syllable, *whoa*.

"So, your parents are murdered, and you dedicate your life to fighting crime. Like Batman."

"Yep," I say, and I smile at her, dip my last dumpling into a rowboat of ginger-scallion sauce. "Like Batman."

They come and clear away the lazy Susan and we go on talking, the neon flashing and flashing and finally flickering off, the ancient married couple who run Mr. Chow's coming around with the long push brooms, just like in the movies, and then, at last, they lift the chairs around us onto the tables, and we go.

* * *

"Okay, Detective Palace. Do you know what a contestability clause is?"

"No, I do not."

"Well, it's kind of interesting. Maybe not. You tell me."

Naomi adjusts herself in her folding beach chair, trying to get comfortable. I would apologize again for the fact that my living room has no proper furniture, just a set of beach chairs in a semicircle around a milk carton, except that I've already apologized repeatedly, and Naomi told me to stop.

"The contestability clause in a life-insurance policy means that if a policy is taken out and the subject dies within two years, for any reason, the company gets to investigate the circumstances of death before paying out."

"Okay," I say. "Do a lot of life-insurance policies have these clauses?"

"Oh, yeah," says Naomi. "They all do."

I refill her wine.

"And are they being enforced?"

"Oh, yeah."

"Huh," I say, scratching my mustache.

"Tell you the truth, people with Merrimack policies are lucky," says Naomi, "because a lot of the bigger companies are totally frozen shut; they're not paying out at all. What Merrimack is saying is, yes, you can get your money, because we issued the policy and that was the deal, asteroid or no asteroid, basically. The big boss, in Omaha, has a Jesus thing, I believe."

"Right," I say. "Right, right." Houdini comes in, sniffs the floor, stares suspiciously at Naomi, and darts out again. I've made a bed for him in the bathroom, just an old sleeping bag I cut open, a bowl for water.

"But the company line is, we're going to make absolutely sure that we're not being bilked, because a lot of people are cheating. I mean, what an easy way to get squared away until the end, right? Fake Mom's death, big payday, off to the Bahamas. So that's the policy, right now."

"What is?"

"Investigate every claim. Every contestable claim, we're contesting."

I stop, the wine bottle frozen in my hand, and suddenly I'm thinking, *Palace, you dunce. You total dunce.* Because I'm picturing the boss, pale jowly Gompers, settled in his big chair, telling me that Peter Zell wasn't doing actuarial work anymore at the time that he died. No one's buying life insurance, so there's no data to analyze, no tables of data to draw up. So Zell, like everyone else in that office, was working on clearing suspicious insurance claims.

"It's kind of harsh policy, when you think about it," Naomi is saying, "for all the people who *weren't* committing insurance fraud, whose husband or whoever really did kill himself, and now they're going to wait an extra month, two months, for the cash? Brutal."

"Right, right," I say, mind rolling, thinking about Peter, Peter in the McDonald's, his eyes bugging out. All along the answer was right there. The first day of my investigation, the first witness I interviewed, it was laid at my feet.

"What I'm wondering is," Naomi says, and I'm right there with her, "I'm wondering if maybe Peter found out something, or he was close to finding out something. . . . I don't know. It sounds silly. He stumbled into something, and it got him killed?"

"Doesn't sound silly at all."

Not at all. Motive. It sounds like motive. Palace, you total absolute dunce.

"Okay," I say to Naomi, sit down in the chair across from her. "Tell me more."

She does; she tells me more about the kinds of cases that Peter was working on, most likely, insurable-interest cases, where a policy isn't taken out by a person on another person, but by an *organization* on a person. A company takes out a policy on its executive director, or its CEO, hedging the risk of financial calamity should that key individual die. I sit down to listen, but then it turns out it's hard to pay attention while sitting down—given the wine, given the late hour, given the redness of Naomi's lips and the pale luminescence of her scalp in the moonlight—so I get up, I'm pacing around the room, from the small television to the door of the kitchen, Naomi with her head craned back, watching me pace with an arch, amused expression.

"Is this how you stay so thin?"

"It helps," I say. "I need to see what he was working on."

"Okay."

"His office—" I close my eyes, think back. "There was no inbox, no pile of active files."

"No," says Naomi. "No, since we stopped using the computers, and everything was on paper. Gompers came up with this whole annoying system. Or maybe the regional office did, I don't know. But every day, at the end of the day, what you're working on goes back in the filing cabinets. You pick it up in the morning."

"Is it filed by worker?"

"What do you mean?"

"Would all of Peter's files be together?"

"Huh. You know—I don't know."

"Okay," I say, and I grin, my cheeks flushed, my eyes flashing. "I like this. This is good."

"What a funny person you are," she says, and I sort of can't believe that she's real, she's sitting in my house, on my crappy old beach chair in her red dress with the black buttons.

"I do, I like this. Maybe I'll make a midlife career change," I say. "Try my luck in the insurance biz. I've got the rest of my life ahead of me, right?"

Naomi doesn't laugh. She stands up. "No. No. Not you. You're a policeman through and through, Hank," she says. She looks at me, right up at my face, and I stoop a little and look right back, I'm suddenly thinking to myself, fiercely, painfully, that this is it. I will never fall in love again. This will be the last time.

"You'll be standing there when the asteroid comes down, with one hand out, yelling, *Stop! Police!*"

I don't know what to say to that, I really don't.

I stoop a little, and she cranes her neck upward, and we kiss very slowly, as if we have all the time in the world. Halfway through the kiss the dog pads in, nuzzles against my leg, and I sort of gently kick him away. Naomi reaches up and puts a hand around my neck, her fingers drifting down beneath the collar of my shirt.

When we're done with the kiss, we kiss again, harder, an onrush of urgency, and when we pull apart again Naomi suggests that we go into the bedroom, and I apologize because I don't have a real bed, just a mattress on the floor. I haven't gotten around to buying one yet, and she asks how long I've been living here and I say five years.

"You're probably not ever going to get around to it, then," she murmurs, pulling me to her, and I whisper, "You're probably right," pulling her down.

* * *

Much later, in the darkness, sleep starting to seep into our eyelids, I whisper to Naomi, "What kind of poetry?"

"Villanelles," she whispers in return, and I say I don't know what that means.

"A villanelle is a poem of nineteen lines," she says, still hushed, murmuring into my neck. "Five tercets, each composed of three rhymed lines. And the first and last lines of the first tercet return over and over again, over the course of the poem, as the last line of each of the subsequent tercets."

"Okay," I say, not really registering all of that, more focused on the soft electric presence of her lips on my neck.

"It ends with a quatrain, which is four rhymed lines, with the second two lines of the quatrain again repeating the first and last lines of the first tercet."

"Oh," I say, and then, "I'm going to need an example."

"There are a lot of really good ones."

"Tell me one of the ones you're writing."

Her laugh is a small warm gust into my collarbone. "I'm only writing one, and it's not done."

"You're only writing one?"

"One great one. Before October. That's my plan."

"Oh."

We're still and quiet then, for a moment.

"Here," she says. "I'll tell you a famous one."

"I don't want the famous one. I want yours."

"It's by Dylan Thomas. You've probably heard of it. It's been in the newspaper a lot lately."

I'm shaking my head. "I try not to read the papers too much."

"You're a strange man, Detective Palace."

"People tell me that."

* * *

At some point late, late at night, I drift awake and there's Naomi standing in the doorframe, in only her underwear, slipping the red dress on over her head. She sees me watching and pauses, smiles, un-embarrassed, and finishes dressing. I can see, even in the pale light from the hallway, that the lipstick is scrubbed from her lips. She looks shorn and lovely, like something newborn.

"Naomi?"

"Hey, Henry." She closes her eyes. "Something." Opens her eyes. "One more thing."

I make my hand a visor against the moonlight, trying to see

her clearly. The bedsheets are scrunched up against my chest, my legs are spilling slightly over the edge of the mattress.

She sits on the bed, down by my feet with her back to me.

"Naomi?"

"Forget it."

She shakes her head rapidly, stands again, speaks, a rush of words in the near darkness. "Henry, just know that no matter what else—no matter how this ends—this was all real and good and right."

"Well, sure," I say. "Yeah. Yes."

"Real and good and right, and I won't forget it," she says. "Okay? No matter how it ends."

"Okay," I say.

She leans over me and kisses me hard on the lips, and she goes.

3.

"Palace."

"What?" I say, sitting up, looking around. "Hello?"

I'm so used to being woken from a dream by the telephone that it takes me a moment to realize that I was dreaming not of Alison Koechner but of Naomi Eddes, and then it's the next moment that I figure out that it was not a dream, not this time—Naomi was real, is real, and then I look around for her, and she's gone. My shades are open, the winter sun is sending wavering yellow rectangles across the crumpled sheets on my old mattress, and there is a woman on my phone yelling at me.

"Are you familiar with the current statutory penalties for impersonating a state official?"

Oh, God. Oh, no. Fenton.

"Yes, ma'am, I am."

The blood, the vial of blood. Hazen Road.

"Well, I'll quote them for you."

"Dr. Fenton."

"Impersonating a state official carries a sentence of ten to twenty-five years and is prosecuted under Title VI, meaning automatic imprisonment pending trial, which will never occur."

"I know that."

"The same penalty pertains for impeding a criminal investigation."

"Can I explain?"

"No, thanks. But if you're not at the morgue in twenty minutes, you're going to jail."

I take two minutes to get dressed and two minutes to remove and replace the wad of paper towels over my eye. Before I close my front door, I take a look around: the beach chairs, the empty bottle of wine. No sign of Naomi's clothes, of her pocketbook, her coat, no traces of her boot heels on the rug. No trace of her scent.

It happened, though. Close my eyes and I can feel it, the trace of her finger tickling the back of my neck, drawing me in. No dream.

Twenty minutes, Fenton said, and she was not kidding. I push the speed limit all the way to Concord Hospital.

* * *

Fenton is precisely as she was when I saw her last, alone with her rolling cart of medical equipment in the stark cold brightness of the morgue. The steel drawers with their gray handles, the strange sad locker room of the damned.

I walk in and she looks at her watch. "Eighteen minutes and forty-five seconds."

"Dr. Fenton, I hope that you—I hope—listen—" There are tears in my voice, somehow, for some reason. I clear my throat. I am trying to formulate an explanation that will satisfy, trying to explain how I could have stolen blood and had it tested under false pretenses—how sure I was that this was a drugs case, how imperative it was to prove or disprove that Peter Zell was an addict—and of course now it doesn't matter, turns out never to have mattered, it was about insurance claims, about insurance all along—and I am meanwhile melting under the combined effect of her glare and the brightness of the lights—and there, too, is Peter, she's taken his body out of its drawer and laid it on the cold slab of the mortuary table, stone dead and staring straight up into the lights.

"I'm sorry," is all I can muster, at last. "I'm really sorry, Dr. Fenton."

"Yes." Her face is neutral, impassive, behind the perfect O's of her glasses. "Me, too."

"What?"

"I said that I am also sorry, and if you think I'm going to say it a third time, you are deeply mistaken."

"I don't understand."

Fenton turns to her cart to pick up a single sheet of paper. "These are the results of the serology tests, and as you will see they have caused me to revise my understanding of the case."

"In what way?" I ask, trembling a little bit.

"This man was murdered."

My mouth drops open, and I can't help it, I am thinking the words and then I am saying them aloud. "I knew it. Oh, my God, I knew it all along."

Fenton pushes up her glasses slightly where they have slipped down the bridge of her nose and reads from the paper. "First. The bloodwork reveals not only a high blood-alcohol level but also alcohol in the stomach itself, which means he had done some heavy drinking in the hours before he died."

"I knew that," I say. J. T. Toussaint, in our first interview: they went to see *Distant Pale Glimmers*. They had a bunch of beers.

"Also present in the blood," Fenton continues, "were significant traces of a controlled substance."

"Right," I say, nodding, mind buzzing, one step ahead of her. "Morphine."

"No," says Fenton, and looks up at me, curious, surprised, a little irritated. "Morphine? No. No traces of opiates of any kind. What he had in his system was a chemical compound called gamma-hydroxybutyric acid."

I squint over her shoulder at the lab report, a thin sheet of paper, decorated with calculations, checked-off boxes, someone's precise backward-slanting handwriting. "I'm sorry. What kind of acid?"

"GHB."

"You mean—the date-rape drug?"

"Stop talking, Detective," says Fenton, pulling on a pair of clear latex gloves. "Come here and help me turn over the body."

We slip our fingers under his back and carefully lift Peter Zell and flip him over onto his stomach, and then we're looking at the broad paleness of his back, the flesh spreading away from the spine. Fenton fits into her eye a small lens, like a jeweler's glass, reaches up to adjust the hallucinogenically bright lamp overhanging the autopsy table, aiming it at a blotchy brown bruise on the back of Zell's left calf, just above the ankle.

"Look familiar?" she says, and I peer forward.

I'm still thinking about GHB. I need a notebook, I need to write all this down. I need to think. Naomi stopped in the doorway of my bedroom, she almost said something, and then she changed her mind and slipped away. I experience a pang of longing so strong that it momentarily buckles my knees, and I lean against the table, grasp it with both hands.

Easy, Palace.

"This is what I really have to apologize for," she says flatly. "In my rush to conclude an obvious suicide case I failed to make thorough survey of the things that could cause a ring of bruises above a person's ankle."

"Okay. And so . . ." I stop talking. I don't know what she means at all.

"At some point in the hours before he ended up where you found him, this man was knocked unconscious and dragged by the leg."

I look at her, unable to speak.

"Probably to the trunk of a car," she continues, placing the paper back on the cart. "Probably to be taken to the scene, and hanged. Like I said, I have significantly revised my understanding of this case."

I catch an inward glimpse of Peter Zell's dead eyes, the glasses, disappearing into the darkness of the trunk of a car.

"Do you have any questions?" Fenton asks.

I have nothing but questions.

"What about his eye?"

"What?"

"The other cluster of old bruises. On his cheek, below his

right eye. He apparently reported that he fell down some stairs. Is that possible?"

"Possible, but unlikely."

"And are you sure there was no morphine in his system? Are you sure he wasn't using it the night he died?"

"Yes. Nor for at least three months beforehand."

I have to rethink this whole thing, go over it again from top to bottom. Rethink the timeline, rethink Toussaint, rethink Peter Zell. Having been right all along, having guessed correctly that he was murdered, provides no joy, no powerful self-righteous rush. To the contrary, I feel confused—sad—uncertain. I feel like *I've* been thrown in a trunk, like I'm surrounded by darkness, peering up toward a crack of daylight. On my way out of the morgue I stop at the small black door with the cross on it, and I reach out and run my fingers along the symbol, remembering that so many people are feeling so awful these days that they had to close down this little room, move the nightly worship service to a bigger space, elsewhere in the building. That's just how things are.

* * *

As soon as I step outside into the Concord Hospital parking lot, my phone rings.

"Jesus, Hank, where have you been?"

"Nico?"

It's hard to hear her, there's a loud noise in the background, a kind of roar.

"I need you to listen to me closely, please."

The noise is intense behind her, like wind whipping through an open window. "Nico, are you on a highway?"

It's too loud in the parking lot. I turn around and go back into the lobby.

"Henry, *listen*."

The wind behind her is growing louder, and I'm starting to hear the distinct menacing whine of sirens, a distant shrieking mixed in with the whoosh and howl of the wind. I'm trying to place the sound of the sirens, those aren't CPD sirens. Are they state cars? I don't know—what are federal marshals driving right now?

"Nico, where are you?"

"I am not leaving you behind."

"What on Earth are you talking about?

Her voice is stiff as steel; it's her voice but not her voice, like my sister is reading lines from a script. The roar behind her stops abruptly, and I hear a door slam, I hear feet running.

"Nico!"

"I'll be back. I'm not leaving you behind."

The line goes dead. Silence.

* * *

I drive 125 miles an hour at full code all the way to the New Hampshire National Guard station, running the dashboard emitter to turn the red lights green as I go, burning precious gasoline like a forest fire.

The steering wheel shudders in my hands, and I'm shouting at myself full volume, *stupid stupid stupid*, should have told her, why didn't I tell her? I should have just told her every single thing that Alison had told me: Derek had lied to her all along about what he was mixed up in, where he was going; he had gotten himself mixed up in this secret-society nonsense; the government considered him a terrorist, a violent criminal, and if she persisted in trying to be with him, she would end up with the same fate.

I make a fist, pound it into the steering wheel. I should have just told her, how little it was worth it, to sacrifice herself for him.

I call Alison Koechner's office, and of course there's no answer. I try to call back, and the phone fails, and I hurl it angrily into the backseat.

"God damn it."

Now she's going to do something stupid, get herself shot up by military police, get herself thrown in the brig for the duration, right alongside that moron.

I squeal to a halt at the entrance of NGNH, and I'm gibbering like an idiot to the guard at the gate.

"Hey! Hey, excuse me. My name is Henry Palace, I'm a detective, and I think my sister is in here."

The guard says nothing. It's a different guard than was at the front the last time.

"My sister's husband was in jail here, and I think my sister is here and I need to find her."

The gate guard's expression doesn't change. "We are holding no prisoners at present."

"What? Yes—oh, hey. Hi. Hello?"

I'm waving my hands, both hands over my head, here comes someone I recognize. It's the tough reservist who was guarding the brig when I came to interview Derek, the woman in camouflage who waited impassively in the hallway while I tried to get some sense out of him.

"Hey," I say. "I need to see the prisoner."

She marches right over to us, to where I'm standing, halfway out of the car, the car in park, stopped at a crazy angle, engine running, by the entrance gatehouse. "Excuse me? Hi. I need to see that prisoner again. I'm sorry, I don't have an appointment. It's urgent. I'm a policeman."

"What prisoner?"

"I'm a detective." I stop, take a breath. "What did you say?"

She must to have known I was here, must have seen the car pull up in a monitor or something, and come out to the gate. The thought is strangely chilling.

"I said, what prisoner?"

I stop talking, look from the reservist to the gatehouse guard. They're both standing there staring at me, both with their hands on the butts of the machine guns slung around their necks. *What is going on here?* is what I'm thinking. Nico's not here. There are no sirens, no frantic alarms sounding. Just a distant rotor hum; somewhere close by, somewhere on this sprawling campus, a helicopter is taking off or landing.

"The kid. The prisoner. The kid who was here, the one with the silly dreadlocks, who was in the . . ." I gesture vaguely in the direction of the brig facility. "In the cell there."

"I don't know what individual to whom you are referring," answers the guard.

"Yeah, but you do," I say, staring back at her dumbly. "You were there."

The soldier never takes her eyes off mine as she slowly raises the machine gun to waist level. The second soldier, the gatehouse man, lifts his AK-47, too, and now it's two soldiers with guns angled upward, the butts of the guns nestled into their waists and the barrels aimed directly at the center of my chest. And it doesn't matter that I'm a cop, and these are United States soldiers, that we're all peacekeepers, there is nothing in the world to stop these two from shooting me dead.

"There was no young man here."

* * *

As soon as I am back in the car, the phone rings, and I scrabble around on the backseat, frantic, until I find it.

"Nico? Hello?"

"Whoa. Easy. It's Culverson."

"Oh." I breathe. "Detective."

"Listen, I think you mentioned a young woman named Naomi Eddes. From your hanger investigation?"

My heart jerks and leaps in my chest, bouncing like a fish on a line.

"Yeah?"

"McConnell just found her, up in the Water West Building. In this insurance office."

"What do you mean, McConnell found her?"

"I mean, she's dead. You want to come and see?"

PART FOUR

Soon, They Will

Wednesday, March 28

Right ascension 19 12 57.9
Declination -34 40 37
Elongation 83.7
Delta 2.999 AU

1.

The best thing I can do at present, in this cramped and narrow storeroom with the low tile ceiling and the three rows of long gray-steel filing cabinets, is concentrate on the facts. This, after all, is the appropriate role for the junior detective who has been called to the scene of the crime, as a courtesy, by his more senior colleague.

This is not my murder, it is Detective Culverson's murder, and so all I'm doing is, I'm standing just inside the door of the dim room, staying out of his way, out of Officer McConnell's way. It was my witness, but it's not my corpse.

So—the victim is a Caucasian female in her mid-twenties wearing a brown wool houndstooth skirt, light brown pumps, black stockings, and a crisp white blouse with the sleeves rolled up. The victim bears a number of distinguishing physical characteristics. Around each wrist there is a wreath of tattoos of art-deco roses; there are multiple piercings along the rim of each ear, and a small gold stud in one nostril; her head is shaved, with a light blonde fuzz just beginning to grow in. The body is slumped in the northeast corner of the room. There are no signs of sexual assault, nor indeed of a physical altercation of any kind—except of course for the gunshot wound, which appears almost certainly to have been the cause of death.

A single gunshot wound to the center forehead, which has left a ragged hole just above and to the right of the victim's left eye.

"Well, it's not a suicide by hanging," says Denny Dotseth, appearing at my elbow, chuckling. Mustache, broad grin, coffee in a paper cup. "Kind of refreshing, isn't it?"

"Morning, Denny," says Culverson, "come on in," and Dotseth steps around me, the small room getting busier, more crowded, coffee smell coming off Dotseth, the smell of Culverson's pipe tobacco, small twists of rug fiber drifting and floating in the dim light, my stomach rising and churning.

Focus, Detective Palace. Easy.

The room is a slim rectangle, six feet by ten, empty of decoration. No furniture except the three rows of squat steel filing cabinets. The lights are flickering a little, two long parallel fluorescent bulbs in a low-hung dusty fixture. The victim is slumped against one of those cabinets, which is slightly ajar, and she died on her knees, head tilted back, eyes open, suggesting that she died facing her killer, perhaps pleading for her life.

I did this. The details are unclear.

But this is my fault.

Easy, Palace. Focus.

Culverson murmuring to Dotseth, Dotseth nodding, chuckling, McConnell scribbling in her notebook.

There is a spray of blood, an upside-down crescent, fanned on the plaster wall behind the victim, unevenly mottled pinks and reds in a seashell pattern. Culverson, with Dotseth hovering over him, kneels and gently eases the victim's head forward and finds the exit wound. The bullet smashed through the fragile porcelain of her skull, just there, between the eyes, ripped through her brain, and burst out again through the back. That's how it looks, Fenton will tell us for sure. I turn away, look out into the hallway. Three Merrimack Life and Fire employees are huddled at the end of the hall, where it bends toward the front door of the suite. They see me looking, look back, hushed, and I turn back into the room.

"Okay," says Culverson. "Killer enters here, the victim is down here."

He rises, walks back to where I am at the door, and then back to the body, slow movements, considering.

"Maybe she's looking for something in the file cabinet?" says McConnell, and Culverson says, "Maybe." I'm thinking, *yes, looking for something in the file cabinet.* Dotseth sips his coffee, makes a satisfied "ah" noise, Culverson continues.

"Killer makes a noise, maybe announces himself. Victim turns."

He's acting it out, playing both parts. He tilts his head first this way, then that, imagining, reenacting, approximating the movements. McConnell is writing it all down, taking furious notes in her spiral flip-top notebook, a great detective someday.

"Killer crouches, the victim backs up, into the corner—the gun is fired—"

Culverson stands in the doorway and makes his hand into a gun and pulls the imaginary trigger, and then with his forefinger he traces the journey of the bullet, all the way across the room, stopping just shy of the entrance wound, where the real bullet continued, penetrated the skull. "Hm," he says.

McConnell, meanwhile, is peering into the filing cabinet. "It's empty," she says. "This one drawer. Cleaned out."

Culverson bends to check it out. I stay where I am.

"So what are we thinking?" says Dotseth mildly. "One of these ancient-grudge cases? Kill her before she dies, kind of thing? You hear about the guy who hung himself in his fourth-grade classroom?"

"I did," says Culverson, looking around the room.

I keep my focus on the victim. The bullet hole looks like a crater torn in the sphere of her skull. I lean against the doorjamb, struggle for breath.

"So, Officer," says Culverson, and McConnell says, "Yes, sir?"

"Talk to all these mopes." He jerks a thumb out into the office. "Then go through the building, floor by floor, starting here and working your way down."

"Yes, sir."

"Interview that old guy at the front desk. Someone saw the killer come in."

"Yes, sir."

"Wowie wowie wow," says Dotseth, talking through a small yawn. "A full investigation. At—what are we? Six months to go? Color me impressed."

"It's the kid," says Culverson, and since he's down on his knees now, hunting the rug for the spent casing, it takes me a second to realize he means me. "He's keeping us honest."

I'm watching a silent movie in my head, a woman looking for

a file, slim fingers walking across the tabs, a sudden click of a door opening behind her. She turns—her eyes widen—*bam!*

"Skip the manager, Officer McConnell. The guy who called this in. I'll talk to him." Culverson flips searchingly through his book.

"Gompers," I say.

"Gompers, right," he says. "You'll join me?"

"Yeah." I stop, grit my teeth. "No."

"Palace?"

I feel bad. A kind of pressure, a horror, is inflating itself in my lungs, like I swallowed a balloon full of something, some kind of gas, a poison. My heart is slamming repeatedly against my ribcage, like a desperate prisoner hurling himself rhythmically against the concrete door of his cell.

"No, thank you."

"You all right there, son?" Dotseth takes a step back from me, like I may vomit on his shoes. McConnell has scooted behind Naomi's body, she's running her fingers along the wall.

"You gotta—" I drag a hand across my forehead, discover that it's slick and clammy. My wounded eye socket is throbbing. "Ask Gompers about the files in this drawer."

"Of course," says Culverson.

"We need copies of everything that would have been in that drawer."

"Sure."

"We need to know what's missing."

"Hey, look," says McConnell. She's got the bullet. She pries it from the wall behind Naomi's skull, and I turn and flee. I stumble down the hallway, find the stairwell, and then I take the stairs two at a time, then three, hurling downward, and I kick open the door, spilling into the lobby, out onto the sidewalk, heaving breaths.

Bam!

* * *

All of this, all of it, what did I think? You go into this hall of mirrors, you chase these clues—a belt, a note, a corpse, a bruise, a file—one thing and then the next, it's this giddy game that you enter into, and you just stay down there, in the hall of mirrors, forever. I'm sitting up here at the counter because I couldn't face my usual booth, where I sat with Naomi Eddes over lunch and she told me about Peter Zell's secrets, his addiction, his grim fleeting joking fantasy about killing himself in the Main Street McDonald's.

The music drifting from the kitchen of the Somerset is nothing I recognize, and it is not to my taste. Pounding and electronic, keyboard-driven, a lot of shrill beeps and whistles and hoots.

My notebooks are lined up in front of me, six pale-blue rectangles in a neat row like tarot cards. I've been staring at their covers for an hour, not interested, unable to open them and read the history of my failure. But I can't help it, the thoughts keep coming, one fact after another shuffling across my brain, like grim refugees trudging along with their packs.

Peter Zell was not a suicide. He was murdered. Fenton confirmed it.

Naomi Eddes was murdered, too. Shot through the head while looking for insurance files, the files that we talked about together last night.

She sat at the foot of my bed before she left; she was going to tell me something and then she stopped herself and went home.

He told her about the McDonald's: if he was going to kill himself, that's where he would do it. But he'd told his sister the same thing. Who knows who else?

Sixty-milligram bottles of MS Contin, in a bag, in a doghouse.

I'm dimly aware of a cup of coffee growing cold in front of me on the counter, dimly aware of the television floating above me, bolted high on a metal arm. A newsman stands in front of some kind of palace, speaking in agitated tones about "a minor confrontation beginning to assume the dimensions of a crisis."

Peter Zell and J. T. Toussaint, Detective Andreas, Naomi Eddes.

"All right, honey," says Ruth-Ann, apron, order pad, one fist around the handle of a coffeepot.

"What's this music?" I say. "Where's Maurice?"

"He quit," she says. "You look terrible."

"I know. More coffee, please."

And then, too, there is my baby sister. Missing, possibly dead, possibly in jail. Another catastrophe I failed to predict or prevent.

The television now shows jerky footage of a line of South Asian men behind a table, green military uniforms with gold epaulets, one of them speaking sternly into a microphone. A guy two stools down from me makes an agitated *harumph*. I take him in, a soft middle-aged man in a Harley jacket, a thick mustache and beard; he says, "You mind?" I shrug, and he climbs up onto the counter, balances awkwardly on his knees to change the channel.

My phone is shivering.

Culverson.

"Hey, Detective."

"How you feeling, Henry?"

"Yeah," I say. "I'm all right."

The Pakistanis on the TV are gone, replaced by a pitchman, grinning obscenely before a pyramid of canned food.

Culverson runs through what he's got so far. Theodore Gompers, in his office with his bottle, heard a shot fired at around 2:15, but by his own admission he was pretty drunk, and it took him several minutes to set out in search of the noise, and then several minutes more to locate the narrow storeroom, where he found Naomi's body and called the police at 2:26.

"What about the rest of the staff?"

"It was just Gompers in there when it happened. He's got three other employees at present, and they were all out, enjoying a long lunch at the Barley House."

"Bad luck."

"Yeah."

I stack the blue books, spread them out, shift them into a square, like a fortification around my coffee cup. Culverson is going to do a ballistics workup on the bullet—on the off chance, the way-off chance, he says, that this gun was bought legally, pre-IPSS, and we can trace it. In the corner of my eye the bearded guy in the Harley jacket mops up egg yolk with a crust of toast. The TV pitchman scornfully tosses the canned food into the garbage, and now he's demonstrating some kind of countertop vacuum sealer, dumping a bowl of strawberries in its stainless-steel funnel. McConnell, says Culverson, canvassed the rest of the Water West Building, four stories of office suites, half of them empty, no one saw anything or heard anything strange. No one cares. The old security guard says no one came in or out that he didn't recognize—but there are two back entrances, and one of them leads directly to the rear stairwell, and the security cameras are long gone.

More clues. More puzzles. More facts.

I stare at the TV screen, where the pitchman dumps out his cardboard carton of blueberries into the funnel and switches on the machine. My counter-mate whistles appreciatively, chuckles.

"And the uh—" I say.

And then I'm just frozen, I'm sitting there, holding my head in my forehead. Right at this moment I have to decide, is the thing, am I going to leave town and go north to Maine and find a house on Casco Bay and sit there and stare out the window with my sidearm and wait, or am I going to stay here and do my work and finish my case. My cases.

"Palace?" says Culverson.

"The files," I say, I clear my throat, I sit up on my stool, stick a finger in my ear to block out the TV and the bad music, reach for a blue book. "What about the files?"

"Ah, yes, the files," says Culverson. "The terribly helpful Mr. Gompers basically says we're up the metaphorical creek, on that front."

"Huh," I say.

"Just eyeballing the file cabinet, he says there are maybe three dozen files missing, but he can't tell me what the claims were, or who was working on them, or anything. They gave up on computer files in January, and there are no backups of the paper files."

"Bad luck," I say, I get out a pen, I'm writing, I'm getting it all down.

"Tomorrow I'm going to try and track down some friends and family on this Eddes girl, give 'em the bad news, see if they know anything."

"I'll do that," I say.

"Yeah?"

"Sure."

"You sure?"

"I'll take care of it."

I get off the phone and pack up my notebooks, sliding them one by one into the pocket of my blazer. The question as before is why. Why does anybody do this? Why now? A murder, calculated, cold blood. To what purpose, for what gain? Two stools over the mustache man makes his agitated harumphing noise again, because the infomercial has been broken into by a news report, women in *abayas* somewhere, running in a panic through a dusty marketplace.

He turns my way with doleful eyes, shakes his head, as if to say, *boy oh boy, huh?* and I can tell he's about to try to talk to me, have some sort of human moment, and I don't have time, I can't do it. I have work to do.

* * *

At home I peel out of the clothes I've been wearing all day— to the morgue, to the National Guard, to the scene of crime—and I stand in the bedroom and look around.

Last night past midnight I woke in this room, in this same darkness, and Naomi was framed in the doorway, slipping her red dress over her head in the moonlight.

I'm pacing, thinking.

She put on the dress and she sat on the mattress and she started to talk—to tell me something—but then she stopped herself, "*Forget it.*"

I walk slowly in a circle in my bedroom. Houdini stands in the doorway, unsure, unsettled.

Naomi started to say something, and then she stopped, and then instead she said that, no matter what happened, it was real and good and right. And she won't forget it, no matter how it ends.

I pace in a circle, snapping my fingers, biting at the ends of my mustache. *Real and good and right, no matter how it ends* is what she said, *but she was going to say something else, instead.*

In my restless dream the bullet that tore through Naomi's skull becomes a ball of fire and rock charging through Earth's fragile crust, gouging trenches into the landscape, blasting away sedimentary rock and soil, goring into the ocean floor and sending up spumes of boiled ocean. Deeper and deeper it goes, plowing forward, releasing its stores of kinetic energy, as a bullet rips through a brain, tearing through warm clots of gray matter, severing nerves, creating blackness, pulling thought and life down around it as it goes.

I wake up with the dead yellow light of the sun filling my bedroom, with the next phase of the investigation having announced itself in my head.

A tiny little thing, a little lie to follow up on.

2.

It's not my murder, it's Culverson's murder, but here I go again back toward downtown, back to the Water West Building, like an animal who's witnessed some scene of violence and keeps on restlessly returning to the place of horrid fascination. There's some goon marching in circles around Eagle Square, big parka and a fur hat and an old-fashioned sandwich board—DO THEY THINK WE'RE STUPID in big cartoon bubble-letters—and he's ringing a bell like a Salvation Army Santa Claus. "Hey," he hollers, "do you know what *time* it is?" I duck my head, ignore him, push open the door.

The old guard isn't here. I take the stairs up to the third floor, and I don't politely call out hello from reception, I just go ahead on in and find Mr. Gompers behind his walnut desk.

"Oh," he says, startled, and half rises, unsteadily, to take me in. "I, uh, I went over everything with the other gentleman last night. About poor Naomi."

"Yeah," I say. He's graduated from a tumbler to a pint glass of gin. "Not everything, though."

"What?"

My insides feel cold, like my organs have been removed, separated from one another, packed back inside me in mud. I slam my hands down on Gompers's desk and lean in; he rears back, fleshy face retreating from my glare. I know what I look like. Unshaven, gaunt, the one dead eye with an uneven halo of brown puffy bruising around the clean white of the gauze.

"When I talked to you last week, you told me that the parent company in Omaha is obsessed with fraud prevention."

"What? I don't know," he mumbles.

"Okay, well, here," I say, tossing the thin blue book on the desk in front of him, and he flinches. "Read it."

Gompers doesn't move, so I tell him what it says. "You claimed that all your company cares about is protecting the bottom line. You said the board chairman thinks he's going to buy his way into heaven. But yesterday you told Detective Culverson that there are no duplicates of those files."

"Yeah, see, we went to an all-paper system," he mumbles. "The servers . . ." He's not looking at me, he's looking at a picture on his desk: the daughter, the one who went off to New Orleans.

"You've got the whole office checking and double-checking those claims, there's no computer backup, and you're telling me there's no hard copies being made? No duplicate set squirreled away somewhere?"

"Well. I mean . . ." Gompers looks out his window, and then back at me, steeling himself to make one more run at it. "No, I'm sorry, there's—"

I grab the glass from his hand and I hurl it against the window pane and it explodes and rains ice and gin and chips of glass onto the rug. Gompers stares at me, gaping like a fish. I picture Naomi—all she wanted was to write one perfect villanelle—see her fetching this man fresh bottles of alcohol from the corner store, and then I'm grabbing him by his lapels and lifting him out of his chair and up onto the desk, his blubbery neck trembling at the pressure of my thumbs.

"Are you out of your mind?"

"Where are the copies?"

"Boston. The regional office. State Street." I slacken my grip, just ever so slightly. "Every night we run off everything and overnight them. The overnights, they keep 'em in Boston." He says the words again, pleading, pathetic. "The overnights . . . okay . . ."

I let go of him, and he drops down onto the desk, slides miserably back into his chair.

"Look, Officer—" he says, and I interrupt him.

"I'm a detective."

"Detective. Variegated, they're shutting the franchises one by one. They're looking for reasons. Stamford. Montpelier. If that happens here, I don't know what I'll do. We have no savings. My wife and I, I mean." His voice is trembling. "We won't make it."

I stare at him.

"If I call Boston and I tell them I need to see the overnights, and they say why, and I—" He breathes, trying to keep it together, I'm just staring at him. "I say, gee, I've got missing files, I've got—I've got dead employees." He looks up at me, his eyes wet and wide, pleading like a child. "Just let me sit here. Just let me sit here until it ends.

Please just let me sit here."

He's weeping, his face dissolving in his hands. It's exhausting. People hiding behind the asteroid, like it's an excuse for poor conduct, for miserable and desperate and selfish behavior, everybody ducking in its comet-tail like children in mommy's skirts.

"Mr. Gompers, I am sorry." I rise. "But you're going to get those files. I want to know everything that's missing, and I want you to tell me, specifically, if any of the missing files were Peter Zell's. Do you understand?"

"I will—" He gets himself together, sits up a little and honks into a handkerchief. "I'll try."

"Don't try," I say, standing, turning. "You have till tomorrow morning. Do it."

*   *   *

I take the steps slowly back down to the first floor, trembling, shot, my energy expended, and while I was upstairs hassling Gompers the sky has decided to send down a miserable frozen drizzle, which slants into my face while I cross Eagle Square on the way back to my car.

The man with the sandwich board is still stalking the plaza, parka and fur hat, and again he hollers, "Do you *know* what *time* it is?" and I ignore him, but then he's planted himself in my path. He's holding up his sandwich board, DO THEY THINK WE'RE STUPID, raising it between us like a centurion's shield, and I mutter, "Excuse me, sir," but he doesn't move, and then I realize it's the guy from last night, from the Somerset, out of his Harley jacket now but still the heavy untrimmed mustache, red cheeks, doleful eyes.

And he goes, "You *are* Palace, right?"

"Yeah," and I realize what's happening too late, I reach for my shoulder holster but he's already dropped the sign and he's got something jammed up into my ribs. I glance down—a pistol, short and black and ugly.

"Do not move."

"Okay," I say.

The rain splatters steadily down over both of us, frozen in the center of Eagle Square. People are walking down the sidewalk, a couple dozen feet away, but it's cold and it's raining hard and everybody's looking at their feet. Nobody notices. Who cares?

"Do not say a word."

"I won't."

"Okay."

He breathes heavily. His mustache and beard are stained in patches, dirty cigarette-yellow. His breath is stale with old smoke.

"Where is she?" he hisses. The gun is pressed painfully into my ribs, angled upward, and I know the path that the bullet will take, gouging through the soft flesh, severing muscles, slamming to a stop in my heart.

"Who?" I ask.

I'm thinking about Toussaint's desperation move, with the ashtray. To make a move like that, Alison said, he would have had to be desperate. And now here is this man with his sandwich board: assaulting a police officer, use of a sidearm in the commission of a felony. Desperate. The gun twists into my side.

"Where is she?" he asks again.

"Where is who?"

"Nico."

Oh, God. Nico. It's raining harder and harder while we're standing here. I'm not even wearing a raincoat, just my gray blazer and blue tie. A rat darts by, out from behind a Dumpster, bounds across the square and out toward Main Street. I track it with my eyes while my assailant licks his lips.

"I don't know where Nico is," I tell him.

"Yes, you do, you do know."

He jams the pistol in harder, digs it deeper into the thin cotton of my dress shirt, and I can feel him itching to fire it, his anxious energy warming the coldness of the barrel. I picture the hole that had been left in Naomi, just above and to the right of her left eye. I miss her. It's so cold out here, my face is soaked. I left my hat in the car, with the dog.

"Please listen to me, sir," I say, raising my voice over the drumbeat of the rain. "I do not know where she is. I've been trying to find her myself."

"Bullshit."

"It's true."

"Bull*shit*."

"Who are you?"

"Don't worry about who I am."

"Okay."

"I'm a friend of hers, okay?" he says anyway. "I'm a friend of Derek's."

"Okay," I say, and I'm trying to remember everything Alison told me about Skeve and his ridiculous organization: the Catchman report, secret bases on the Moon. All nonsense and desperation, and yet here we are, and if this man twitches just one finger just a little bit, I'll be dead.

"Where's Derek?" I ask, and he snorts, angrily, says, "You *asshole*," and heaves back with his other hand, the one not holding the gun, and punches me closed-fist on the side of my head. Instantly, the world loses focus, blurs, and I double over and he hits me again, an undercut rushing up into my mouth, and I bounce backward against the wall of the plaza, my head banging against the bricks. The gun is immediately back in place, grinding into my ribcage, and now the world is spinning, swimming, rain overflowing around my eye patch and flooding my face, blood oozing from my upper lip into my mouth, my pulse roaring in my head.

He comes in close, hisses into my ear. "Derek Skeve is dead, and you know that he's dead because you killed him."

"I didn't—" my mouth fills with blood, I spit it out. "No."

"Oh, okay, so you *had* him killed. That is a pretty cutthroat technicality."

"I promise you. I don't know what you're talking about."

It's funny, though, I'm thinking, as the world slowly stops rotating, the furious face of the mustache man comes back into focus with the cold desolation of the plaza behind him, I sort of *did* know. I probably would have said that Skeve was dead, if you'd asked. But I haven't really had time to think about it. God, you wake up one day and everybody is dead. I turn my head, spit out another black stream of blood.

"Listen, friend," I say, bringing my voice to an easy place. "I promise you—no, wait, look at me, sir. Will you look at me?" He jerks his head up, his eyes are wide and scared, his lips twitching under the heavy mustache, and for a second we're like grotesque lovers, gazing into each other's eyes in this cold wet public square, a gun barrel between us.

"I do not know where Nico is. I do not know where Skeve is. But I might be able to help you, if you tell me what you know."

He thinks it over, his fearful inner debate playing out in his big, dolorous eyes, his mouth slightly open, breathing heavily. And then, suddenly and too loudly he says, "You're lying. You do know. Nico said her brother had this plan, some secret policeman plan—"

"What?"

"To get Derek out of there—"

"What?"

"Nico says her brother has this plan, he gets her a car—"

"Slow down—wait—"

The rain is pounding.

"And then Derek gets shot dead, and I barely get out of there, and when I get out she's nowhere."

"I don't know about any of this."

"Yes, you *do*."

A cold metal snap as he clicks off the safety. I yelp twice and clap my hands, and Mustache Man says, "Hey—" and then there's a ferocious bark from the street side of the square, and he turns his head toward it, and I raise my hands and shove him hard in the face, and he stumbles backward and lands on his rear end. "Shit," he says from the ground, and I draw my sidearm and aim, right down at his thick torso, but the sudden motion has thrown off my balance, and it's dark and my face is soaked, I'm seeing double again, and I must be pointing the gun at the wrong man, because the kick comes out of nowhere—he swipes out with his feet and catches me in the heel, and I topple like a statue being pulled down with ropes. I roll over, look wildly around the plaza. Nothing. Silence. Rain.

"Shoot," I say, sitting up and drawing out my handkerchief and holding it up to my lip. Houdini comes over and stands in front of me, bouncing back and forth, growling tenderly, and I hold out my hand, let him sniff it.

"He's lying," I tell the dog. Why would Nico have told some story about me having a prison-break plan? Where would Nico get a vehicle?

The problem is, a person like this guy doesn't have the brains to lie. A person who really thinks that the United States government somehow, over the last half decade, secretly constructed a warren of habitable bases on the dark side of the Moon, that we would have dedicated that level of resources toward mitigating the risk of a 1-in-250-million event.

It's weird, I think, struggling to my feet. My sister is too smart for this nonsense.

I wipe my mouth on the back of my sleeve and start to lope back to the car.

The thing is, she really is. She really is too smart for this nonsense. "Huh," I say. "Huh."

* * *

An hour later I'm down in Cambridge, in the sunken plaza across from Harvard Yard, where there's a group of ragged college-age homeless kids in a drum circle, and a couple of hippies dancing, and a man selling paperback books from a shopping cart, and a woman in a halter top on a unicycle, juggling bowling pins, singing "Que Sera Sera." A very old woman in a silver pantsuit is smoking a marijuana cigarette, trading it back and forth with a black man in thrift-store fatigues. A drunk snores loudly, sprawled across the steps, his lower half soaked with urine. A Massachusetts state trooper keeps a wary eye on the scene, his big mirrored sunglasses propped atop his ranger-style hat. I nod at him, a fellow policeman's nod, but he doesn't nod back.

I cross Mt. Auburn Street and find the little green kiosk with the boarded-up windows. I still have no idea where Alison Koechner works, and there is no one answering the phone at the old number, so this is all I've got: one place I know she goes a lot

"Well, well," says the Coffee Doctor in his hat and beard. "If it isn't my old nemesis."

"I'm sorry?" I say, narrowing my eyes, looking around at the dark room, empty but for me and the kid. He puts his hands up, grins. "Just kidding, man. Just something I say." He points at me with both hands, a big boisterous two-finger point. "You look like you could use a latte, friend."

"No, thank you. I need information."

"I don't sell that. I sell coffee."

He bustles around behind his counter, swiftly and efficiently, inserting the conical base of the portable filter into the espresso machine and pulling it out again, a light *ka-chunk*. He levels off the ground beans, tamps them down.

"I was in here a couple days ago."

"Okay," he says, eyes on his machine. "If you say so."

The paper cups are still lined up along the counter, one for each continent, step right up and place your bets. North America has only one or two beans in there—Asia a handful—Africa a handful. Antarctica remains in the lead, overspilling with beans. Wishful thinking. As if the thing would just plow into the snow, snuff out like a candle.

"I was here with a woman. About this tall, short red hair. Pretty."

He nods, pours milk from a carton into a metal jug. "Sure." He sticks a wand into the jug, flicks a switch, it begins to foam. "Coffee Doctor remembers all."

"Do you know her?"

"I don't *know* her, but I see her a lot."

"Okay."

For a moment I lose my train of thought, entranced by the frothing of the milk, staring along with the Coffee Doctor into his jug, and then he flicks the thing off with a sharp, birdlike movement, exactly at the moment before it would have foamed over.

"Ta-da."

"I need to leave her a message."

"Oh, yeah?"

The Coffee Doctor cocks an eyebrow. I massage my side, where the assailant's gun barrel has left me with a patch of tenderness, just below the ribs.

"Tell her that Henry was here."

"I can do that."

"And let her know that I need to see her."

"I can do that, too." He lifts a white ceramic demitasse off a hook and fills it with espresso, layers in the foamed milk with a long-handled spoon. There's a kind of genius at work here, a delicate sensibility being applied.

"You didn't always do this," I say. "Coffee, I mean."

"No." He keeps his eyes on his work, he's got the demitasse cradled in his palm and he's delicately jostling it, conjuring a pattern of dark coffee and cloudy foam. "I was a student of applied mathematics," he says, and very lightly inclines his head to indicate Harvard, across the street. He looks up, beaming. "But you know what they say," he concludes and presents me my latte, which bears a perfect and symmetrical oak leaf in milk foam. "There's no future in it."

He's smiling, and I'm supposed to laugh, but I don't. My eye hurts. My lip is throbbing where I got punched.

"So, you'll let her know? That Henry was here?"

"Yes, dude. I'll tell her."

"And please tell her—" You know what? At this point, why not? "Tell her Palace needs to know what all this Jules Verne moonshot hokum is covering up. Tell her I know there's more to this, and I want to know who these people are, and what it is they want."

"Wow. See, now, that's a message."

I'm pulling my wallet out of my pocket, and the Coffee Doctor reaches up and stills my hand.

"No, no," he says. "On the house. I gotta be honest, friend. You don't look so good."

3.

Detectives must consider all possibilities, consider and weigh each conceivable set of events that might have led to a crime, to determine which are most likely, which might prove to be true.

When she was murdered, Naomi was looking for Peter's insurable-interest files because she knew I was intrigued by them, and she was helping me in my investigation.

When she was murdered, Naomi was looking for the files to hide them before I could find them.

Someone shot her. A stranger? An accomplice? A friend?

For one hour I'm driving back from Cambridge to Concord, an hour of dead highway and vandalized exit signs and deer standing tremulously along the lip of 93 North. I'm thinking about Naomi in the doorway of my bedroom, Monday night. The more I think of that moment, the more certain I become that whatever she had to tell me—whatever she started to say and then stopped—it was not merely sentimental or interpersonal. It was relevant to the mechanics of my ongoing investigation.

But do you stand in the moonlight half-dressed and tell somebody *one more thing* about contestability clauses and insurable interest?

It was something else, and I'll never know what it was. But I
want to.

Normally, when I arrive at CPD headquarters on School Street,
I park in the lot and enter through the back door that leads to the
garage. This afternoon for some reason I go around to the front and
use the main door, the public entrance, which I first walked through
when I was four, maybe five years old. I say hey to Miriam, who
works at the desk where my mother used to work, and I go upstairs
to call Naomi Eddes's family.

Only thing is, now I'm up here, and the landline's not working.

No dial tone, no nothing. Dead plastic. I lift the cord, trace it
back to the jack and then back to the desk, click the switch hook a
few times. I look around the room, bite my lip. Everything is the
same: the desks are in place, the piles of papers, filing cabinets, sandwich wrappers, soda cans, the wan winter light tilting in through the
window. I travel around the room to Culverson's desk, lift up his receiver. It's the same: no dial tone, no life. I place the receiver back
gently in the cradle.

"Something's fucked," says Detective McGully, appearing in the
doorway with his arms crossed, sleeves of his sweatshirt pushed up,
cigar jabbing out of the side of his face. "Right?"

"Well," I say. "I can't get a line."

"Tip of the fucking iceberg," he growls, digging in the pockets of his sweatpants for a matchbox. "Something's up, New Guy."

"Huh," I say, but he is serious, dead serious—in all the time I've known him I've never seen an expression like this one on McGully's face. I go over and take Andreas's chair down off his desk, give his phone a try. Nothing. I can hear the Brush Cuts in the little coffee room two doors down, loud voices, someone guffawing, someone going, "So I say—I say—listen, wait." Somewhere a door slams; footsteps are rushing this way and that way outside.

"I ran into the chief when I came in this morning," McGully says, wandering into the room, leaning against the wall by the radiator, "and I said, 'hey, asshole,' like I always do, and he just walked right past me. Like I was a ghost."

"Huh."

"Now there's some kind of meeting going on in there. Ordler's office. The chief, the DCO, the DCA. Plus a bunch of jerks I don't recognize." He puffs on the cigar. "In wraparound sunglasses."

"Sunglasses?"

"Yeah," he says, "*sunglasses*," like it signifies something, but whatever the drift is I'm not catching it, and I'm only half listening, anyway. There's a small tender swelling on the back of my head, where it slammed against the brick wall in Eagle Square this morning.

"You mark my words, kid." He points at me with his unlit cigar, gestures with it all around the room, like the Ghost of Christmas Future. "Something is going the fuck on."

* * *

In the lobby of the main branch of the Concord Public Library is a neat display of classics, the greatest hits of the Western canon arranged in a tidy pyramid: *The Odyssey, The Iliad*, Aeschylus and Virgil providing the foundation, Shakespeare and Chaucer the second row, upward and forward in time all the way through *The Sun also Rises* at the capstone. No one has felt it necessary to provide a title for the display, although the theme is clearly *things to read before you die*. Somebody, maybe the same joker who put the R.E.M. song on heavy rotation on the Penuche's jukebox, has slipped a paperback copy of *On the Beach* into this display, shoehorned between *Middlemarch* and *Oliver Twist*. I take it out and carry it over to Fiction and refile it before going down to the basement to find the reference section.

This is what it must have meant to be a policeman in a predigital age, I'm thinking, enjoying the experience in a visceral way, digging out the fat phonebook for suburban Maryland, thumping it open along the spine, running my forefinger along the tiny columns of type, flipping through the tissue-thin pages for a name. Will there be policemen afterward, I do not know. No—there won't—eventually, maybe—but not for a while.

There are three listings for *Eddes* in Gaithersburg, Maryland, and I carefully copy the numbers into my blue book and go back up to the lobby, past the Shakespeare and John Milton, to where they have an old-fashioned phone booth by the front entrance. There's a line, and I wait for about ten minutes, gazing out the tall deco windows, my eyes resting on the skinny branches of a little gray musclewood tree outside the library entrance. I get in there, take a breath, and start dialing.

Ron and Emily Eddes, on Maryland Avenue. No answer, no machine.

Maria Eddes, Autumn Hill Place. She answers, but first of all she sounds very young and second she speaks only Spanish. I manage to ask her if she knows a Naomi Eddes, and she manages to reply no, she does not. I apologize and hang up.

It's drizzling out there again. I dial the last number and while it rings I watch a single lonesome ovular leaf, alone on the farthest reach of a twisting branch, get pelted by the raindrops.

"Hello?"

"William Eddes?"

"Bill. Who's this?"

My teeth clench. I clutch my forehead with my palm. My stomach is a tight black knot.

"Sir, are you related to a woman named Naomi Eddes?"

The pause that follows is long and painful. This is her father.

"Sir?" I say at last.

"Who is this?" he says, his voice tight and cold and formal.

"My name is Detective Henry Palace," I say. "I'm a policeman, in Concord, New Hampshire."

He hangs up.

The musclewood leaf, the one I was watching, is gone. I look and I think I can see where it landed, a black smear in the slush of the lawn. I call Bill Eddes back and I do not get an answer.

There's someone outside the phone booth, an agitated-looking old lady, bent over a small wire-frame shopping cart, the kind you get from the hardware store. I hold up one finger, smile apologetically, and I call Bill Eddes a third time, and I'm not surprised at all when there's no answer, and that the phone abruptly stops ringing entirely. Naomi's father, in his living room or kitchen, has yanked the phone from the wall. He's slowly winding the slim gray cord around the phone, placing the phone on the shelf of a closet, like you put away something not to be thought of again.

"Sorry, ma'am," I say, holding open the door for the old lady with the cart, and she asks, "What happened to your face?" but I don't answer. I'm leaving the library, I'm chewing on an end of my mustache, holding one hand over my heart, palming it, feeling it beat— holy moly—this is it—holy moly—hurrying, running now, through the sodden lawn and back to the car.

* * *

It's such a small town, Concord, sixty square miles taking in all the outskirts, and to drive just from downtown to the hospital with no other cars on the road? Ten minutes, which is not time enough to figure it all out, but is time enough to be sure that I *will* figure it out, that I've got it, that I will solve this murder—these murders—two murders, one murderer.

Here I am already, at the intersection of Langley Parkway and Route 9, looking up at Concord Hospital, where it sits like a child's model of a castle on a hill, surrounded by its outbuildings and sprawling parking lots and office suites and clinics. The new wing, unfinished and never-to-be finished, piles of timber, panes of glass, frames of scaffolding hidden under tarps.

I pull in, sit in the parking lot, drum my fingers on the wheel.

Bill Eddes reacted how he did for a reason, and I know what the reason is.

That fact implies a second fact, which leads me on to a third.

It's like you walk into a dark room, and there's a sliver of pale light under a doorway on the opposite side. You open that door and it leads on to a second room, slightly brighter than the last, and there's another door on the other side, with light under that one. And you keep going forward, one room after the other, more and more rooms, more and more light.

There's a bank of spherical lights over the main doors, and all were lit the last time I was here, and now two are out, and that's just it. The world is decaying bit by bit, every piece degrading at its own erratic rate, everything trembling and crumbling in advance, the terror of the coming devastation a devastation of its own, and each minor degradation has its consequences.

There's no volunteer behind the horseshoe desk in the lobby today, just a family sitting on the couches in a small anxious knot, a mom and a dad and a kid, and they look up as I walk past, as if I might have the bad news they're waiting for. I nod apologetically and then I stand there, turning in all directions, trying to orient myself, looking for Elevator B.

A nurse in scrubs rushes past me, stops at a doorway, mutters, "Oh, shoot," and turns back the other way.

I think I've figured out which way I'm going, and I take two steps and experience a pulse of intense pain from my bandaged eye. I gasp, raise my hand to it, shake it off, no time just now.

The pain, because—what was it that Dr. Wilton told me while winding gauze around my head? *The hospital is experiencing a shortage of palliative resources.*

Facts are connecting themselves, glowing to life in my memory and then connecting themselves, one to the other, forming pictures like constellations. But there is no joy, I feel no pleasure at all, because my face hurts, and my side where the gun barrel dug into it, the back of my head where it banged against the wall, and I'm thinking, *Palace, you dunce*. Because if I could just go back in time and see things clearer, see them correctly quicker, I would have solved the Zell case—and there would be no Eddes case. Naomi would not be dead at all.

The elevator door slides open and I step inside.

No one else gets on; it's just me, the tall quiet policeman with one eye, running his fingers up and down the sign, like a blind man reading Braille, trying to read the answers off the sign.

I ride it for a while, a few times up, a few times down. "Where," I mutter to myself, "where could you be keeping it?" Because somewhere in this building is a place analogous to the doghouse at J. T. Toussaint's, where presale product and ill-gotten gains are being hoarded. But a hospital is a place full of places—storerooms and surgeries, office suites and hallways—especially a hospital like this one, chaotic, chopped up, frozen midrenovation, it's a place *full* of places.

At last I call it quits and get off in the basement and find Dr. Fenton in her office, down a short hallway from the morgue, a small and immaculate office decorated with fresh flowers and family pictures and a print of Mikhail Baryshnikov, the Bolshoi Ballet, 1973.

Fenton looks surprised and not pleased to see me, like I'm a garden pest, a raccoon maybe, she thought she was rid of.

"What?"

I tell her what I need done and ask her how long that takes, typically. She scowls, and says, "Typically?" like the word no longer has meaning, but I say, "Yes, typically."

"Typically, between ten days and three weeks," she says. "Although, the Hazen Drive staff being what it is, at present, I imagine it would be more like four to six weeks."

"Okay—well—can you do it by the morning?" I ask, and I'm waiting for the scornful bray of laughter, bracing myself, thinking how I'm going to beg for it.

But she takes off her glasses, gets up from her chair, and looks at me carefully. "Why are you trying so hard to solve this murder?"

"I mean—" I hold up my hands. "Because it's unsolved."

"Okay," she says, and tells me she'll do it, as long as I promise never to call her or seek her out again, for any reason, forever.

And then, on my way back to the elevator, I find it, the place I was looking for, and I gasp, my jaw drops open and I literally gasp, and I say, "Oh, my God," my voice echoing down the concrete basement hallway, and then I turn and run back to ask Fenton for one more thing.

* * *

My cell phone isn't working. No bars. No service. It's getting worse.

I can picture them in my mind: untended cell towers tilting over slowly and then falling, connecting cables drooping, dead.

I drive back to the library, put quarters in the meter. I wait in line for the phone booth, and when it's my turn I reach Officer Mc-Connell at home.

"Oh, hey, Palace," she says. "You work upstairs. You want to tell me what on earth is going on over there? With the chiefs?"

"I don't know." Mysterious men in sunglasses. McGully, *some-*

thing's fucked. "I need your help with something, Officer. Do you have any clothes that aren't pants?"

"What?"

McConnell writes down where she's supposed to go and when, where Dr. Fenton will meet her in the morning. There's a line forming outside the phone booth. The old lady with the wire cart from the hardware store is back, waving her arms at me, like, *hello*, and behind her is a businessman type in a brown suit, with a briefcase, and a mom with twin girls. I flash my badge through the glass of the phone booth and duck down, trying to arrange myself comfortably in this tiny wooden room.

I raise Detective Culverson on the CB and I tell him that I solved the case.

"You mean, your hanger?"

"Yeah. And your case, too. Eddes."

"What?"

"Your case, too," I say. "Same killer."

I run over the whole thing for him, and then there's a long pause, radio crackling in the silence, and he says that's quite a lot of police work I've been doing.

"Yeah."

He says the same thing I said to McConnell last week: "You're going to be a great detective one day."

"Yep," I say. "Right."

"Are you coming back to headquarters?"

"No," I say. "Not today."

"Good," he says. "Don't."

4.

Even in the most quiescent policing environments, there is that occasional violent and random incident, where someone is murdered for no good reason in broad daylight on a busy street or in a parking lot.

The entire Concord Police Department was on hand for my mother's funeral, and they all rose and stood at attention as the coffin was carried in—fourteen staff members and eighty-six officers in their uniform blues, stiff as statues, saluting. Rebecca Forman, the force's certified public accountant, a sturdy middle-aged lady with salt-and-pepper hair, seventy-four years old, dissolved into sobs and had to be escorted out. The only person who remained seated was Professor Temple Palace, my father; he sat slackly in his pew throughout the short service, dull-eyed, eyes staring straight ahead, like a man waiting for a bus, his twelve-year-old son and six-year-old daughter standing wide-eyed on either side of him. He sat there, just sort of slumped against my hip, looking more perplexed than grief-stricken, and you could tell right there—I could tell—he wasn't going to make it.

I am sure that in retrospect what was hard for my father the English professor was not just the simple fact of her death, but the irony: that his wife, who sat from nine to five Monday through Friday behind bulletproof glass in a police station, should be shot through the heart by a thief in the T.J. Maxx parking lot on a Saturday afternoon.

Just to give you a sense of how low the crime rate was in Concord at that time: in the year in question, 1997, according to FBI records, my mother was the only person killed. Which means that, retrospectively, my mother's odds of falling victim to a murderer in Concord, in that year, came in at one in forty thousand.

But that's how it works: no matter what the odds of a given event, that one-in-whatever-it-is has to come in at some point, or it wouldn't be a one-in-whatever chance. It would be zero.

After the wake, my father looked at the kitchen, his glasses sitting on his nose, his eyes large and confused, and said to his children, "Well, now, what *are* we going to do for dinner?" and he meant not just tonight but forever. I smiled uneasily at Nico. The clock was ticking. He wasn't going to make it.

Professor Palace slept on the sofa, unable to go up there and deal with the fact of my mother's absence from the bed, with going through her closet full of things. I did all that. I packed up her dresses.

The other thing I did was hang around the police station a lot, asked the young detective leading the investigation to please let me know how it was going, and Culverson did: he called me when they had analyzed the footprints lifted from the gravel of the T.J. Maxx parking lot; he called when they located the vehicle identified by witnesses, a silver Toyota Tercel subsequently abandoned in Montpelier. When the suspect was in custody, Detective Culverson stopped by the house, laid out the files for me on the kitchen table and walked me through the case, the chain of evidence. He let me see everything except the photographs of the corpse.

"Thank you, sir," I said to Culverson, my father leaning in the doorway of the kitchen, pale, tired, mumbling "thank you" also. In my memory Culverson says, "Just doing my job," but I have my doubts whether he really would have said something so cliché. My memory is cloudy—it was a difficult time.

On June 10 of that same year they found my father's body in his office at St. Anselm's, where he had hung himself with the window cord.

I should have told Naomi the whole story, about my parents, the truth of it, but I didn't, and now she's dead and I never will.

5.

It's a beautiful morning, and there's something galling about it, how suddenly, just like that, the winter ends and springtime begins—rivulets of snowmelt and twists of green grass pushing up from under the rapidly thinning layer of snow in the farmland outside my kitchen window. This is going to be trouble, just in terms of law enforcement. It will work like black magic on the public spirit, this new season, the dawn of the last springtime we're going to get. We can expect a ratcheting up of desperation, fresh waves of anxiety and terror and anticipatory grief.

Fenton said that if she could pull it off, she would call me at nine o'clock with her report. It's 8:54.

I don't really need Fenton's report. Don't need the confirmation, I mean. I'm right, and I know I'm right. I know that I've got it. It'll help though. It'll be necessary in court.

I watch one perfect white cloud drift across the blue of the morning, and then, thank God, the phone rings, and I snatch it up and say hello.

No answer. "Fenton?"

There's a long silence, a rumbling of deep breathing, and I hold my breath. It's him. It's the killer. He knows. He's toying with me. Holy moly.

"Hello?" I say.

"I hope you're happy, Officer—excuse me, Detective." There's a noisy cough, a tinkling noise, ice in a glass of gin, and I look up at the ceiling and exhale.

"Mr. Gompers. This is not a good time."

"I found the claims," he says, as if he hadn't heard me. "The mysterious missing claims you wanted me to find. I found them."

"Sir." But he's not going to stop, and anyway I did tell him he had twenty-four hours, and here he is, reporting in, the poor bastard. I can't just hang up. "Right," I say.

"I went to the overnight cabinet, and I pulled that stretch of case numbers. There's only one in the bunch with Zell's name on it. That's what you wanted to know, right?"

"That's right."

His voice sloshes with drunken sarcasm. "Hope so. Because it's all going to happen, just like I said it was. Just like I said."

I'm looking at the clock. 8:59. What Gompers is telling me doesn't matter anymore. It never mattered in the first place. This case was never about insurance fraud.

"I'm in the conference room in Boston, digging through the overnights, and who sidles in but Marvin Kessel. Do you know who that is?"

"No, sir. I appreciate your help, Mr. Gompers."

It was never about insurance fraud. Not even for one second.

"Marvin Kessel, for your information, is the assistant regional manager for the Mid-Atlantic and Northeast regions, and he was *awfully* interested in what the heck is going on up in Concord. And so now he knows, and now Omaha knows, we've got missing files, we've got suicides. We've got it all!" He sounds like my dad: *Because it's Concord!*

"And so *now* I am going to lose my job, and everybody in this branch, they're going to lose their jobs, too. And we'll all be out on the street. So, I hope you have a pen handy, Detective, because I've got the information."

I do have a pen, and Gompers gives me the information. The claim that Peter was working on when he died was filed in mid-November by a Ms. V. R. Jones, a director of the Open Vista Institute, a nonprofit corporation registered in the state of New Hampshire. Its headquarters are in New Castle, which is on the coast, near Portsmouth. It was a comprehensive life-insurance policy on the executive director, Mr. Bernard Talley, and Mr. Talley committed suicide in March, and Merrimack Life and Fire was exercising its right to investigate.

I write it all down, old habit, but it doesn't matter and it never mattered, not even for a second.

Gompers is done and I say, "Thanks," looking at the clock, it's 9:02—any minute Fenton will call, she'll give me the confirmation I need, and I'll get in the car and go get the killer.

"Mr. Gompers, I recognize that you have made a sacrifice. But this is a murder investigation. It's important."

"You have no idea, young man," he says morosely, "You have no idea what's important."

He hangs up, and I almost call him back. I swear to God, with all that's going on, I almost get up and go over there. Because he's not—he's not going to make it.

But then the landline rings again, and I snatch it up again, and now it is Fenton, and she says, "Well, detective, how did you know?"

I take a breath, close my eyes, and listen to my heart pounding for a second, two seconds.

"Palace? Are you there?"

"I'm here," I say, slowly. "Please tell me exactly what you've found."

"Why certainly. I'd be happy to. And then at some point you are going to buy me a steak dinner."

"Yep." I say, opening my eyes now, peering at the crisp blue sky just beyond the kitchen window. "Just tell me what you've found."

"You're a lunatic," she says. "MassSpec on the blood of Naomi Eddes confirms presence of morphine sulfate."

"Right," I say.

"This does not come as a surprise to you."

"No, ma'am," I say. *No, it does not.*

"Cause of death is unchanged. Massive craniocerebral trauma from gunshot wound in mid-forehead. But the victim of this gunshot had ingested a morphine derivative within the six- to eight-hour period prior to her death."

It does not surprise me at all.

I close my eyes again, and I can picture Naomi leaving my house in her red dress in the middle of the night and going home to get high as a satellite. She must have been getting toward the end of her stash, too, must have been getting anxious about that, because now her dealer was dead. McGully had shot him. My fault.

Oh, Naomi. You could have told me.

I pull out my SIG Sauer from its holster and lay it on the kitchen table, open the magazine, empty out and count the dozen .357 bullets.

In the Somerset Diner, a week before, Naomi eating French fries, telling me that she *had* to help Peter Zell when she saw that he was suffering, that he was in withdrawal. She *had* to help him, she said, looked down, looked away.

I could have known it right then, had I wanted to know.

"I wish I could tell you more," Fenton says. "If the girl had some hair on her head, I could tell you if she's been using morphine for a long time."

"Oh, yeah?"

I'm not really listening. Here's a girl who felt compelled to help this random coworker, this man she barely knew, when she saw that he was suffering. Here's a girl with her own long experience of drug addiction, who's put her parents through hell, so much so that her father hangs up the phone as soon as he hears her name, hears the word *policeman.*

"If you've got a long enough piece of hair, you can cut it into quarter-inch sections, break them down and test them one by one," Fenton says, "figure out what substances were metabolized, month by month. Pretty fascinating stuff, actually."

"I'll see you over there," I say. "And I will. I'll buy you that dinner."

"Sure you will, Palace," she says. "Around Christmas, right?"

I know what the hair test would have revealed. Naomi had been using, this time, for three months. I don't know about her past usage, her periods of addiction and recovery and relapse, but this time she was using for almost three months exactly. Since Tuesday, January 3, when Professor Leonard Tolkin of the Jet Propulsion Lab went on television and gave her the same bad news he gave everybody else. My guess is, if she didn't renew her active use of controlled substances that night, it was the day after, or the day after that.

I reload the magazine, snap it into place, depress the safety, and return my sidearm to the holster. I've already done this exercise in its entirety—open the magazine, check the bullets, close it up—several times since waking this morning at seven thirty.

Peter Zell had made his risk assessment and taken his plunge months before, gone through his whole cycle of attraction, experimentation, addiction, and withdrawal as the odds climbed steadily through the months. But Naomi, along with a lot of other people, took her own plunge only when it was official, when the odds of impact jumped all the way to one hundred percent. Millions of people all around the world deciding to get high as satellites and stay that way, scrambling for whatever they could—dope or junk or NyQuil or whippets or stolen bottles of hospital painkillers—and slip into pure pleasure mode, tune out the terror and the dread, in a world where the idea of *long-term consequences* had magically disappeared.

I will myself back in time, back to the Somerset Diner, reach across the table and take Naomi's hands in my own, and I tell her to go ahead and tell me the truth, tell me about her weakness, and I'd tell her I don't care and I'm going to fall for her anyway. I would have understood.

Would I have understood?

My father taught me about irony, and the irony here is that in

October, when it was still fifty-fifty, when there was still hope, it was Naomi Eddes who had helped Peter Zell kick his stupid habit—helped him so well that when the end of the world was officially announced he fought through it, stayed clean. But Naomi, whose own addiction was deeper bred, whose habit was lifelong, not the result of a cold calculation of the odds . . . Naomi wasn't that strong.

Another irony: it wasn't so easy, in early January, to get ahold of drugs, especially the kind Naomi needed. New laws, new cops, demand spiking wildly, new choke points on supply, all the way up and down the line. But Naomi had known just where to go. She knew from her nightly conversations with Peter about his ongoing temptation: his old pal J. T. was still dealing, still getting morphine, in some form, from somewhere.

So that's where she went, to the squat dirty house on Bow Bog Road, started buying, started using, never told Peter, never told anyone, and the only people who knew were Toussaint and the person who was his new supplier.

And that person—that person is the killer.

In the dark, at my house, frozen in the doorway, she almost told me the whole truth. Not only the truth about her addiction, but the truth about insurable interest, fraud claims, *I thought of something that might be helpful to you, in your case.* If I'd gotten out of bed, taken her wrists, kissed her and pulled her back into bed, she'd still be alive.

If she'd never met me, she'd still be alive.

I feel the weight of the gun in the holster, but I don't take it out, not again. It's ready, it's loaded. I'm ready.

* * *

My Impala rolls through the gigantic parking lot, the asphalt painted black and wet with runoff. It's 9:23.

There is only one thing left that I don't understand, and that's *why*. Why would someone do something like this—why would *this* person do *these things*?

I get out of the car and walk into the hospital.

I have to apprehend the suspect. And even more so, I have to know the answer.

In the crowded lobby I loiter behind a column, hunched over to minimize my height, my bandaged face hidden behind the *Monitor* like a spy. After a few minutes I see the murderer coming, striding purposefully down the hall, right on time. It's urgent, important, work to be done in the basement.

I'm hunched in the hospital hallway, twitching with nervousness, ready for action.

The motive, on the one hand, is obvious: money. The same reason anybody steals and then sells controlled substances and commits murders to cover up those activities. Money. Especially now, high demand, low supply, the cost-benefit analysis on drug sales is skewed, someone is going to take the risk, someone is going to put together a small fortune.

But—somehow—it's wrong. For this killer, for these crimes. These risks. Murder and then double murder, and worse than murder, and for what, for money? The risk of jail, of execution, of throwing away what little time is left? Just money?

Soon I'll know all the answers. I'm going to go down there, it's going to work, and then this will be over. The thought of it, the whole thing being over, rolls over me, inevitable, joyless, cold, and I clutch my newspaper. Peter's killer—Naomi's killer—gets on the elevator, and a few seconds later, I go down the stairs.

* * *

The morgue is cold. The autopsy lights are off, and it's dim and hushed. The walls are gray. It's like being inside a refrigerator, inside a coffin. I step into the chilling silence just in time to see Erik Littlejohn shake hands with Dr. Fenton, who gives him a curt, businesslike nod.

"Sir."

"Good morning, Doctor. As I believe I mentioned on the phone, I do have a visitor coming at ten, but in the meantime I am happy to be of service."

"Of course," says Fenton. "Thanks."

Littlejohn's voice is hushed and sensitive and appropriate. The director of Spiritual Services. The gold beard, the big eyes, the aura of respect. A handsome new-looking jacket of creamy mahogany leather, a gold watch.

But money's not enough—a gold watch—a new jacket—to do all that he's done, the horrors that he has committed. It's not enough. I can't accept it. I don't care what's coming toward us in the sky.

I tuck myself against a wall, in a far corner, close by the door, the door leading back down the hallway, to the elevator.

Littlejohn turns now and nods his head deeply, respectfully, to Officer McConnell, who is supposed to be looking bereaved, in character, but who instead looks irritated, probably because she is following my instructions, wearing a skirt and blouse and carrying a black pocketbook, wearing her hair down, no ponytail.

"Good morning, ma'am," says Peter Zell's murderer. "My name is Erik. Dr. Fenton has asked me to be present this morning, and I understand that that is your wish."

McConnell nods gravely and launches into the little speech we wrote for her.

"My husband, Dale, he went and he shot himself with his old hunting rifle," says McConnell. "I don't know why he did it. I mean, I do know, but I thought—" and then she plays at being unable to continue, her voice trembles and catches, me thinking, *there you go, very impressive, Officer McConnell.* "I thought we'd have the rest of it together, the rest of our time together."

"The wound is rather severe," says Dr. Fenton, "and so Ms. Taylor and I agreed that she might benefit from your presence in viewing her husband's body for the first time."

"Of course," he murmurs, "absolutely." My eyes flicker over his body, top to bottom, looking for the bulge of a firearm. If he's got one, it's well hidden. I don't think he does.

Littlejohn smiles at McConnell with radiant kindness, places a reassuring hand on her shoulder, and turns to Fenton.

"And where," he asks in a delicate undertone, "is Ms. Taylor's husband now?"

My stomach tightens. I place a hand over my mouth to control the sound of my breathing, to control myself.

"This way," Fenton answers—and here we are, this is the pivot point of the whole affair, because now she's leading the two of them—Littlejohn with his gentle hand guiding McConnell, the fake widow—leading the two of them across the room, toward where I am, toward the hallway.

"We've laid the body out," explains Dr. Fenton, "in the old chapel."

"What?"

Littlejohn hesitates, a small stutter step, his eyes flashing with fear and confusion, and my heart catches in my throat, because I'm right—I knew I was right, and yet I cannot believe it. I'm staring at him, imagining those soft hands winding a long black belt around Peter Zell's neck, slowly tightening. Imagining a pistol trembling in his hand, Naomi's big black eyes.

A moment more, Palace. A moment more.

"I believe you are mistaken, Doctor," he says quietly to Fenton.

"No mistake," she replies briskly, smiling tightly, reassuringly at McConnell. She's enjoying this, Fenton. Littlejohn keeps pushing, what choice does he have? "No, you are incorrect, that room is out of service. It is locked."

"Yes," I say, and Littlejohn jumps, in this instant he knows exactly what's going on, he looks around the room and I step out of the darkness with my sidearm raised. "And you have the key. Where is the key, please?"

He looks at me, dumbstruck.

"Where is the key, sir?"

"It's—" he closes his eyes, opens them again, the blood draining from his face, hope dying in his eyes. "It's in my office."

"We'll go there."

McConnell has drawn her weapon from her black pocketbook. Fenton stays put, her eyes glinting behind her round glasses, enjoying every second.

"Detective." Littlejohn steps forward, he's making an effort, his voice trembling, but he's trying. "Detective, I can't imagine—"

"Quiet," I say. "Quiet, please."

"Yes, but Detective Palace, I don't know what you're thinking, but if you . . . if you think . . ."

Feigned confusion distorts his handsome features. It's there, the truth is there, even in the fact that my name comes so easily to mind: he's known exactly who I am since the day I caught this case, since I called his wife to arrange an interview, he's been on to me, tailing me, interposing himself between me and my ongoing investigation. Encouraging Sophia, for example, to evade my questions, selling her on the attenuated notion that it would upset her father. Selling *me* on how depressed his brother-in-law was. Watching outside the house, waiting, while I interviewed J. T. Toussaint. And then, a Hail Mary, unhooking the chains on my snow tires.

And he was at Toussaint's again, the house on Bow Bog Road, scrabbling around looking for the leftover merchandise, the phone numbers, client lists. Looking for the same things I was, except he knew what we were looking for and I didn't, and then I chased him off before he could think to search the doghouse.

But he had one more trick to play, one more way to shove me in the wrong direction. One more brutal trick to play, and it almost worked.

Officer McConnell steps forward, drawing handcuffs from the small pocketbook, and I say, "Wait."

"What?" she asks.

"I just—" my gun still leveled on Littlejohn. "I'd like to hear the story first."

"I am sorry, Detective," he says, "but I don't know what you're talking about."

I release the safety. I think that if he keeps lying, I might kill him. I might just do it.

But he does, he talks. Slowly, softly, his voice dead and toneless, staring not at me but into the barrel of my firearm, he tells the story. The story that I already know, that I already figured out.

After October, when Sophia discovered that her brother had stolen her prescription pad and was using it to score pain pills—after she confronted him and cut him off—after Peter slipped into the brief painful period of withdrawal, and Sophia thought the whole thing was at an end—after all of that, Erik Littlejohn went to J. T. Toussaint and made him a proposition.

At that time, with Maia in conjunction and the odds of impact hovering at an agonizing fifty percent, the hospital was working at half staff: pharmacists and pharmacists' assistants were quitting in droves, and new people were being hired, glad for a salary backed by government money. Security was, and remains, all over the map. Some days, armed guards with machine guns; other days, the doors to locked wards propped open with folded-over magazines. Pyxis, the state-of-the-art mechanized pill dispensary, stopped working in September, and the technician assigned by the manufacturer to Concord Hospital could not be located.

The director of Spiritual Services, in this time of desperation and wildness, has remained at his post, a trusted and constant figure, a rock. And he was, as of November, stealing vast quantities of medicine from the hospital pharmacy, from the nurses' stations, from patients' bedsides. MS Contin, Oxycontin, oxytocin, Dilaudid, half-empty bags of liquid morphine.

Through all of this, my gun does not waver, pointed at his face: his golden eyes half closed, the mouth set, expressionless.

"I promised Toussaint that I would keep him supplied," he says. "I told him I would take the risk of procuring the pills, if he would take the risk of selling them. We split the risk, and we split the profit."

Money, I'm thinking, just stupid money. So small, so squalid, so dull. Two murders, two bodies in the ground, all those people suffering, doing with half doses of their pills, with the world about to end? I gape at the murderer, looking him up and down. Is this a man who does all that for gain? For a gold watch and a new leather jacket?

"But Peter found out," I say.

"Yes," Littlejohn whispers, "he did," and he lowers his head and shakes it slowly, sadly, back and forth, as if remembering some regrettable act of God. Someone had a stroke, someone fell down the stairs. "He—it was last Saturday night—he showed up at J. T.'s house. It was late. I only went there very late."

I exhale, grit my teeth. No escaping the fact that if Peter was at J. T.'s very late on a Saturday night—a meeting J. T. had not mentioned to me—then he was there for a fix. He had his nightly call with Naomi, his support system who was herself secretly using morphine; he told her he was doing fine, holding up, and then he went to J. T.'s to get high as a satellite; and then his brother-in-law of all people shows up, his brother-in-law who, unbeknownst to him, is delivering a fresh supply.

Everybody with secrets, squirreled away.

"He sees me, I'm holding a duffel bag for God's sake, and I just said, 'please, please, please don't tell your sister.' But I knew—I knew he——" He stops himself, brings a hand to his mouth.

"You knew you had to kill him."

He moves his head very slightly up and down.

He was right: Peter would have told Sophia. In fact, he had called her for that purpose the next day, Sunday, March 18, and again on Monday, but she didn't answer. He sat down to write her a letter, but couldn't find the words.

So, on Monday night, Erik Littlejohn went to see *Distant Pale Glimmers* at the Red River, where he knew he would find his brother-in-law, the quiet insurance man. And there he is with their mutual friend J. T. Toussaint, and after the movie Peter tells J. T. to take off, he wants to walk home—Littlejohn caught a break on that one—because now Peter is alone. And what do you know, here's Erik, and Erik says, let's have a beer, let's catch up—let's make amends before everything happens.

And they're drinking their beers, and from his pocket he takes a small vial, and when Peter has passed out he drags him from the theater, nobody notices, nobody cares, he takes him to the McDonald's to hang him in the bathroom.

* * *

McConnell puts the suspect in the handcuffs and I guide him by the bicep to the elevator, Fenton trailing behind us, and we ascend in silence: coroner, murderer, cop, cop.

"Holy crap," says Fenton, and McConnell says, "I know."

I don't say anything. Littlejohn doesn't say anything.

The elevator stops and the doors open onto the lobby and it's crowded and among the crowd is a preadolescent boy, waiting there on one of the sofas, and Littlejohn's whole body goes tense, and mine does, too.

He had told Fenton that he could come down to the morgue to help with a body at 9:30, but he had a visitor coming at 10.

Kyle looks up, stands up, stares, wide-eyed and baffled, his father in handcuffs, and Littlejohn can't take it, he hurls his body out of the elevator, and I'm holding fast to his arm, and the force of his body in motion pulls me forward, too, both of us together. We land on the floor and go into a roll.

McConnell and Fenton spill out of the elevator, the lobby is full of people, doctors and volunteers, dodging out of the way and hollering as Littlejohn and I go end over end. Littlejohn bangs his forehead up and slams it into mine just as I'm drawing for my sidearm, and the force of the impact sends an explosion of pain into my wounded eye, throws a sky full of stars up in front of the other one. I slump down on top of him, he's wriggling underneath me, McConnell is shouting, "Freeze!" and then someone is yelling, too, a small scared voice saying, "Stop, stop." I look up, my vision is wavering back into place, and I say, "Okay." He's got my sidearm, the kid has got it, the service-issue SIG 229, pointed right at my face.

"Son," says McConnell, and she's got her gun out, but she doesn't know what to do with it. She aims it, uncertainly, at Kyle, then at Littlejohn and me, slumped together on the floor, and then back at the boy.

"Let him—" Kyle sniffs, whimpers, and I'm seeing myself, I can't help it, of course, I was eleven once. "Let him go."

God.

God, Palace.

You dunce.

The motive was staring me in the face the whole time, not just money but what you can get for it. What you can get for money, even now. Especially now. And here's this funny-looking kid, the wide smile, a princeling, the boy I first saw the second day of my investigation, tromping across a lawn of unbroken snow.

I saw it in Littlejohn's eyes when he was hollering affectionately up the stairs, telling his boy to go ahead and get ready, boasting quietly about what a whiz he is out there on the ice.

Let's say, in our present unfortunate circumstances, I was the father of a child; what would I not do to shield that child, to whatever degree I could, from the coming calamity? Depending on where that thing comes down, the world is either ending or descending into darkness, and here is a man who would do anything—who has done awful things—to prolong and protect the life of his child should the latter eventuality arise. To mitigate the hazards of October and after.

And no, Sophia wouldn't have called the police if she had found out, but she would have taken him, taken the boy and gone away, or at least that's what Erik Littlejohn was afraid of—that the mother would not have understood what the father was doing, how important it was, how it *had to be done*, and she would have snatched him away. And then what would have become of him—and her—in the aftermath?

And tears are welling up and falling from the boy's eyes, and tears are falling from Littlejohn's eyes, and I wish I could say, being a professional detective in the middle of an extraordinarily difficult arrest, that I maintain my composure and focus, but they are, they are, tears are rolling down my face like the flood.

"Give me the gun, young man," I say. "You should give the gun to me. I'm a policeman."

He does. He walks over, and he puts it in my hand.

* * *

The little chapel in the basement is stacked with boxes.

They are labeled as containing medical supplies, and, in fact, some of them do: three boxes of syringes, six score to a box, two boxes of protective face masks, a small box of iodine pills and saline solution. IV bags, drip chambers. Tourniquets. Thermometers.

There are pills, too, the same variety I found at the doghouse. Stored here till he had enough to be worth smuggling them out of the hospital and to Toussaint's.

There is food. Five boxes of canned goods: chipped beef and baked beans and chunky soup. Cans like this disappeared many months ago from the supermarket, and you can find them on the black market if you've got the money, but no one has the money. Not even cops. I lift a can of Del Monte pineapple chunks and feel its familiar weight in my hand, comforting and nostalgic.

Most of the boxes, however, are full of guns.

Three Mossberg 817 Bolt Action hunting rifles with twenty-one-inch barrels.

A single Thompson M1 submachine gun, with ten boxes of .45 caliber bullets, fifty bullets in a box.

A Marlin .30-06 with a scope on the top.

Eleven Ruger LCP .380s, little ten-ounce conceal-carry automatic handguns, plenty of ammunition for these, too.

Thousands and thousands and thousands of dollars' worth of guns.

He was just getting ready. Getting ready for afterward. Although, when you look at it from inside this cramped room with the cross on the door, full of boxes of guns and canned foods and pills and syringes, you start to think: well, afterward has started already.

In one long box, of the kind that might have been used to package and ship a vanity mirror or a large picture frame, lies an over-sized cross-bow, with ten aluminum bolts tied in a neat bundle at the bottom of the box.

* * *

We're in the unit, the suspect is in the backseat, we're on the way back to headquarters. It's a ten-minute drive, but that's time enough. Time enough to know whether I've got the rest of the story straight, or don't I.

Instead of waiting for him to tell me, I tell him, my gaze flicking back and forth to the rear-view mirror, watching Erik Little-john's eyes to see if I'm right.

But I am—I know I'm right.

May I please speak to Ms. Naomi Eddes?

That's what he said, that gentle and mellifluous voice, a voice she didn't recognize. It must have been strange, much like the time I called her from Peter Zell's phone. Now here was a strange voice calling from J. T. Toussaint's phone. A number she knew by heart, the number she'd been calling for a few months now, every time she needed to get high, to get lost.

And now the strange voice on the other end began to give her instructions.

Call that cop, said the voice—call your new friend, the detective. Gently remind him of what he's overlooked. Suggest to him that this sordid drug-murder case is about something else entirely.

And boy, did it work. Holy moly. My face burns at the thought of it. My lips curl back in self-disgust.

Insurable interest. False claims. It sounded like just the sort of thing that someone gets killed for, and I dove right in. I was a kid playing a game, overheated, ready to jump for the brightly colored ring dangled in front of me. The dumb detective pacing in excited circles around his house, a fool, a puppy. Insurance fraud! A-ha! That must be it. I need to see what he's working on!

Littlejohn isn't saying anything. He's done. He's living in the future. Surrounded by death. But I know that I'm right.

Kyle has remained at the hospital, sitting in the lobby with Dr. Fenton, of all people, awaiting Sophia Littlejohn, who is now hearing the news, who is about to begin the hardest months of her life. Like everybody else, but worse.

I don't need to ask anymore, I've really got the whole picture, but I can't help it, it can't be helped. "The next day, you came to Merrimack Life and Fire, and you waited, right?"

I linger at a red light at Warren Street. I could blow the light, of course, I have a dangerous suspect in custody, a murderer, but I wait, my hands at ten and two.

"Answer me, please, sir. The next day, you came to her office, and you waited?"

"Yes." A whisper.

"Louder, please."

"Yes."

"You waited in the hallway, outside her cubicle."

"In a closet."

My hands tighten on the wheel, my knuckles white, practically glowing white. McConnell looking at me from the shotgun seat, looking uneasy.

"In a closet. And then when she was alone, Gompers drunk in his office, the rest of them at the Barley House, you showed her the gun, you marched her into the storeroom. Made it look like she was digging for files, too, just to—to what? Turn the screw one more time, for me, make sure I thought what you wanted me to think?"

"Yes, and . . ."

"Yes?"

McConnell, I notice, has placed one of her hands over mine, on the wheel, to make sure I don't run off the road.

"She would have told you. Eventually."

Palace, she said, sat on the bed. *Something.*

"I had to," moans Littlejohn, fresh tears in his eye. "I had to kill her."

"No one has to kill anyone."

"Well, soon," he says, looking out the window, staring out. "Soon, they will."

* * *

"I *told* you something was fucked."

McGully, in Adult Crimes, sitting on the floor with his back against the wall. Culverson sits on the opposite side of the room, somehow radiating dignity and poise though he is cross-legged, pant legs hitched up slightly.

"Where is everything?" I say.

The desks are gone. The computers are gone, the phones, the trash cans. Our tall bank of filing cabinets is gone from its space beside the window and has left behind an irregular pattern of rectangular indentations in the floor. Cigarette butts litter the ancient pale blue carpeting like dead bugs.

"I told you," says McGully again, his voice a chilling echo in the hollowed-out room.

Littlejohn is outside, still cuffed in the backseat of the Impala, being babysat by Officer McConnell with a reluctant assist from Ritchie Michelson, until we do the official booking. I came into the station alone, ran upstairs to get Culverson. I want us to process the perp together—his murder, my murder. Teammates.

McGully finishes the cigarette he's working on, twists it out between his fingers, and flicks the dead butt into the center of the room to join the others.

"They know," says Culverson quietly. "Somebody knows something."

"What?" asks McGully.

But Culverson doesn't answer, and then Chief Ordler comes in.

"Hey, guys," he says. The chief is in street clothes, and he looks tired. McGully and Culverson look up at him warily from their respective squats; I straighten up, bring my heels together and stand there expectantly, I am conscious of the fact that I have a suspected double-murderer downstairs in a parked unit, but strangely, after all this, it feels like it doesn't matter anymore.

"Guys, as of this morning, the Concord Police Department has been federalized."

Nobody says anything. Ordler's got a binder under his right arm, the seal of the Justice Department stamped on the side.

"Federalized? What does that mean?" I ask.

Culverson shakes his head, slowly gets up, lays a steadying hand on my shoulder. McGully stays where he is, tugs out a fresh cigarette and lights it.

"What does that mean?" I ask again. Ordler looks at the floor, keeps talking.

"They're overhauling everything, putting even more kids on the street, and they say I can keep most of my patrol officers, if I want and they want, but all under Justice Department jurisdiction."

"But what does it *mean*?" I ask a third time, meaning, for us? What does it mean for us? The answer is obvious. I'm standing in an empty room.

"They're shutting down the investigative units. Basically—"

I shake Culverson's hand off my shoulder, drop my face down into my hands, look up again at Chief Ordler, shaking my head.

"—basically the feeling is that an investigative force is relatively unnecessary, given the current environment."

He goes on for a while—it all gets lost for me, after that, but he goes on—and then at some point he stops talking and asks if there are any questions. We just look at him, and he mumbles something else, and then he turns and leaves.

I notice for the first time that our radiator has been shut off, and the room is cold.

"They know," Culverson says again, and we both pivot our heads toward him, like marionettes.

"They're not supposed to know for more than a week yet," I say. "April 9, I thought."

He shakes his head. "Somebody knows early."

"What?" says McGully, and Culverson says, "Somebody knows where the damn thing is going to come down."

* * *

I open the front shotgun-seat door of the Impala, and Mc-Connell says, "Hey. What's the story?" and I don't say anything for a long time, I just stand there with one hand on the roof of the car, looking in at her, craning my neck to look at the prisoner in the backseat, slouched down, staring up. Michelson is sitting on the hood, smoking a butt, like my sister did that day in the parking lot.

"Henry? What's going on?"

"Nothing," I say. "Nothing. Let's go ahead and take him in."

McConnell and Michelson and I remove the suspect from the backseat and stand him up in the garage. There's a little crowd watching us, Brush Cuts and a few of the vets, Halburton, the old mechanic who's still kicking around the garage. We pull Littlejohn from the car in his handcuffs, in his sharp leather jacket. A concrete stairwell leads from this area directly down to the basement, to Booking, to be used in exactly this circumstance: the perp is brought in, in a squad car, and handed directly to the duty officers to be taken down for processing.

"Stretch?" says Michelson. "What's up?"

I'm just standing there, one hand on the suspect's arm. Someone wolf-whistles at McConnell, she's still in the skirt and blouse, and she says, "Up yours."

I've used the staircase for pickpockets, once for a suspected arsonist, for countless drunks. Never before for a murderer.

A double-murderer.

I feel nothing, though, I feel numb. My mother would have been proud of me, I think dumbly; Naomi might have been proud of me. Neither is here. In six months none of this will be here, this'll be ash and a hole.

I start moving again, leading the little group in step toward the staircase. The detective brings in his man. My head hurts.

What happens next, under normal circumstances, is this: The on-duty processing officers take custody of the suspect and walk him down the steps to the basement, where the suspect is fingerprinted and reminded of his rights. Then he would be searched, photographed, the contents of his pockets collected and labeled. His options for legal counsel would be presented to him; someone like Erik Littlejohn, a man of means, would presumably have private counsel he could retain, and he would be afforded an opportunity to make those arrangements.

This top step of this concrete staircase, in other words, is in fact just the next step in a long and complicated journey that begins with the discovery of a corpse on a dirty bathroom floor and ends ultimately at justice. That's under normal circumstances.

We're lingering a few steps from the stairhead, Michelson says it again, "Stretch?" and McConnell says, "Palace?"

I don't know what happens to Littlejohn once I give him over to the two kids, maybe seventeen, eighteen years old, who are waiting with their dull eyes and their hands outstretched to guide my suspect down the stairs.

The due-process rules have been adjusted several times under IPSS and the corresponding state laws, and the truth is I don't know what's in the new statutes. What's in the binder Chief Ordler was holding just now—what other provisions are included along with the suspension of detective-level criminal investigation?

I haven't confronted the question, in my heart, of what happens next to the alleged murderer once he's been brought in. Tell you the God's honest truth, I don't think I ever believed I'd be standing here.

But now—I mean—what're the options? That is the question.

I'm looking at Erik Littlejohn, and he's looking at me, and then I say, "I'm sorry," and I hand him over.

EPILOGUE

....

Wednesday, April 11

....

Right ascension 19 27 43.9
Declination 35 32 16
Elongation 92.4
Delta 2.705 AU

I'm rolling on a ten-speed bicycle down the sun-washed side-walks of New Castle, New Hampshire, in search of Salamander Street. The sun is up there slipping in and out of patchy cloud cover, the breeze is warm and kind and salt-smelling, and I decide, what the heck, and I take a right and coast down a side street toward the water.

New Castle is a small and charming summer town out of sea-son, with the chained-up souvenir shops, the ice-cream-and-fudge place, the post office, the historical society. There's even a boardwalk, running for a quarter mile or so along the beach, a handful of happy beachgoers out on the dunes. An elderly couple hand in hand, a mom tossing a Nerf football with her son, a teenager sprinting, trying to get a bulky box kite up and off the ground.

A path from the far end of the beach leads back to the town square, where a green lawn surrounds a handsome dark-wood gazebo festooned with bunting and American flags. It looks like there was a small-town celebration last night, and it looks like there's going to be another one tonight. A couple of locals are wandering into the square, even now, unpacking brass instruments and making small talk, shaking hands. I chain up my ten-speed bike by an overflowing garbage can surrounded by paper plates, uneaten bites of funnel cake drawing happy lines of ants.

There was a parade in Concord last night, also, and there were even fireworks launched from a barge in the Merrimack, bursting majestically and sparkling around the golden dome of the state house. Maia, we now know, is going to land in Indonesia. They can't or won't name an impact spot with a hundred percent certainty, but the vicinity is the Indonesian archipelago, just east of the Gulf of Boni. Pakistan, with its eastern border just four thousand kilometers from the impact site, has renewed its promise to blast the rock from the sky, and the United States has renewed its objections.

In America, meanwhile, across the country, parades and fireworks and celebrations. And, at a suburban shopping mall outside Dallas, looting, followed by gunfire, ending in a riot; six people dead. A similar incident in Jacksonville, Florida, and one in Richmond, Indiana. Nineteen people dead at a Home Depot in Green Bay, Wisconsin.

* * *

Four Salamander Lane does not look like the headquarters of any kind of institute. It's a little Cape Cod–style single-family residence, old wood painted in blue pastel, close enough to the water that I can smell the salt breeze, here on the front steps.

"Good morning, ma'am," I say to the tremendously old woman

who answers my knock. "My name is Detective Henry Palace." It's not, though. "Sorry, my name is Henry Palace. Is this the Open Vista Institute?"

The old woman turns silently and goes into the house, and I follow her, and tell her what I want, and at last she speaks.

"He was an odd duck, wasn't he?" she says, of Peter Zell. Her voice is strong and clear, surprisingly so.

"I actually never met him."

"Well, he was."

"Okay."

I just figured it couldn't hurt to find out a little more about this file, this last claims investigation that my insurance man was up to, before he was killed. I've had to return my department-issued Impala, so I just biked out here, broke out my mother's old Schwinn. It took me a little over five hours, including a stop to eat my lunch at an abandoned Dunkin' Donuts at a highway rest stop.

"An odd duck. And he didn't need to come here."

"Why not?"

"Because." She gestures to the file I brought, which rests on the coffee table between her and me, three pieces of paper in a manila folder: a claim, a policy, a summary of supporting documents. "There was nothing he asked that he couldn't have asked me on the phone."

Her name is Veronica Talley, it's her signature on the files, hers and that of her husband, Bernard, now deceased. Mrs. Talley's eyes are small and black and beady, like doll's eyes. The living room is small and tidy, the walls lined with seashells and delicate seaweed still lifes. I am still seeing zero evidence that this is the headquarters of any kind of institute.

"Ma'am, I understand that your husband committed suicide."

"Yes. He hung himself. In the bathroom. From the thing—" She looks irritated. "The thing? That the water comes out of?"

"The showerhead, ma'am?"

"That's right. Excuse me. I'm old."

"I am sorry for your loss."

"Shouldn't be. He told me he was going to do it. Told me to go for a walk along the water, talk to the hermit crabs, and when I got back he'd be dead in the bathroom. And that's how it happened."

She sniffs, appraises me with her tiny hard eyes. Bernard Talley's death, I know from having read the papers on the table between us, netted her one million dollars, personally, and an additional three million for the Open Vista Institute, if there is such a thing. Zell had authorized the claim, released the money, after his visit to this place three weeks ago—though he had left the file open, as if he might have been intending to come back, follow up.

"You're a bit like him, aren't you?"

"Excuse me?"

"You're like your friend, the one that came out here. Sat right there where you're sitting."

"As I said, ma'am, I never knew Mr. Zell."

"Still, you're like him though."

There are wind chimes hung right out the back window, behind the kitchen, and I just keep still for as second, listen to their gentle crystal tolling.

"Ma'am? WIll you tell me about the Institute? I would like to know what all that money will go toward."

"That's just what your friend wanted to know."

"Oh."

"It's not illegal. We're a registered nonprofit. 501(c)3, whatever it's called."

"I'm sure."

She doesn't say anything else. The wind chimes go again, and then a drift of parade music, tubas and trumpets from the gazebo, warming up.

"Mrs. Talley, I can find out in other ways if I must, but it would be easier if you could just tell me."

She sighs, stands up and shuffles out of the room, and I'm following her, hoping we're going somewhere so she can show me, because that was pure bluff—I have no real way of finding out anything. Not anymore.

* * *

The money, as it turns out, has gone in large part for titanium.

"I'm not the engineer," says Mrs. Talley. "Bernard was the engineer. He designed the thing. But the contents we chose together, and we solicited the materials together. We started in May, as soon as it became clear that the worst was a real possibility."

On a worktable in the garage is an unadorned metal sphere, a few feet in diameter. Mrs. Talley tells me the outer layer is titanium, but that is only the outer layer: there are several layers of aluminum, levels of a thermal coating of Mr. Talley's own design. He had been an aerospace engineer for many years, and he felt certain that the sphere would be resistant to cosmic radiation and to damage from space detritus, and it could survive in orbit around Earth.

"Survive for how long?"

She smiles, the first time she has done so in my presence.

"Until humanity recovers sufficiently to retrieve it."

Packed carefully inside the sphere are a brick of DVDs, draw-
ings, rolled-up newspapers in glass cases, and samples of various materials. "Salt water, a clump of clay, human blood," says Mrs. Talley.
"He was a smart cookie, my husband. A smart cookie."

I go through the inventory in the little satellite for a few minutes, turning over the odd assemblage of objects, holding each thing
in my hand, nodding appreciatively. The human race, human history,
in a nutshell. While putting the collection together, they had con-
tracted with a small private aerospace company to do the launch,
scheduled it for June, and then they'd run out of money. That's what
the insurance claim was for; that's what the suicide was for. Now the
launch, says Mrs. Talley, is back on schedule.

"Well?" she says. "What do you want to add to the capsule?"

"Nothing," I say. "Why do you ask that?"

"That's what the other man wanted."

"Mr. Zell? He wanted to put something in here?"

"He did put something in there." She reaches into the accu-
mulated materials, shifts through and removes an innocuous manila
envelope, thin and small and folded over. I hadn't noticed it before.
"I actually think this is why he came up here, to tell you the truth.
He pretended that he needed to investigate our claim in person, but
I had told him everything, and then he showed up here anyway.
Came up here with that little tape, and then he asked, kind of mum-
bling, if could he put it in here."

"Do you mind?"

She shrugs. "He was your friend."

I lift the small envelope and shake out what's inside: a microcas-
sette tape, the kind that was once used for answering-machine messages, the kind on which senior executives would make their dictations.

"Do you know what's on it?"

"Nope."

I stand there looking at the tape. It might take me some effort to
find something that could play this tape, is what I'm thinking, but I
could definitely make it happen. At the station house, in one of the
storerooms, there were a couple of old answering machines. They might
still be there, and Officer McConnell could maybe dig one out for me.
Or I'm sure I could find a pawn shop, or maybe at one of the big out-
door markets they're having down in Manchester now, every week, big
public-space flea markets—I could find one, play the tape. Be interesting, if nothing else, just to hear his voice—be interesting—

Mrs. Talley is waiting, watching me with her head at an angle, like
a bird. The little tape rests in my palm like my hand belongs to a giant.

"Okay, ma'am," I say, slipping the tape back into the envelope,
laying it back in the capsule. "Thanks for your time."

"Okay."

She walks me to the door and waves goodbye. "Watch yourself
on the steps, there. Your friend slipped on the way out, banged up his
face pretty bad."

* * *

I unchain my bike from the green central square of New Castle, now crowded with merrymakers, and start out for home, the

joyful clamor of the parade fading behind me until it sounds like a music box, and then is gone.

I ride along the shoulder of highway 90, feeling the breeze in my pant legs and up the sleeves of my coat, wavering in the wake of the occasional delivery truck or state vehicle. They suspended mail delivery last Friday, with a rather elaborate ceremony at the White House, but private companies are still delivering packages, the FedEx drivers with armed heavies riding shotgun. I have accepted an early retirement from the Concord Police Department, with a pension equal to eighty-five percent of my full salary at the time of retirement. In total, I served as a patrol officer for one year, three months, and ten days, and as a detective in the Criminal Investigations Unit for three months and twenty days.

I go ahead and take my bike right down the middle of I-90, ride it right along the double yellow lines.

You can't think too much about what happens next, you really can't.

* * *

I don't get home until the middle of the night and there she is waiting for me, sitting on one of the overturned milk crates I keep on the porch for chairs: my baby sister in a long skirt and a light jean jacket, the strong bitter smell of her American Spirits. Houdini is giving her the evil eye from behind the other milk crate, teeth bared, trembling, thinking somehow that he's invisible.

"Oh, for heaven's sake," I say, and I rush up toward her, leaving the bike in the dirt at the bottom of the porch steps, and then we're hugging, laughing, I'm pressing her head into the bones of my chest.

"You total jerk," I say, when we pull apart, and she says, "I'm sorry, Hen. I'm really sorry."

She doesn't need to say any more, that's all I need to hear, in terms of a confession. She knew all along what she was doing, when she begged me, in tears, to help spring her husband.

"It's okay. To be honest, I guess I'm rather impressed, retrospectively, with your cleverness. You played me like a—how did dad used to say it? Like an oboe? Something?"

"I don't know, Henry."

"Sure you do. Something about an oboe, with a bonobo, and—"

"I was only six, Henry. I don't know any of the sayings."

She flicks the butt of her cigarette off the porch and pulls out another one. Reflexively I scowl at her chain-smoking, and reflexively she rolls her eyes at my paternalism—old habits. Houdini gives a little tentative *woof* and pokes his snout out from under the milk crate. Officer McConnell has informed me that the dog is a bichon frisé, but I still like to think of him a poodle.

"So all right, but now you need to tell me. What did you need to know? What information did I unwittingly provide for you by worming my way into the New Hampshire National Guard?"

"Somewhere in this country there is a secret project under construction," Nico begins, slowly, her face turned away from mine. "And it's not going to be somewhere obvious. We've narrowed it down, and now our goal is to find the seemingly innocuous facility where this project is taking place."

"Who's 'we'?"

"Can't tell you. But we have information—"

"Where'd you get the information?"

"Can't tell you."

"Come on, Nico."

I feel like I'm in the Twilight Zone. I'm arguing with my little sister, like we used to over the last Popsicle, or over her boosting my grandfather's car, except this time we're fighting about some preposterous geopolitical conspiracy.

"There is a certain level of security in place to protect this project."

"And, just so I'm clear, you don't really believe that it's a shuttle to take people to the Moon."

"Well," she says, draws on her cigarette. "Well. Some of us do believe that."

My mouth drops open, the full ramifications of this thing—what she's done, what she's doing here, why she's apologizing—all of it only now sinking in. I look at her again, my sister, and she even looks different, a lot less like my mother than she used to. She is thinner than before, and her eyes are sunken and serious, not an ounce of baby fat to soften the hard lines of her face.

Nico, Peter, Naomi, Erik—everybody hoarding secrets, changing. Maia, from 280 million miles, having her way with us all.

"Derek was one of the saps, huh? You were on the inside, but your husband really thought we were escaping to the Moon."

"He had to. He had to believe he had a purpose in riding his ATV onto the base, but he couldn't know the real purpose. Too untrustworthy. Too—you know."

"Too stupid."

She doesn't answer. Her face is set, her eyes gleaming now with something familiar, something chilling, something like the aggressive religious types in Police Plaza, like the worst of the Brush Cuts, rousting their drunks for the thrill of it. All the true believers batting away the reality of all of this.

"So, the level of security you mentioned. If that had been the real facility, the place you're looking for, I would have found him, what, in shackles?"

"No. You would have found him dead."

Her voice is cold, brutal. I feel like I'm standing here with a stranger.

"And you knew he was going to be taking this risk when you sent him in there. He didn't know, but you did."

"Henry, I knew it when I married him."

Nico looks off into the distance and smokes her cigarette, and I'm standing here shivering, not even because of what happened to Derek, not because of this crazy science-fiction madness that my sister has let herself become involved in, not even because I was unknowingly dragged into it, too. I'm shivering because this is it—when Nico takes off, tonight, we're done—I'm never going to see her again. That'll leave me and the dog, together, waiting.

"All I can tell you is that it was worth it."

"How can you say that?" I'm remembering the last part of the story, too, the botched jailbreak, Derek left behind, left for dead. Expendable. A sacrifice. I pick up my bike, heave it onto my shoulder, and walk past her to the door.

"I mean—wait—do you want to know what it is we're looking for?"

"No, thank you."

"Because it's worth it."

I'm done. I'm not even angry, so much as exhausted. I've been biking all day. My legs hurt from my ride. I'm not sure what I'm doing tomorrow, but it's late. The world keeps turning.

"You have to trust me," says Nico to my back, I'm at the door now, the door is open, Houdini is at my heels. "It's all worth it."

I stop, and I turn and look at her.

"It's *hope*," she says.

"Oh," I say. "It's hope. Okay."

I close the door.

THANK YOU

Dr. Tim Spahr, director of the Minor Planet Center at the Harvard-Smithsonian Center for Astrophysics

Dr. Cynthia Gardner, forensic pathologist

The Concord Police Department, especially Officers Joseph Wright and Craig Leveques

Andrew Winters, Esq.

Jeff Strelzin, New Hampshire assistant attorney general

Steve Walters at Loyola University Maryland

Binyamin Applebaum at the *New York Times*

Dr. Judy Greene

David Belson at Akamai Technologies

Dr. Nora Osman and Dr. Mark Pomeranz

Jason and Jane and Doogie and Dave and Brett and Mary Ellen and Nicole and Eric and everyone else at Quirk Books

Molly Lyons and Joelle Delbourgo

Early readers Nick Tamarkin, Erik Jackson, and Laura Gutin

Michael Hyman (and Wylie the Dog)

And thanks very, very, very much to Diana and Rosalie and Isaac and Milly

* * *

Rusty Schweickart, former NASA astronaut and asteroid expert, urged me not to write this book, suggesting I take on instead the vastly more likely scenario of a sub-apocalyptic but still-devastating impact. I failed to honor this request, but I can recommend that everyone visit his work at the B612 Foundation (www.B612Foundation.org).

Turn the page

for a sneak preview of

COUNTDOWN CITY

THE LAST POLICEMAN BOOK II

By Ben H. Winters

Available Wherever Books Are Sold

July 2013

PART ONE

....

A Man with a Woman on His Mind

....

WEDNESDAY, JULY 18

Right Ascension 20 08 05.1
Declination -59 27 39
Elongation 141.5
Delta 0.873 AU

1.

"It's just that he *promised*," says Martha Milano, pale eyes flashing, cheeks flushed with anxiety. Grieving, bewildered, desperate. "We both did. We promised each other like a million times."

"Right," I say. "Of course."

I pluck a tissue from the box on her kitchen table and Martha takes it, smiles weakly, blows her nose. "I'm sorry," she says, and honks again, and then she gathers herself, just a little, sits up straight and takes a breath. "But so Henry, you're a policeman."

"I was."

"Right. You were. But, I mean, is there . . ."

She can't finish, but she doesn't need to. I understand the question and it floats there in the air between us and slowly revolves: Is there anything you can do? And of course I'm dying to help her, but frankly I'm not sure whether there is anything that I can do, and it's hard, it's impossible, really, to know what to say. For the last hour I've just been sitting here and listening, taking down the information in my slim blue exam-taker's notebook. Martha's missing husband is Brett Cavatone; age thirty-five; last seen at a restaurant called Rocky's Rock 'n' Bowl, on Old Loudon Road, out by the Steeplegate Mall. It's her father's place, Martha explained, a family-friendly pizza-joint-slash-bowling-alley, still open despite everything, though with a drastically reduced menu. Brett has worked there, her father's right-hand man, for two years. Yesterday morning, about 8:45, he left to do some errands and never came back.

I read over these scant notes one more time in the worried silence of Martha's neat and sunlit kitchen. Officially her name is Martha Cavatone, but to me she will always be Martha Milano, the fifteen-year-old kid who watched my sister Nico and me after school, five days a week, until my mom got home, gave her ten bucks in an envelope, and asked after her folks. It's unmooring to see her as an adult, let alone one overturned by the emotional catastrophe of having been abandoned by her husband. How much stranger it must be for her to be turning to me, of all people, whom she last laid eyes on when I was twelve. She blows her nose again, and I give her a small gentle smile. Martha Milano with the overstuffed purple JanSport backpack, the Pearl Jam T-shirt. Cherry-pink bubblegum and cinnamon lip gloss.

She wears no makeup now. Her hair is an unruly brown pile; her eyes are red rimmed from crying; she's gnawing vigorously on the nail of her thumb.

"Disgusting, right?" she says, catching me looking. "But I've been smoking like crazy since April, and Brett never says anything even though I know it grosses him out. I have this stupid feeling, like, if I stop now, it'll bring him home. I'm sorry, Henry, did you—" She stands abruptly. "Do you want tea or something?"

"No, thank you."

"Water?"

"No. It's okay, Martha. Sit down."

She falls back into the chair, stares at the ceiling. What I want of course is coffee, but thanks to whatever byzantine chain of infrastructural disintegration is determining the relative availability of various perishable items, coffee cannot be found. I close my notebook and look Martha in the eye.

"It's tough," I say slowly, "it really is. There are just a lot of reasons why a missing-persons investigation is especially challenging in the current environment."

"Yeah. No." She blinks her eyes, closed and then open again. "I mean, of course. I know."

Dozens of reasons, really. Hundreds. There is no way to put out a description on the wires, to issue an APB or post to the FBI Kidnappings and Missing Persons List. Witnesses who might know the location of a missing individual have very little interest or incentive to divulge that information, if they haven't gone missing themselves. There is no way to access federal or local databases. As of last Friday, in fact, southern New Hampshire appears to have no electricity whatsoever. Plus of course I'm not a policeman anymore, and even if I was, the CPD as a matter of policy is no longer pursuing such cases. All of which makes finding one particular individual a long shot, is what I tell Martha. Especially—and here I pause, load my voice with as much care and sensitivity as I can—especially since many such people left on purpose.

"Yeah," she says flatly. "Of course."

Martha knows all of this. Everybody knows. The world is on the move. Plenty still leaving in droves on their Bucket List adventures, going off to snorkel or skydive or make love to strangers in public parks. And now, more recently, whole new forms of abrupt departure, new species of madness as we approach the end. Religious sects wandering New England in robes, competing for converts: the Doomsday Mormons, the Satellites of God. The mercy cruisers, traveling the deserted highways in buses with converted engines running on wood gas or coal, seeking opportunities for Samaritanship. And of course the preppers, down in their basements, hoarding what they can, building piles for the aftermath, as if any amount of preparation will suffice.

I stand up, close my notebook. Change the subject. "How is your block?"

"It's fine," says Martha. "I guess."

"There's an active residents association?"

"Yes." She nods blankly, not interested in the line of questioning, not ready to contemplate how things will be for her alone.

"And let me ask, hypothetically, if there were a firearm in the home . . ."

"There is," she begins. "Brett left his—"

I hold up one hand, cut her off. "Hypothetically. Would you know how to use it?"

"Yes," she says. "I can shoot. Yes."

I nod. Fine. All I needed to hear. Private ownership or sale of firearms is technically forbidden, although the brief wave of house-to-house searches ended months ago. Obviously I'm not going to bike over to School Street and report that Martha Cavatone has her husband's service revolver under the bed—get her sent away for the duration—but neither do I need to hear any details.

Martha murmurs "excuse me" and gets up, jerks open the pantry door and reaches for what looks like a carton of cigarettes. But then she stops herself, slams the door, and spins around to press her fingers into her eyes. It's almost comical, it's such a teenage set of gestures: the impetuous grab for comfort, the immediate and disgusted self-abnegation. I remember standing in our front hallway, at seven or eight years old, just after Martha went home in the evenings, trying to catch one last sniff of cinnamon and bubblegum.

"Okay, so, Martha, what I can do is go by the restaurant," I say—I hear myself saying—"and ask a few questions." And as soon as the words are out she's across the room, hugging me around the neck, grinning into my chest, like it's a done deal, like I've already brought her husband home and he's out there on the stoop, ready to come in.

"Oh, thank you," she says. "*Thank you*, Henry."

"Listen, wait—wait, Martha."

I gently pry her arms from around my neck, step back and plant her in front of me, summon the stern hardheaded spirit of my grandfather, level Martha with his severe stare. "I will do what I can to find your husband, okay?"

"Okay," she says, breathless. "You promise?"

"Yes." I nod. "I can't promise that I will find him, and I definitely can't promise that I will bring him home. But I'll do what I can."

"Of course," she says, "I understand," and she's beaming, hugging me again, my notes of caution sliding unheard off her cheeks. I can't help it, I'm smiling, too, Martha Milano is hugging me and I'm smiling.

"I'll pay you, of course," she says.

"No, you won't."

"No, I know, not with *money* money, but we can figure out something . . ."

"Martha, no. I won't take anything from you. Let's have a look around, okay?"

"Okay," she says, wiping the last of the tears from her eyes.

*   *   *

Martha finds me a recent picture of her husband, a nice full-body snapshot from a fishing trip a couple years back. I study him, Brett Cavatone, a short man with a broad powerful frame, standing at the bank of a stream in the classic pose, holding aloft a dripping wide-mouth bass, man and fish staring into the camera with the same skeptical and somber expression. Brett has a black beard, thick and untrimmed, but the hair on his head is neat and short, a crew cut only slightly grown out.

"Was your husband in the military, Martha?"

"No," she says, "he was a cop. Like you. But not Concord. The state force."

"A trooper?"

"Yes." Martha takes the picture from me, gazes at it proudly.

"Why did he leave the force?"

"Oh, you know. Tired of it. Ready for a change. And my dad

was starting this restaurant. So, I don't know."

She murmurs these fragments—*tired of it, ready for a change*—as if they require no further explanation, like the idea of leaving law enforcement voluntarily makes self-evident sense. I take the photograph back and slip it into my pocket, thinking of my own brief career: patrolman for fifteen months, detective on Adult Crimes for four months, forcibly retired along with my colleagues on March twenty-eighth of this year.

We walk around the house together. I'm peering into the closets, opening Brett's drawers, finding nothing interesting, nothing remarkable: a flashlight, some paperbacks, a dozen ounces of gold. Brett's closet and dresser drawers are still full of clothes, which in normal circumstances would suggest foul play rather than intentional abandonment, but there is no longer any such thing as normal circumstances. At lunch yesterday, McGully told us a story he heard, where the husband and wife were out for a walk in White Park, and the woman just runs, literally runs, leaps over a hedge and disappears into the distance.

"She said, can you hold my ice cream a sec?" McGully said, laughing, bellowing, pounding the table. "Poor dummy standing there with two ice creams."

The Cavatones' bedroom furniture is handsome and sturdy and plain. On Martha's night table is a hot-pink journal with a small brass lock, like a child's diary, and when I lift it I get just the lightest scent of cinnamon. Perfect. I smile. On the opposite night table, Brett's, is a miniature chess board, pieces arranged midgame; her husband, Martha tells me with another fond smile, plays against himself. Hung above the dresser is a small tasteful painting of Christ crucified. On the wall of the bathroom, next to the mirror, is a slogan in neat block all-capital letters: IF YOU ARE WHAT YOU SHOULD BE, YOU WILL SET THE WORLD ABLAZE!

"Saint Catherine," says Martha, appearing beside me in the mirror, tracing the words with her forefinger. "Isn't it beautiful?"

We go back downstairs and sit facing each other on a tidy brown sofa in the living room. There's a column of deadbolts along the front door and rows of iron bars on the windows. I flip open my notebook and gather a few more details: what time her husband left for work yesterday, what time her father came by, said "have you seen Brett?" and they realized that he was gone.

"This may seem like an obvious question," I say, when I'm done writing down her answers. "But what do you think he might be doing?"

Martha worries at the nail of her pinky. "I've thought about it so much, believe me. I mean, it sounds silly, but something *good*. He wouldn't be off bungee jumping or shooting heroin or whatever." My mind flashes quickly on Peter Zell, the last poor soul I went in search of, while Martha presses on. "If he really left, if he's not . . ."

I nod. If he's not dead. Because that possibility, too, hovers over us. A lot of missing people are missing because they're dead.

"He'd be doing something, like, *noble*," Martha concludes. "Something he thought was noble."

I smooth the edges of my mustache. Something noble. A powerful thing to think about one's husband, especially one who's just disappeared without explanation. A pink bead of blood has appeared at the edge of her fingernail.

"And you don't feel it's possible—"

"No," says Martha. "No women. No way." She shakes her head, adamant. "Not Brett."

I don't press it; I move on. She tells me that he was getting around on a black ten-speed bicycle; she tells me no, he didn't have any regular activities outside of work and home. I ask her if there's anything else she needs to tell me about her husband or her marriage, and she says no: He was here, they had a plan, and then he went away.

Now all that's left is the million-dollar question. Because even if I do track him down—which I almost certainly will not be able to do—it remains the case that abandoning one's spouse is not illegal and never has been, and of course I have no power at this point to compel anyone to do anything. I'm unsure exactly how to explain any of this to Martha Milano, and I suspect she knows it anyway, so I just go ahead and say it:

"What do you want me to do if I find him?"

She doesn't answer at first, but leans across the sofa and stares deeply, almost romantically into my eyes. "Tell him he has to come home. Tell him his salvation depends on it."

"His . . . salvation?"

"Will you tell him that, Henry? His salvation."

I murmur something, I don't know what, and look down at my notebook, vaguely embarrassed. The faith and fervency are new; they weren't an aspect of Martha Milano when we were young. It's not just that she loves this man and misses him; she believes that he has sinned by abandoning her and will suffer for it in the world to come. Which is coming, of course, a lot sooner than it used to be.

I tell Martha I'll be back soon if I have any news and where she can find me, in the meantime, if she needs to.

As we stand up, her expression changes.

"Jeez, I'm sorry, I'm such a—I'm sorry. Henry, how's your sister doing?"

"I don't know," I say.

I'm already at the door, I'm working my way through the series of deadbolts and chains.

"You don't know?"

"I'll be in touch, Martha. I'll let you know what I can find."

* * *

The current environment. That's what I said to Martha: *A missing-persons investigation is especially challenging in the current environment.* I sigh, now, at the pale inadequacy of the euphemism. Even now, fourteen months since the first scattered disbelieving sightings, seven months after the odds of impact rose to one hundred percent, nobody knows what to call it. "The situation," some people say, or "what's going on." "This craziness." On October third, seventy-seven days from today, the asteroid $2011GV_1$, 6.5 kilometers in diameter, will plow into planet Earth and destroy us all. *The current environment.*

I trot briskly down the stairs of the Cavatones' porch in the sunlight and unchain my bike from their charming cement birdbath. Their lawn is the only one mowed on the street. It's a beautiful day today, hot but not too hot, clear blue sky, drifting white clouds. Pure uncomplicated summertime. On the street there are no cars, no sound of cars.

I snap on my helmet and take my bike slowly down the street, right on Bradley, east toward Loudon Bridge, heading in the direction of Steeplegate Mall. A police car is parked at the end of Church with an officer in the driver's seat, a young man sitting upright in black wraparound shades. I nod hello and he nods back, slow, impassive. There's a second cop car at Main and Pearl, this one with a driver I slightly recognize, although his wave in return to mine is cursory at best, quick and unsmiling. He's one of the legions of inexperienced young patrol officers who swelled the ranks of the CPD in the weeks before its abrupt reorganization under the federal Department of Justice—the same reorganization that dissolved the Adult Crimes Unit and the rest of the detective divisions. I don't get the memos anymore, of course, but the current operating strategy appears to be one of overwhelming presence: no investigations, no neighborhood policing, just a cop on every corner, rapid response to any whiff of public disturbance, as with the recent events on Independence Day.

If I *were* still on the force, it would be General Order 44-2 that would be relevant to Martha's case. I can call up the form in my mind, practically see it: Part I, procedures; Part VI, Unusual Circumstances. Additional investigative steps.

There's a guy at Main and Court, dirty beard and no shirt, whirling in circles and punching the air, earbuds in place, though I'd be willing to bet there's no music coming out of them. I raise my hand from my handlebars and the bearded man waves back then pauses, looks down, adjusting the volume on his nonexistent music. Once I'm over the bridge I make a small detour, weave over to Quincy Street and the elementary school. I chain my bike to the fence surrounding the playing field, take off my helmet and scan the recess yard. It's the height of summer but there's a small army of kids hanging out here, as there has been all day, every day, playing four-square and hop-scotch, chasing one another across the weeds of the soccer field, urinating against the wall of the deserted brick school-house. Many spend the night here too, camping out on their beach towels and *Star Wars: The Clone Wars* bed sheets.

Micah Rose is sitting on a bench on the outskirts of the play-ground, his legs drawn up and hugged to his chest. He's eight. His sis-ter Alyssa is six, and she's pacing back and forth in front of him. I take the pair of eyeglasses from my coat pocket and hand them to Alyssa, who claps her hands delightedly.

"You fixed them."

"Not me personally," I say, eyeing Micah, who is looking stonily at the ground. "I know a guy." I jab a thumb at the bench. "What's wrong with my man?"

Micah looks up and scowls warningly at his sister. Alyssa looks away. She's wearing a sleeveless jean jacket I gave her a couple weeks ago, two sizes too big, with a Social Distortion patch sewn on the back. It belonged to Nico, my own sister, many years ago.

"Come on, guys," I say, and Alyssa glances one last time at Micah and launches in: "Some big kids from St. Alban's were here and they were being all crazy and pushing and stuff, and they took things."

"Shut *up*," says Micah. Alyssa looks back and forth from him to me and almost cries, but then keeps it together. "They took Micah's sword."

"Sword?" I say. "Huh."

Their father is a feckless character named Johnson Rose, whom I went to high school with, and who I happen to know went Bucket

List very early on. The mother, unless I got the story wrong, subsequently overdosed on vodka and pain pills. A lot of the kids spending their days out here have similar stories. There's one, Andy Blackstone—I see him right now, bouncing a big rubber medicine ball against the school—who was being raised, for one reason or another, by an uncle. When the odds rose to a hundred percent, the uncle apparently just told him to get the fuck out.

A little more gentle prodding of Alyssa and Micah, and it emerges, to my relief, that what has been lost is a toy—a plastic samurai sword that once upon a time came with a ninja costume, but which Micah had been wearing at his belt for some weeks.

"Okay," I say, squeezing Alyssa's shoulder and turning to look at Micah in the eye. "It's not a big deal."

"It just sucks," says Micah emphatically. "It sucks."

"I know that."

I flip past the details on Brett Cavatone to the back of my notebook, where I've got certain small tasks laid out for myself. I cross out *A's glasses* and pencil in *samurai sword* with a couple of question marks beside it. As I straighten awkwardly out of my squat, Andy Blackstone bounces the medicine ball my way, and I turn just in time for it to sproing up off the pavement and hit my outstretched palms with a satisfying, stinging *whap*.

"Hey, Palace," hollers Blackstone. "Play some kickball?"

"Rain check," I say, winking at Alyssa and clipping my helmet back on. "I've got a case I'm working on."

WHAT WOULD YOU DO ...

... with just six months until the
end of the world?

Author Ben H. Winters posed this question to a variety
of writers, artists, and notable figures.

Visit QuirkBooks.com/TheLastPoliceman to:

• Read their answers

• Share your own responses

• Watch the book trailer

• Read a Q&A with Ben H. Winters

• Discover the science behind the science fiction

And much more!